The Dark Side of Tranquility

by

Susana Aclan

The Dark Side of Tranquility

Cover Art by *Kristian Norris*

The Wild Rose Press, Inc.
PO Box 708
Adams Basin, NY 14410-0708
Visit us at www.thewildrosepress.com

Publishing History
First Edition, 2021
Trade Paperback ISBN 978-1-5092-3624-4
Digital ISBN 978-1-5092-3625-1

Published in the United States of America

Engulfed in a grief stupor, I take a few tentative steps forward. As my feet sink into the warm mass of beings, I cover my mouth to stifle a scream. I continue with my unsteady walk, stopping at times to avoid falling on my classmates.

When the carpet of bodies transitions into one of rubble, I am already facing the Praying Room. Just this morning, we all gathered here for our daily prayers. As I now stand above the ruins and amidst a ring of menacing flames, life feels surreal.

My recent brush with danger during the mongrels' rebellion had left a deep dent in my courage, and I can't stop dreading the perils that lie ahead.

All sorts of hazardous debris cover the floor. After a few seconds of indecisiveness, I slowly take a step on the hard and uneven surface. When an image of Mom pops in my head, I overcome fear and pick my way to the other end of the room.

How am I going to find Mom? Fire and rubble are everywhere. Even if I am lucky enough to see the needle in the haystack, Mom is probably dead.

Dedication

This book is dedicated to world peace. Hoping individual differences are cherished rather than frowned upon.

Majestic mountains and roaring rivers
The great wonders of Earth lie in Tranquility
The gift of the sun's rays rising over the valley
It is peace
The vast reaches of the unknown shine over all that is true
The starlight falls upon the island of red, green, and blue
On the island, a colony of beings
Divided in expression but united in purpose
The truth, as it seems, is just like the night
Dark and unclear, but faith brings the light
It is peace
But the warmth of society is made from glittering gold
Most who will seek it will find themselves cold
The order is broken, and the mountains fall
Rivers are emptied for the sake of one town
Truths are created, ideas are made
The minds are deluded with each and every trade
The few will be happy with lavish gold and fame
But the rest will bow their heads in shame
For every gain, there must be a cost
But can we make up for what will be lost?

Marten the Seer

Introduction

I was born on Tranquility in the year 2400. Tranquility is among a cluster of planets circling Trappist—a distant sun—and can support human life. Like everybody else on this planet, I am a true believer in Marten the Seer.

Marten is our beloved martyr. Back in the day, the Seer had predicted greed would fatally infect Earth, and his people—known as Followers—had seen the signs of doom. People feared Marten's prophetic words and repelled them as mere blasphemy, distrusting everyone who carried his symbol, an eye with a black skull at the center.

In the year 2330, Earth became a living hell when world leaders ordered the mass extermination of Followers to exorcise the demon and rid the planet of Marten's intellectual poison.

Intolerance forced our people to choose between accepting death or risking new challenges beyond planet Earth. Those who ventured into space vowed to embody Marten's doctrines by establishing peaceful communities to overcome the sorrow of lifelong persecution and alienation.

My ancestors arrived on Tranquility after a long interstellar flight. Tranquility was barren and had harsh, unpredictable weather, but it was peaceful. The bird-like natives who inhabited this land were welcoming, which helped a small colony thrive and multiply into thousands.

As the colony grew in numbers, Followers ventured onto the neighboring planets. Expeditions to Placidity, Serenity, Comity, Harmony, Quietude, Amity, Peace, Equilibrium, and Equanimity soon gave birth to new colonies where the Seer's doctrines took root.

It was not until decades later that the self-governed colonies agreed to establish a council to administer the entire array of settlements. Since then, the Council has resided in Tranquility. A handful of representatives supervise the rest of the colonies, which are in more inhospitable locations and far less crowded.

Our communities adhere to the Seer's restrictive rules. Our people are cordial but distant, and physical intimacy is prohibited unless within the realm of marriage. Our behavior and modest dress code discourage immoral thoughts and help us focus on our religious obligations.

My life is frugal, but I accept the many restrictions willingly. It is a small token compared to the many sacrifices endured by our ancestors in the early years. I am a proud Follower, and I love Tranquility—my piece of Heaven.

Chapter 1

I wait underneath the ledge of a massive structure while the frenzied skydiving of gobblers continues above my head. Each one of their ear-piercing vocalizations sends instant chills down my spine.

I have been sprinting from building to building, crossing small alleyways to stay out of sight. However, the distance between buildings is growing, and I am becoming an easier target. Under these treacherous conditions, the natives will track me down soon.

My entire body aches, and my heart pounds at an abnormally fast pace while I stare at the darkness as if hypnotized. My beloved Tranquility is unrecognizable. The gobblers have always been welcoming to our people, but there is no denying it—they want to kill me.

The night is a double-edged sword. A total blackout hinders my ability to distinguish safe from treacherous. I have been making little headway despite my steadfast attempt to reach the Beacon, the source of our communications and defense systems.

Thankfully darkness also works to my advantage as the gobblers' inferior night vision is keeping them away.

The warehouse across the road looks like a safe place to rest for a while, but I have to cross a two-lane street first.

"I must get to the Beacon, or Dad will die," I repeat

a hundred times to harness the courage to step into the open.

The shrieks momentarily fade, and I dart forward, but three seconds into the run, my heart skips a beat when I step into a giant puddle. Water splashes everywhere, and almost instantly, the squeals intensify as the gobblers search for the source of the noise.

With no time to spare, I dive inside the building headfirst, rolling on the cold tiles until my momentum is gone. When I confirm there is no danger inside, I crawl to the entrance and collapse against the door.

Nobody had groomed me for such a chaotic event, and I am unequipped to survive it. My eyes become blind with tears, and I keep wiping them away with the cuff of my sleeve.

I dry the last teardrop and walk to the opposite end of the building to look out the window. My heart sinks when there is no visible shelter ahead. Only one big rock sits fifty feet away.

Without stopping to consider the risk, I abandon my refuge and dart toward the rock. But as I step foot in the open, two gobblers that are quietly surveying the territory from a nearby roof squeal feverishly.

I bolt in a zigzag pattern, hoping to confuse them, but despite my efforts, they head straight to me.

Fear has hijacked my brain. I can't come up with any good idea to keep me alive. When the gobblers are about three feet away, I halt.

Unbelievably, the natives can't adjust their trajectory and miss me by a foot, violently crashing on the ground.

Holding my breath, I dash around their crumpled bodies to the rock. However, I soon regret leaving the shelter; the stone has nowhere to hide.

On my hands and knees, I explore the base of the spiky mineral formation. As the seconds pass and I can't secure a haven, my movements become desperate and uncoordinated.

The crushed gobblers are back in pursuit and will catch me in seconds.

I am about to trace my steps back to the shelter when my fingers slide over an opening on the rock's north side. The hole looks way too small to fit my entire body, but I lie down flat on the ground and squeeze my way in.

This rock is the perfect hiding spot. The opening is completely hidden from plain view, and the gobblers will not find it. Under the protection of the rock, I remain quiet, waiting for the gobblers to fly away. My inability to move gives way to restlessness as my thoughts whirl with memories of my sick father.

My father's illness came on abruptly and at the worse time in our colony's history. Soon after we arrived at the hospital, the gobblers launched a rebellion, their first uprising ever. Just as the doctor was completing his examination, the power went out in the complex.

Dad did not look too sick when we arrived at the hospital, and Mom had assured us it was just a bad case of influenza. No wonder the doctor's prognosis shook me to the core.

"Your husband has a rare and aggressive infection," the doctor conveyed to my mother. "We must transfer him to the Outpost Hospital immediately to run tests to determine the right treatment, or he might not survive."

But requesting even emergency medical transport during the blackout was impossible.

"The Beacon has its power source and communications system. I will go to call for help," Mom said, pulling the doctor aside and walking away from my younger siblings.

Even after the doctor uttered a stern warning about the complex's inactive defense system, I still volunteered to go in Mom's place.

"That is out of the question. I will do it," Mom decreed, holding my arm tight.

"You must look after my baby brothers. Tonight, they need you more than ever."

"No, Clara. You stay and take care of the little ones."

What if Mom went after me once she realized I had disobeyed her?

The stabbing pain in my chest soon subsides. Mom had no option but to stay with the boys and pray for my safe return.

It is freezing, and my inactivity triggers uncontrollable shivering.

Now that the gobblers' shrieks have subsided, it is time to leave my refuge. It has been more than two hours, and I have yet to cover half the distance to the elusive Beacon. However, my survival instinct urges me to stay still, particularly now that there are fewer places to hide along my route.

A gobbler is circling the rock, scanning the ground for the slightest movement. Suddenly, he sniffs the air with his prominent nose and lands by the opening to continue his search on foot.

Long nails scratch the soles of my shoes all of a

sudden.

I hasten to lift my legs to my chest as much as the space allows, but the gobbler keeps scratching at my shoes relentlessly. After a few seconds, we are at a standoff. I can't lift my legs any farther, and my attacker can't stretch his arm any longer.

Suddenly, the scratching on my feet stops, followed a few seconds later by hefty thwacks on the other side of the rock. The gobbler is looking for other entry points.

I crawl quickly from my refuge, scraping my knees in the process. I tiptoe my way toward the Beacon, praying to remain unnoticed. After about a hundred feet, I race ahead.

Five minutes into my run, my heart resumes its usual tempo, and I regain control of my breathing. Although there are no buildings ahead, I am not being followed, and I am grateful for my good fortune.

My precarious security suffers a sudden blow when my skirt gets tangled between my legs, and I fall hard on my knees.

"Ouch!" A painful yell escapes my mouth before I can hold it back.

Instantly, the gobblers shriek in the distance. The short cry was loud enough to alert them of my location, and two of them are already in pursuit and will catch me soon unless I find refuge.

In desperation, I scrutinize the horizon for a miracle. Suddenly, the silhouette of a small house emerges on the horizon.

Is that a mirage, or is it really there?

Without waiting for an answer, I gather my skirt up and race toward hope.

The gobblers' screams become deafening as the distance between us decreases. My only chance of survival is getting inside the building.

Adrenaline propels me forward, ahead of the gobblers. When I arrive, the door refuses to budge. "Help! Is anybody in there?"

The run-down structure is vacant, and nobody comes to my aid.

Fighting rising panic, I repeatedly kick the door until it finally succumbs to the pressure and swings open.

I dash inside the dark building and slam the door closed just as the gobblers are about to swoop down on me.

I am not strong enough to keep these powerful beings at bay. As I search for the door lock, I can feel my body shivering in a cold sweat. I am about to give up hope when my fingers find the metal bolt.

Marten's prayer provides me with fortitude while the gobblers beat the door viciously.

The wood is old and cracks after the first few blows. The crack deepens with each consecutive whack, and the door will soon split in half.

Suddenly, the gobblers stop to sniff the air inside the building. Then they instantly disappear.

The cabin's interior is pitch black, which makes the search for something to protect me against imminent danger exceedingly tricky. I have moved fewer than ten feet when my left foot gets tangled, and I almost trip.

The place is not as empty as it seems. Hesitantly, I lift my leg to take another step. When there are no impediments to my movement, I resume my walk. Just as I am about to step forward, something tightens around my ankle.

My stomach clenches—the pressure feels like a hand. I give my foot a yank, but the pressure remains steady.

I want to scream in fear, but shock numbs my voice. I raise my free foot and prepare to kick.

"Help…" The weak voice is human, a man.

I get down on my knees.

"Oh no! What have they done to you?"

The man is covered in blood. He must have been walking when the power outage hit. A gang of natives must have attacked him and left him for dead.

"Water." The whisper is almost inaudible.

"Sorry. I don't have any."

The man writhes in pain, moving me to action.

"Don't worry. I'll get some."

I know I should not waste precious time helping a stranger. However, my moral compass points to a person in need, and the Seer would disapprove of me turning a blind eye.

I comb the darkness for water but find nothing resembling a tap. I am on the verge of giving up when I come across a door. Still, I hesitate to open it; the door might lead me back to the gobblers.

"Praise the Seer!"

The door leads to a bathroom. The sink is right by the door. While I wait for the water to run, I grab my metal cup from a clasp strapped to my leather belt.

But the pipes are silent; there is no running water.

As I search the wall for the shut-off valve, I come across a light switch.

A soft light flickers on and off above the bathroom cabinet.

I let a deep sigh out instantly. The shut-off valve is under the sink a few feet away.

Weird sounds come from the pipe as soon as I turn the knob on. Seconds later, a thin stream of water flows from the tap.

I let the water run for a minute before filling the cup to the rim. I gulp a mouthful and hurry to the injured man.

The soft flickering light from the bathroom guides my way back without spilling a drop of water.

The man is unresponsive, and his breathing is very shallow.

I lift his head carefully, but he moans in agony. Then he opens his eyes and screams.

"The gobblers are gone." I try to reassure him.

He meets my gaze and recoils noticeably.

"Please drink."

The man's eyes light up at the sight of the cup, but he refuses to drink when I hold it against his lip.

"Medicine...pants' front pocket."

The man is delirious. Doesn't he know it's against our rules to touch someone of the opposite sex? I held his head only because I thought he was dying.

Unaware of my hesitation, the man lies motionless, hardly breathing.

"Wait! Don't sleep! I'll get your medicine."

All I can do is use my hands as guides. The man has a thick jacket over his shoulders, so I open it a little to allow room for my hands. Then I pretend the man is my ill father, and the make-believe helps alleviate the awkwardness.

The man recoils with each brush of my fingers. Still, I do not move away. He is boiling, and his body is soaking wet.

I trace my hands down his chest with increased desperation. I doubt the medicine will help but doing something feels better than letting him die without easing his suffering.

Once I reach his pants, I find his left pocket on my first attempt. But the pocket is empty. The man must have his medicine in his other pocket, which is far less accessible.

"Can you turn a little?"

When I get no response, I put my fingers inside the pocket.

The man is too heavy, and only the tip of my fingers slide in.

"This will hurt."

The man moans in agony but offers no resistance when I push him until he is flat on his back. Once his pocket is accessible, I try to retrieve his medicine.

Elation fills my heart when I find the pouch tucked deep within, but it will be impossible to remove it painlessly.

I tug the bag gently, each small movement sharply hurting the man. The groans continue, and I have to fight back tears until the small leather sack is in my hand.

I squeeze the bag between my fingers to discern its contents—it is powdery. A long leather string keeps the pouch closed, and it takes some time to remove it.

Once the sack opens, I pour some of its contents into my palm. I recognize the gray powder right away; it is Tranquility's soil. Still, I have no idea what the man wants me to do with it.

Suddenly, he opens his eyes and sees the pouch.

When the man notices my clueless expression, he instructs me to pour the sack's content into the water.

The powder dissolves instantly.

I offer the cup to the man, but he passes out before taking a sip. Gently, I shake his shoulders until he opens his eyes again. I then hold his head up while he swallows the mixture.

The man is too weak, and his head keeps drooping. After a few grueling attempts, he gathers enough strength to keep his head up long enough to swallow a mouthful of the solution.

With extreme effort, I repeat the process until the man swallows all his medicine.

"I must leave."

"Go…"

"I hope this keeps you warm until help comes."

I remove the warmest of my sweaters and spread it over his body.

"I'll request transportation for two. One for Dad, and one for you."

My words fall on deaf ears. The man has passed out.

Quietly, I pray to Marten to protect him. If the gobblers return, the man will be defenseless.

I dash to the door and press my ear against the cracked wood to listen for gobblers. There is no sound. I grab my cup and hold it against the door and listen again—still nothing.

It is time to leave my refuge.

Chapter 2

I stand outside the door, letting my lungs adjust to the freezing night air. I dart into the vast emptiness for the hope of a Beacon I can't see.

An eerie silence fills the air as I traverse the rugged terrain. I keep pressing forward, only stopping when exhaustion overcomes me.

I scan the darkness for a miracle.

Am I even going in the right direction?

I study my surroundings for a second time. A distant flickering light catches my attention, the soft glow taunting me from beyond my vantage point. Energized, I dash toward the light faster than ever.

I arrive at the massive structure, exhausted but unharmed.

I scan the perimeter to look for what might lie in wait. Though all appears quiet, I feel that something is dreadfully wrong—the place looks abandoned. My gaze goes up to the Beacon, rising into the dark sky for more than three hundred feet.

The flickering light at the top is the only one on the entire tower.

Panic strikes me when I find the entrance ajar, and my legs refuse to walk any further.

I fill my thoughts with the words of the Seer to find strength. But I still lack the courage to tackle the last few steps keeping me away from peril.

When memories of my loving dad consume me, my hands curl into fists. I slowly enter the pitch-black building.

The main floor is devoid of life. I creep across the room in search of stairs while hundreds of droplets reverberate on the mosaic tile floor.

I have only covered ten feet when I bump into something. I shove it out of the way, but the object bounces back and strikes my head with force.

I realize it is hanging from the ceiling when liquid drips on my shoulders. As I try to push it aside, the object moans—it is a man.

I leap back in terror. The repulsive smell of blood fills my nostrils, and I try to get away.

The odor triggers a memory of my grandmother. It reminds me of one of my last visits to her house before she died. Granma was holding an old jar of pennies to my nose.

"This is the source of all tragedies and the reason why money is forbidden in Tranquility. Remember the scent and stay away from this Evil."

The pennies in Grandma's jar had smelled just like fresh blood.

The man groans, and again I feel compelled to help someone in distress.

"Stay still. I'll get help."

"Run!" The man pleads and succumbs to death.

Feeling sick to my stomach, I rush ahead in search of a way to the top.

As I move toward the light trickling down the stairs, an area to my right comes into view. My glance snaps from left to right in an irregular frenzy, capturing glimpses of a colossal massacre—dozens of bodies hang from the ceiling, head down.

The natives have extinguished all life—only the scent of Evil lingers in the shadows.

My body convulses violently as I stand in the sea of blood. I hasten to the stairs and almost instantly feel a powerful urge to puke. I keep my mouth and nose buried in my sleeve all the way to the top.

The spiral stairs are structurally sound, and there is enough light to climb quickly to the top. I remain hidden in the shadows of the stairway to examine the doors leading from the landing.

The floor is silent, and my beating heart takes center stage.

The door closest to me leads to the Command Center. I take a deep breath and storm inside.

The gobblers have destroyed the communications equipment, reducing a state-of-the-art facility to rubbish.

My body goes numb, and I drop to my knees and weep. The savages have sealed my dad's death sentence.

Grief wanes as anger fills the void. I take the remnants of a keyboard and smash it with hateful determination. I am about to destroy a computer monitor when my leg brushes against something soft.

A woman's foot is protruding from under the desk.

I pull her out, whispering a few words of the gospel to guide her to the afterlife.

I recognize her as her eyes slightly open.

"Mrs. Brown! You are alive!" I have known her since kindergarten. Her son, Thomas, goes to my school.

I gently hold her head in my hands and lower my

ear to her face.

"Emergency protocol…Emergency Room."

She points to the wall with a shaky index finger.

But there is no door.

"…behind the wall," Mrs. Brown whispers as she slips in and out of consciousness.

I search for irregularities that could reveal the existence of a secret room, but there are none.

"Mrs. Brown, can you hear me? How do you open the door?"

"Hurry! You are our only hope to survive these monsters."

My head spins, and I have to hold on to the desk to remain standing.

I'm now responsible not only for Dad's life but for our entire colony's survival.

"Please, tell me what to do."

"Help me up."

"You will bleed out."

"I'm way beyond hope. I'm doing this for Thomas."

"Yes, for Thomas…" *And the rest of humanity.*

Mrs. Brown can hardly walk, and I carry most of her weight, occasionally stopping to catch my breath.

"There is a switch under the desk."

The secret door is damaged but opens on command, revealing a small room in immaculate condition with the radio readily available.

"Praise the Seer!"

"Praise…the…Seer. Take me inside."

I sit the woman at the desk across from the radio.

With trembling hands, Mrs. Brown activates the equipment.

"I can't believe the gobblers didn't find it. They have such a good sense of smell."

Mrs. Brown does not respond. Her focus has shifted to making contact. "Citrus, this is Colony Ten…We are under attack!"

But the line is silent.

Mrs. Brown clutches the microphone. "Citrus, please respond!"

"Colony Ten. Citrus is listening."

"We have no power! You must send help immediately," I say, taking over the radio communication. "You must transfer two patients to the Outpost."

"Colony Ten, who attacked you?"

"The gobblers…"

But Mrs. Brown interrupts and says, "The mongrels have launched a rebellion."

As soon as she gets the words out, a piercing noise shakes the floor.

Mrs. Brown grabs my arm so hard it hurts. "Get the hell out, and don't you dare come back."

Sweating with fear, I run out of the Emergency Room and into the Command Center. The loud shriek is coming from the hallway, so I hide under the remnants of a desk.

A few seconds later, the noise stops.

I am about to crawl my way back to Mrs. Brown when I see the silhouette of a man by the entrance.

My shoulders drop as I exhale a deep sigh of relief.

"Come get me, you bastard!"

Mrs. Brown is delirious. I am about to expose myself when the man pounces on the helpless woman.

As he starts to strangle her, the radio voice replies

with a sense of urgency. "Colony Ten, can you hear me?"

"Bitch, what have you done?"

His big nose flares at the sight of the radio.

In the bright light of the Emergency Room, I can observe the man in detail. Although he has the body of a human, his face is quite different. He has a broad forehead that reaches the top of his head, and his eyes are visibly smaller and closer together than those of our kind.

"I ruined…your parade." Mrs. Brown infuriates the creature on purpose. She is giving me a chance for survival.

The odd-looking creature removes his shirt, revealing a robust pair of wings. He snatches Mrs. Brown with one hand and flies out of the Emergency Room.

My limbs have grown roots, and I can't move; all I do is gawk as the mongrel flies in circles, crushing Mrs. Brown viciously against four walls.

"Sullu, stop!" A native—a female—screams at the flying monster.

"I love you, Thomas!" Mrs. Brown expresses her last message for her son.

I pray for the chance to deliver it.

On my hands and knees, I rush to the door with the image of the creature smashing Mrs. Brown to the floor to forever haunt my dreams.

"You shouldn't enjoy killing." The female scolds the creature. "Or have you become what you hate the most?"

I dart to the stairs without a backward glance. After only a few steps, the creature kicks me brutally in the back.

A stabbing pain spreads through my chest. I fly down the stairs, each step hammering a different part of my body.

Eventually, the momentum of the drop ends, and all goes black.

Chapter 3

The air inside the cave smells like goat manure. The place is freezing, and the blanket that covers me is barely enough to keep me warm. I want to tuck my head under the bedspread, but my arms hurt too much to complete this simple task.

"Hello!"

My voice echoes in the crevices of the rock but remains unanswered.

My right eye hardly opens, and the left one is swollen shut. All my three hundred pairs of muscles hurt, particularly my backbone, which stings when I attempt to turn to the side. Regardless of my condition, I am grateful to be alive. The vicious mongrel had intended to kill me, of that I am sure.

Praying does not release me from the pain. The scent of Evil still lingers in my nostrils, and fear creeps over me like a platoon of a thousand ants. Soon, my anxiety becomes too intense, and I shiver, making my muscles hurt even more.

A small candle by the door is enough to light the entire room. I reach out from under the blanket and press my hand flat on the slimy rock to stifle my rising panic. As I rub my hand back and forth on its distinct texture, I feel like I have become a grain of oxygen and silicon in the sea of minerals that shape Tranquility. Astonishingly, a strong sense of belonging overtakes me, and I fall into a deep sleep.

****

When I wake up, my hand is still touching the rock. Although my muscles are sore, the crippling pain has disappeared.

A man and a woman are arguing by the door, and their voices are very much like ours.

"Mom, what have you done? Why did you save the human?"

The cave shakes each time the man speaks, sending chills down my spine.

"I couldn't let her die. I had to help her."

The female begins to weep.

"Mom, don't worry. She won't survive the night, anyway."

"Shhh. The poor girl will hear you."

"I wouldn't bet on it; she is in terrible shape. Now, stay here."

"Can I see her one last time?"

"Mother, there is no point in going through such pain. Giving her false hope does the human no favor."

"Rem, please!"

"Take five minutes. Then I'll finish her up," the man says, stomping away.

After a few seconds of silence, the female takes a few steady steps but falters once she reaches the door.

"Hello? Are you awake?"

I remain silent, pretending to be asleep, but I fear my trembling will give me away.

Once Rem's steps vanish, the female hurries to the cot.

"Can you hear me? You must listen."

The female is my only ally, and it would be a big

mistake to upset her.

"Hello."

"What's your name?"

"Clara."

"Clara, look at me. I won't hurt you."

A beautiful face greets me, but it is quite apparent that the female is not human. Her eyes are unusually dark blue, and her head has a distinctive crest of short and pointy hair.

"Excuse my rudeness, but what are you?"

"Your people call us mongrels."

"Mongrels? I've never heard of your kind."

"That's because your leaders keep us segregated."

The female turns her head toward the door.

"We don't have much time. He's coming."

"Who's coming?"

"Rem, and he's going to kill you."

This time the message carries a sense of indisputable fatality that shakes me all over.

"I'll take you to a place where he won't find you."

"Why are you helping me?"

"I must."

I hurry out of bed.

"I don't know how to thank you."

"Don't bother. You aren't safe yet."

I am limping because of my injured leg, and as I hobble along the dark hallway, my shoe scrapes the floor.

The mongrel, noticing my distressed condition, gets closer to support most of my weight.

I can hardly believe I was doing the same for Mrs. Brown a short while back.

When we come to a fork in the tunnel, the woman

stops briefly to catch her breath. Then she leads me into a much narrower corridor.

The air in this tunnel feels denser and reeks of mold. In some spots, space is so limited that my shoulder rubs against the slimy rock.

"We'll arrive soon. You should be safe in this section of the tunnel. Nobody ever uses it."

A strong hand suddenly grabs my neck and viciously crushes me against the rock. The mongrel has the strength to keep me suspended in the air with only two fingers. I do not bother resisting him. I have no strength to fight.

"Rem, please stop!"

"I warned you. You only had five minutes."

However, Rem unexpectedly eases his deathly grip. As I struggle to catch my breath, he bends and smells my hair.

"It isn't possible!" Rem throws me over his shoulders, my head bumping against the rock. "I need to see her face in the light."

Rem carries me back to the cave where I was held captive and drops me by the flickering candle.

I can barely stand, but I endure it without complaint. The mongrel is enormous, and there is no point in provoking him.

The female keeps getting in the way, but each time, Rem pushes her aside.

"Mom, stop! Please, stay away and let me see the girl."

Overwrought with fear, I keep my head down, my gaze fixed on the floor.

"Look at me!"

Rem's yell echoes menacingly throughout the

small room.

I slowly obey. Rem is exceptionally tall, and it takes some effort to face him.

"This is impossible."

A familiar face looks at me.

"Crap!"

Rem marches out of the room, leaving his mom and me breathless.

The mongrel looks at me with her eyebrows raised high, waiting for me to solve the mystery.

A few seconds pass before I recover enough to disclose the information.

"I met your son when on my way to the Beacon. I thought he was a man."

"Rem is only twenty-five percent mongrel. It would be difficult to notice the difference unless you see his wings."

"She saved my life," Rem intervenes, returning to the room abruptly. Although his demeanor is calm, he still terrifies me.

Rem's mom is quiet, waiting for Rem to explain, but he remains silent, gazing at me with loathing.

I slowly slip closer to his mom.

"Don't move!"

His scream is so loud that it makes me convulse violently.

"Rem, Clara deserves your gratitude."

"Clara? I will have to update the Council."

Rem strides out of the room, leaving me on the verge of collapse. Thankfully, his mom catches me in time.

"Thank you. You are way too kind."

The mongrel seems startled by Rem's behavior.

"Please, tell me what happened between you two."

"Can I sit first?"

Once I am sitting on the cot, the mongrel sits beside me. Comforted by her affectionate demeanor, I share the story of our peculiar encounter.

"I see."

The mongrel walks to the door, rubbing her chin with her hand.

"I don't get it. I thought Rem was dying."

"He was. Rem is alive because of your timely intervention."

"But all I gave him was some water mixed with dirt."

"Yes, and it was all the medicine he needed. Tranquility's soil has healing properties."

"Would the soil have a similar effect on humans?"

"To some degree but never quite as effectively. It is the gobbler's blood with Rem, you see?"

"Could I try some?" Although hopeful, I expect a firm negative response.

"Sure. Should I get some?"

"Yes, ma'am."

"Please, call me Rosh."

"Rosh…Thank you."

As soon as Rosh leaves the room, my mind fills with thoughts of running away. However, I hesitate to leave the room. The tunnels extend too deep inside the mountain, and I might find myself in even worse trouble.

Rosh returns holding a big cup.

Indecision has ruined my only chance of survival. Rem will soon arrive to erase all trace of my existence.

Rosh hands me the cup. The liquid is darker than

the one I had prepared for her son, but I gulp it all at once. The metallic taste activates my gag reflex, but the sensation subsides once I swallow the last drop.

"You should lie down for a while. You are still very weak."

"I'm fine."

"Don't be silly. I'll make sure you are safe."

She walks out of the room but keeps guard by the door. Her rhythmic footsteps soothe me to sleep.

****

The candle has burned out, and the room is in absolute darkness. The drink must have had some potent sedatives. It knocked me out almost instantly.

Fear flutters in my stomach as I poke my head from under the blanket. Rosh has stopped pacing, but the sound of her breathing remains.

"Rosh, are you there?"

The sound of rushed footsteps precedes the appearance of a silhouette by the door.

"I'm so glad you are still here," I say to Rosh, sitting up.

"Someone has to keep an eye on you," Rem barks back at me.

I quickly back up against the rock.

"Mom needed some rest. I promised her I would not harm you."

I remain quiet. The last time I saw Rem, he almost strangled me.

Rem sits in the middle of the cot. Unlike his mom, Rem's closeness makes me very uneasy.

I slide to my left, as far away as possible, but he is still less than a foot away.

"Am I making you uncomfortable?"

When I do not respond, Rem adds, "You were friendlier when you thought I was human."

"It's not because you are a mongrel," I say, fixing my gaze on the rock. "No woman should sit this close to a man."

"Whose rule is that? It sounds stupid."

"It isn't. Your behavior is inappropriate."

"Am I improper? What's so bad about sitting beside you?"

Rem has a valid point. I have never pondered on the reasons behind the rule. I just follow them without hesitation, as everybody else does.

"I don't buy your excuse. Now, be honest. Would you have helped me if you knew I was a mongrel?"

"Certainly not. I would have fled."

"I am guessing honesty is another one of your rules," Rem says condescendingly.

"Of course. Isn't it one of yours?"

"Surprisingly, it is."

Rem stands in a flash and walks to the door.

"I guess we can agree on a few sets of values."

Rem ignores my comment. He turns around and faces the rock.

"After I presented the new evidence to the Council members, they decided to spare your life."

However, saving Rem had not been good enough to set me free. It had only merited life in prison.

"They might as well kill me." I can't imagine surviving a day within these caves. "But truly, why do you hate me?"

"Don't take it personally. The Council is making you pay for all the atrocities your people commit daily."

"What atrocities are you talking about? We are

peaceful people, and our main rule is not to harm others."

"There is no time to educate you. However, you should know that humans are responsible for our existence."

"What do you mean?"

"We must go. Mom convinced the Council to allow you to live under our roof. We must leave before they change their minds."

"Your mom is very generous."

"I tell you one thing: if you ever betray her trust, I'll kill you."

"I've already guessed that much."

As I follow Rem through the tunnels, I feel no pain—the soil has completely healed me.

I am lost in thought when Rem grabs me by the waist and throws me over his shoulders.

"I feel much better. Please, put me down."

"Why should I? Is this against your rules?"

"You know it is."

"Our home, our rules." Rem keeps marching ahead, disregarding my pathetic kicks. "You are way too slow, and I'm done guarding you. A life-for-a-life kind of deal is good enough for me, and I refuse to babysit you from this point forward."

"You must take after your father. You are nothing like your mom."

My kicks will leave no mark on Rem's muscular chest. However, I keep kicking as a protest against his uncivilized behavior.

"I can't say. I never met the bastard. All I can say is that I'm proud of my native origins."

As I hang head down over Rem's shoulders, I

notice his coat is old and has many holes in it. The biggest one instantly catches my attention—something feathery is poking from under the fabric.

I stretch as far as possible to peek through the fabric. I remember Sullu taking off inside the Emergency Room.

"Are those feathers?"

In response, Rem throws me over his opposite shoulder, where there are no holes in the fabric.

I keep pulling at his coat to get closer to the opening, but Rem smacks my butt. Then, with his terrifying voice, he says, "If I were you, I would immediately stop this nonsense."

For the rest of the journey, I hang from his shoulders like a rag doll.

We meet several mongrels along the way, but the most I see of them is their unusually pointy shoes.

After crossing a network of passages for more than ten minutes, my tiny hope of escaping this prison vanishes. The labyrinth is longer than I anticipated, and it would be impossible to find the way out.

We are passing along a more remote section of the tunnel when an explosion shakes the caves.

"What is going on?"

I hold on to Rem's coat so as not to fall.

"Nothing you should care about."

Rem keeps his steady pace, seemingly undisturbed by the blast.

"Are we fighting back? I thought your rebellion had succeeded."

"We had a huge setback," Rem says between his teeth.

"Really? What happened?"

A flicker of hope lights up in my heart.

Rem remains quiet, not willing to discuss the revolution.

"There are zero risks in you telling me. You know I'm not going anywhere."

Rem turns his head to me and says, "Your people managed to call for help."

"Then, did it work? Did Citrus come?"

Rem becomes tense underneath me, and I immediately regret my recklessness. Now nothing will stop him from extinguishing my life.

Chapter 4

"How do you know about Citrus?"

I freeze, shivering from head to toe.

"I asked you a question!"

Still, I do not say a word. If I tell Rem that I am responsible for the call, he will strangle me right away.

Rem grabs my waist and violently sets me on the ground in front of him. Then he shoves me by my shoulders against the rock.

"Do I need to repeat the question?"

Rem's menacing demeanor is apparent even in the dim light of the tunnel. The mongrel will do whatever it takes to get an answer.

"I might have helped a little."

"What do you mean?"

Rem's hand moves dangerously close to my neck.

"I told you I would get help."

I close my eyes and wait for the imminent blow, but a few seconds pass, and nothing happens. When I harness the courage to look up, I find Rem rubbing his chin.

"How did you call Citrus with broken communication equipment?"

"Mrs. Brown had access to an emergency radio, which your friends missed."

"Did any of us see you by the radio?"

"No, Mrs. Brown took the blame before Sullu

killed her."

Rem narrows his eyes to the point that they are hardly visible. Then he says, "Don't you ever tell anyone. If someone finds out you were responsible for contacting Citrus, all of us will be in danger."

"I won't tell, I promise."

Rem pushes me forward, forcing me to trot ahead.

"Who is Citrus?"

"You are kidding me, right?"

"It was yesterday that I learned about its existence."

"Citrus is your Satellite Command Center. Thanks to you, your Council launched a counterattack using resources from neighboring colonies."

We traverse the tunnels in silence until we reach a fancy bronze door.

"This door is beautiful."

Rem shrugs his shoulders and says, "There are only a handful of them in the tunnels. It was a gift to Mom."

"Aren't you proud of your mom?"

"It's not that. I just hate politics, one of our inherited human traits."

Without waiting for a response, Rem leads me inside his home. He signals me to sit on a wooden bench by the door.

My hosts have painted the rocky walls with a bright cream color. The floor remains untouched like every other underground space I have seen in the caves.

The place's monastic atmosphere is only broken by a few colorful pillows placed over the bench and a small red carpet by the entrance door.

"I'm so glad that you are here."

Rosh warmly welcomes me. Then she says,

"Remember, I can only guarantee your safety if you remain inside these walls."

"Understood. Thank you. I appreciate your efforts very much, particularly knowing this situation is troublesome for both of you."

I rest my gaze on Rem, who is bent over the table.

"Don't worry about Rem. He knows he must obey me if he wants to remain in this house," Rosh says, grabbing my hand and leading me to an adjacent chamber. "This will be your room."

"Rosh, you are too kind. I don't want to disrupt anyone's life. I'll sleep on the bench outside."

"Don't be silly. This room is empty. You aren't imposing on anyone."

"Are you sure?"

"Absolutely."

Rosh walks to a small dresser, and after opening one of the drawers, she says, "You can use these clothes if you like; they should fit you perfectly."

"I don't know how to thank you."

Rosh gives me a short but tender embrace. "Please rest. I'll call you when dinner is ready."

I collapse on the bed as soon as Rosh leaves the room.

She had left a large pail of water and a small soap in one of the corners. I touch the water with my finger and find it warm.

Under these dire circumstances, having water to spare must be a luxury for my hosts. My mental state is so delicate that Rosh's thoughtfulness makes me cry.

I take off my dirty clothes and kneel in front of the pail to wash. My body has completely healed. There are no visible bruises, and even the deep cuts on my knees have already mended.

The room is freezing, and my teeth chatter uncontrollably. But the lack of comfort is understandable as heating this labyrinth of tunnels while under a massive artillery attack must be a challenge.

By the time I finish washing my body, I am as cold as an ice cube. I search the drawers for something warm to wear and find an ankle-long dress remarkably similar to mine.

The dress fits perfectly. Although the fabric is a little rough, it immediately warms me without a coat.

I lie in bed and stretch my tired legs. I want to sleep, but there is too much electricity running through my body. Dad's life now lies in the hands of Citrus, and all I can do is pray for the medical vehicle to arrive on time.

Suddenly, my hosts start a heated argument.

"Mom, you shouldn't have offered to look after the girl. How are you going to guard her all day long?"

"That isn't what I have in mind."

"What do you mean? If the girl leaves the house, they'll kill her."

"That won't happen. You are going to keep an eye on her."

"Me? No way!" Rem erupts in angry laugher. "This is your mess. You fix it."

"Clara saved your life, and you will not fight me on this issue."

Rem walks to his room, slamming the door shut.

"You might be big and scary, but I'm still your mother!"

A few minutes later, Rosh knocks on my door.

"Clara, are you awake?"

"Yes."

"Will you join us for dinner?"

"One minute, please."

I am not hungry, but I do not want to offend Rosh, who has been amazingly kind throughout this madness.

Rosh's demeanor changes as soon as she lays eyes on the clothes, becoming gloomy and on the verge of crying.

"Oh, sorry. I'll go change."

I am about to hurry back to the room when Rosh stops me. "Please, stay. I'm glad…the dress fits you."

Rem sits at the table. When he sees me, he rises to his feet and pushes his chair away. "I should go. I lost my appetite."

"Rem, be polite to our guest." Rosh points to the chair.

Rem violently moves the chair to its original position and sits.

Rosh ignores his childish behavior and says, "Clara, tell us about yourself."

"I live in the complex with my parents and my two brothers," I answer, even when I would rather remain as quiet as a mouse.

"Her father is gravely ill," Rem interjects, keeping his gaze fixed on his food.

"Clara, is this true?"

"Your son is right. My dad's illness is the reason why I went to the Beacon and requested a—"

Rem slams his hand on the table and says, "You don't listen, do you?"

"I didn't know your ultimatum of not telling anyone included your mom." I move my chair close to

Rosh for protection. "After all, she was the one who rescued me."

"Don't worry about Rem. He isn't going to hurt you." Rosh waits until Rem calms down to ask, "Are you the one responsible for all this madness?"

"Yes. I did it for Dad and…for him."

"Please, keep me out of your mess."

"Clara, you meant well, but Rem is right. Let this be our secret."

"Yes, ma'am."

"What were your dad's symptoms?" Rem lifts his head from his plate and fixes his gaze on Clara.

"Dad vomited around-the-clock for almost a day before developing a high fever."

"Did his neck hurt too?"

"Yes, and it was as stiff as a log."

"He must have caught *Manachea*." Rosh looks to Rem for confirmation.

"Excuse me?"

"*Manachea* is an illness caused by a local fungus that feeds off the Nema trees. Humans are such idiots!" Rem's nose flares while he drills me with his gaze. He is unwilling to accept that a minor illness has put a halt to the revolution. "There was no need to seek help. Your dad should have recovered with a single dose of soil."

Disregarding Rem's mood, I turn around and face Rosh. "Is that true? Would the powder work on my father?"

"It worked on you, didn't it?" Rosh responds, grabbing my hand in hers.

"Yes, but I wasn't dying."

"They just need to increase the dose." Rem barks at

me, acting as if I am a toddler who knows nothing.

Such a simple solution. Still, my people would never try it. I remember when Rem asked me to pour the powder into the water, and I thought he was delusional.

"Why are you so sad?" Rosh keeps holding my hands tenderly.

"Is there a way to communicate with the outside to inquire about Dad's health?"

"Sorry, Honey. There is no way to contact them."

"Mom must be terrified. First, Dad fell sick, and then I disappeared into thin air. When I left the hospital without telling anyone, Mom must have guessed I left for the Beacon. Now, after all this time without news, she must be assuming the worst." My eyes become watery, so I fixed my gaze on the floor.

"Why don't you write them a letter? We will do our best to deliver it," Rosh hurries to say, tightening her hold on my hand.

"Are you sure? I could send her the soil treatment too."

"Of course."

"Rosh, thank you. You are wonderful."

"I know how your mom must feel. Unfortunately, your people didn't offer the same courtesy when I needed it the most."

I want to make eye contact with Rosh, but she purposely looks away. Rosh is thinking about someone longingly, but she is not ready to open up to me yet.

"Mom, it isn't safe out there." Rem points to the ceiling after an explosion shakes the room.

Rosh hands me a paper and a small pencil. "Take ten minutes to write the note. Rem will deliver it

37

tonight."

"Are you out of your mind?" Rem stares at Rosh with a stern expression.

"Rem will drop it off during his next round."

"Are you sure? I don't want to put your son in harm's way."

"Honey, don't you worry. Rem is a big boy, and he can take care of himself."

"It didn't look that way last night. Is Rem even recov—?"

"Do I look unwell to you?" Rem springs to his feet, smashing his fists on the table.

"Yesterday was out of the ordinary. Don't worry about Rem. He has nine lives, like Earth's cats," Rosh interjects, placing her hand on Rem's chest to keep him away.

Is Rosh telling the truth? I keep quiet; I would much rather not upset Rem even further. I have done my Good Samaritan duty by raising my concerns, but it is up to them to decide if my apprehension is relevant.

I spend half the allotted time wondering what to write. Then, with only five minutes to spare, I hurry to write a goodbye letter. After I spend a few seconds reassuring my family that I am in good health, I write a thorough description of the soil treatment and urge Mom to try it.

Once I finish writing, I fold the paper in half and give it back to Rosh.

"Clara, where should Rem drop it?"

"Could he deliver it to the hospital?" When Rosh nods, I gaze at Rem and add, "Thank you. Your help means a lot."

Rem snatches the letter from Rosh's hand and puts

it in his pocket. He stomps out of the room without finishing his food.

"Don't worry, sweetie. Rem's girlfriend is a nurse, and if your parents are still at the hospital, she'll deliver the letter right away."

"Bless the Seer."

"Sweetie, what did you say?"

"Rosh, thank you."

"You are more than welcome."

I swallow back the tears, not to worry my host. My last twenty-four hours have been terrifying, and I can hardly eat, but I force myself to finish the food just for Rosh's sake.

"Do these vegetables grow in Tranquility?"

The food tastes nothing like ours, which comes from Earth in large cargo transports every month.

"Of course, dear. We don't have the resources to purchase your food. But the variety of vegetables that grows on Tranquility would surprise you, and even if quite different from your diet, they can be tasty."

Rosh offers to teach me how to cook, and I eagerly accept the offer. It appears that I have been living my life in complete ignorance. If I am going to live among the mongrels, I might as well learn about their habits. The natives keep arguing that humans are monsters, and I have no real facts to refute their claim.

"Sweetie, you should rest."

"I would rather wait for Rem to come back."

"Rem has a few errands to run and might not return until morning."

"Honestly, don't you worry about him?"

"There is no point in worrying. Life in Tranquility has always been chaotic. Rem is a big boy, and I trust his judgment."

"I hope you are right. Goodnight. Thank you for keeping me safe."

"Clara, you are a good person. Letting you die would be a terrible loss for all of us."

Chapter 5

I waited for Rem to return but ended up falling asleep. I am so exhausted that it takes an explosion to wake me.

Rosh and Rem are having yet another heated disagreement. Not wanting to get involved, I remain in bed, pondering on the chaotic state of Tranquility.

Tranquility has always been my peaceful haven, and I find the thought of the Followers killing the natives repugnant. I search for reasons not to believe my hosts' accusations. However, I can't deny that the Council has kept us in the dark about the mongrels' existence. Still, my body and soul reject all wrongdoings as, in the end, it would be too painful to accept responsibility for such actions.

At school, teachers barely mention the gobblers. A handful of lectures centered on the natives, but no one discussed them in detail. The message was always the same: the Seer, in his great wisdom, had foreseen the Followers would thrive on Tranquility. Somehow, Marten had predicted the natives would welcome his people.

What were his actual words?

I draw a blank, which is odd, considering the message is plastered all over the school walls as a constant reminder of our good fortune.

Kindred spirits!

I have always dreamed of both cultures living in harmony—us humans in the complex and the gobblers choosing to make the mountains their domain. The natives interact with us daily while performing manual labor around the complex. Their peaceful behavior has always fully supported our narrative.

However, the fact that we have an aerial defense system against them is quite telling. It would explain why the natives never attacked us—all part of the make-believe.

The mere fact we named the natives after animals should have alerted me about our belief in human supremacy. I feel like puking.

Another more-powerful explosive hits the ground, and the room trembles. In a flash, I get up in case we must evacuate the caves. I tiptoe to the door but stop short of opening it. Making no sound, I put my ear against the door.

"Madness has consumed Tranquility. I was right about warning the Council about this outcome. Unfortunately, nobody cared to listen," Rem says in a loud voice.

"There's no point in blaming anyone," Rosh says.

"How did they miss the emergency radio when even a child could find it? You would be outraged if you had seen the corpses dumped by the sidewalks like cockroaches. The rebellion was short-lived. Now, those of us who are lucky enough to survive the counter-offensive will pay for the Council's mistakes for years to come."

"Let's not dwell on what we can't change."

Rem walks to his room in silence and slams the door behind him.

I peek outside the room and find Rosh bent over the kitchen table, her gaze fixed on a map.

"Rosh, are you all right?"

"Yes, don't worry." Rosh avoids my gaze. It is not difficult to guess she is hiding tears.

"I'll return later."

"Please, stay," Rosh says, hugging me tightly. When I return her embrace, she adds, "He suffers dearly."

"Who?"

"Rem hates violence. He even offered the Council peaceful ways to improve our lives."

I had misread Rem, assuming the opposite was the case. It is comforting to learn that we have a few things in common.

Memories return in a flash of the time I had joined a group of students to the ice cream parlor. Owen, the school bully, was part of the group, but I did not mind it much; he usually behaved when in public. Unfortunately, he soon proved me wrong. We were on our way back to school when we crossed paths with an old gobbler. The native was part of the cleaning crew and had stopped to rest.

"Get back to work, you lazy ass!" Owen yelled, kicking the native with contempt.

"Owen, leave him alone!" I urged him to stop.

Owen did not listen. Instead, he kept screaming insults. When the old native did not move, Owen interpreted his lack of cooperation as defiance. He became enraged, punching the poor gobbler incessantly.

I could not remain idle, so I kicked Owen until he released the injured gobbler. Although I succeeded, my volatile reaction still worries me; Owen ended up with blood gushing from his head.

I shake my head to get rid of the unsettling memory. Then I say, "Rosh, is there anything I can do to help?"

"Unfortunately, not a thing."

Rosh signals me to sit at the table.

A feeling of panic spreads through me as I sit on the chair. "Is there something wrong with Dad?"

"The medical transport wasn't able to land yet."

Suddenly, I can hardly breathe. "Is my dad all right?"

"Your dad is alive. Rem's girlfriend was there, and she promised to deliver the letter to your mom."

My father must be putting up a big fight. His survival now hinges on the effectiveness of the soil treatment.

I look away. As the salty taste of teardrops reaches my lips, Rosh hurries to dry them with a cloth.

"You must trust the healing power of Tranquility," Rosh says in a soft tone of voice.

"But what if they don't try it?"

"Don't worry. Rem persuaded his friend to do it." Rosh gives me a little smirk. "The nurse will make sure your father drinks the mix."

I have already experienced Rem's persuasive behavior firsthand. "Did he threaten her?"

"Oh, no." Rosh stops to laugh wholeheartedly. "For some staggering reason, girls find Rem irresistible."

"Really?"

When Rosh notices my skepticism, she says, "Believe me. Rem can be quite a charmer."

I have not seen this side of Rem, and I am

confident I will never witness it, not even if I spend the rest of my life stuck in this house. "I hope you are right."

"Darling, you should sleep. You still look tired."

"But what about the explosions? Aren't you in danger?"

"Our homes are deep inside the mountain. We are safe."

"Is this the first time we attacked you?"

"Of course. It would have been impossible for your authorities to hide something of this magnitude. We never before rebelled against human oppression."

"Why is Rem blaming humans for the mongrels' existence?"

"It is because we came into existence soon after the Followers settled in Tranquility."

According to Rosh, mongrels were the unexpected outcome of humans having intercourse with gobblers.

But the information makes no sense to me; the gobblers look so different from us. Although I try to wrap my head around the idea, I fail.

"I never thought our species could fall in love."

"Honey, the mongrels are the unfortunate outcome of ravish."

"You mean rape? How can gobblers be such monsters?"

"Honey, you got it all wrong. The gobblers' good nature was what made them easy prey for your kind."

"I can't accept it."

"Clara, I wish it wasn't true." Rosh holds my hand tenderly.

Was Rem born out of rape? I am too afraid to ask the question.

"You should go to bed. If the explosions worsen, I'll get you out."

"But what about you?"

"We can't leave these caves. Your people would kill us on the spot."

The mongrels knew about the possible repercussions of the attack. Now that the rebellion has failed, Rosh has already accepted her fate.

My head spins around, and I must sit to avoid collapsing on the floor.

Would I have saved Dad at the expense of so many others?

"Honey, don't fret about us. Your people don't know about these caves' locations, and they are bombing several miles away. Let's hope this information remains a secret." Rosh points to a small bookshelf by the kitchen wall and adds, "Honey, why don't you grab a book?"

I do not want to read, but I approach the bookshelf to make Rosh happy.

There is a thick layer of dust covering the books.

At first glance, I recognize a copy of Marten's doctrines. I have read this book countless times to the point where I know several passages by heart.

"Are these books yours?"

"Rem found them during his rounds. His friend is teaching him how to read."

"I see." My hosts are illiterate. That explains why they would keep such a book.

I continue my review, but they all look unappealing. I am about to go straight to bed when the last book catches my eye. My heart skips a beat when I read the title: The Mongrels.

I keep my back to Rosh while I flip through its pages. The document contains all sorts of confidential information. I put the report under my arm and walk to my room.

"Goodnight, Rosh."

"Goodnight, Clara. Sleep well. There's no danger here."

I hide the report under the mattress for future reading. I try sleeping, but the relentless attack keeps shaking the cave.

The blasts suddenly increase in magnitude and frequency, making the house tremble. Portions of the ceiling occasionally come loose, floating aimlessly around the room before settling on the ground—a visual reminder of the fragility of my situation.

I grab the report, hoping it will put me to sleep. Unfortunately, the information in the document is atrocious and has the opposite effect.

The document looks a lot like a goat report I once read at school. Goats were the only domestic animals versatile enough to adapt to Tranquility's steep terrain and extreme daily temperature fluctuations. Hence, they became our single local source of meat and milk.

"Number of heads under captivity…estimated number of free-ranged heads." Reading the words chosen to describe the mongrels makes me nauseous. Whoever wrote the report lacks empathy for the natives.

I flip through the pages trying to figure out why the Council keeps such a close eye on their population. Soon, I come across a chart presenting some intriguing facts.

The graph represents a comparison of kilowatts

produced by males, females, and even pregnant mongrels. There is even a graph comparing the gobblers' energy output to that of the mongrels—the mongrels' production being twofold higher.

However, there is no indication as to how energy is produced.

I flip back to the cover to read who authored the report. The author's name is in plain sight.

My heart sinks to my stomach, and cold sweat slowly trickles down my spine as I read Dad's name for a second time, A. Fitzgerald.

My grandparents were among the first settlers, and as such, part of the elite. This could have granted Dad access to all sorts of confidential information.

Against my gut feeling, I abandon this train of thought. The possibility of my father being part of this deception is too unsettling, and I discard it as a coincidence. There must be others in the colonies who carry a similar last name. Besides, the 'A' could stand for Adam or Alex, and not Dad's name, Anthony. The author could even be a woman with a name like Anastasia or Anna.

But the existence of this document fully supports my hosts' stand on humans. For my safety, I should never reveal my identity, especially not to Rem. If my family is involved in these atrocities, my last name must be a well-known commodity among the resistance.

From now on, my name is Clara. Just Clara.

Chapter 6

I wake up determined to find a way out before someone figures out my identity.

I kneel by the pail of water to wash my face. A thin layer of ice had formed during the night, but it breaks as soon as I poke it with my finger. The water is cold and instantly refreshes me.

Dinner had been small, and my stomach is gurgling with hunger. As I am about to leave the room to eat, I see the report lying on the floor. I hurry to hide it under the mattress before walking out.

"Rosh?"

The house is quiet, and she is nowhere in sight. I call again, this time a bit louder. "Rosh, are you here?"

My glance at the kitchen countertop fails to reveal something resembling food.

"Can I help you?"

Rem is standing behind me.

"No, thank you."

"Are you hungry?" When I remain silent, Rem adds, "I'll fix you something to eat."

I stand still by the kitchen table, my arms crossed in front of my chest, watching Rem cook breakfast.

"You don't need to fear me."

"I don't," I say, avoiding his gaze.

"Yes, you do. I could smell your fear from a mile away."

"I don't believe you."

"Your stench is particularly strong."

"How is that possible?"

"Having an enhanced sense of smell is one of the perks—or in this case—a huge disadvantage of being mongrel."

"I don't believe you." But then memories of the gobblers using their noses to find me soon come to mind. "I didn't know."

"Of course you didn't."

"No doubt you were blessed with some of our most negative traits, too," I whisper to myself.

Rem's smirk disappears in a flash.

I step backward to increase the distance between us, but Rem reaches forward and holds my hand.

"Don't touch me!"

"Sorry. I forgot all about your 'don't touch' rule." But Rem resumes his cooking without letting go of my hand.

"Clara, you need to chill. The house is too small, and for obvious reasons, it has no windows. The air quality is already bad as it is. This is what we call the Shock Treatment."

"The Shock Treatment?"

"That's right. Trust me. It will benefit all of us."

I keep trying to release my hand from his grip, but Rem does not budge. I eventually stop resisting but extend my arm as much as possible to keep him away.

"You should pay attention to what I'm doing. I won't cook for you tomorrow."

For the next little while, Rem introduces me to a variety of food, none of which can be eaten raw.

"Will you get sick if you don't cook the vegetables

first?"

"No, but they are rubbery and tough to digest unless you boil them first. Only very sturdy vegetables grow on this planet."

Rem cuts a vegetable into small pieces before throwing them into a frying pan. He then adds a white liquid to the mix.

"Is that milk?"

"Yes, we also keep goats."

Rem adds some grains to the pan before placing it over the burning stove. "You must mix the mixture constantly for five minutes. Let it sit for a few minutes before you eat it, or you'll burn your tongue."

"Sure, what is it?"

"It's our kind of porridge. The only type we can afford."

"Thank you for the food." I might not trust Rem, but I appreciate the work they have taken upon themselves for volunteering to host me.

"Regardless of what you might think, we aren't savages."

"I never said you were. I appreciate your hospitality, especially when you are fighting a war on the surface."

Rem stares at me for a while. He must be satisfied with whatever he reads on my expression, because he goes back to the porridge, serving me a few spoonfuls.

"Can you let go of my hand?"

"Nope."

"Do I still smell bad?"

"Awful."

I rush to issue an apology and sit at the table beside him.

Susana Aclan

"If you don't stop staring at me, I'll stink even more."

Rem roars with laughter. Carefully, I look up to see if he has complied with my request, but his eyes are still fixed on me.

"The Shock Treatment, remember?"

It feels awkward eating while being this close to Rem, but I am famished, and my stomach is hurting badly.

Without wasting more time, I swallow a spoonful of the mixture. The porridge texture is rough, but it is still quite tasty, so I quickly eat the entire bowl.

"I'm glad you liked it," Rem says, chuckling aloud. This time, his laughter sounds relaxed, even amicable.

Rem's sudden change in tone surprises me, and I look up. However, as soon as he notices my gaze, he stops laughing and puts his guard up again.

"Heads up, you might get flatulence."

"Excuse me?"

"The cereal causes flatulence until your gut gets used to it."

"You better release my hand before I pass gas, or you will suffer from even worse air quality."

Rem lets out a sudden burst of laughter.

As I witness Rem's hidden personality for the first time, my cheeks burn. Rosh was right; this version of him would drive girls to fall madly in love with him.

Rem has fired his two secret weapons: an entire set of white teeth framed by a beautiful wide smile and his boyish dimples hardly visible from under his untrimmed beard. Rem exudes masculinity.

Feeling butterflies in my stomach, I look away. I have never met someone like him, and my body soon acknowledges it by accelerating my pulse. I wish I could go to my room, but Rem keeps holding my hand.

I desperately think about the Seer, expecting his image to cool me down, but it is a futile exercise; Rem's presence is too powerful.

"I'll never stop reeking."

"Clara, what's wrong?" Rosh asks, returning from her rounds. When she finds Rem laughing like a maniac, she adds, "Rem?"

"Rem is helping me out. He is giving me the Shock Treatment to make my smell go away."

"The Shock Treatment, eh? Rem, is this right?" Rosh creases her forehead as she stares at Rem. "Clara, you don't have to worry. Unlike the gobblers, mongrels don't have an enhanced sense of smell. Rem's ability to detect scents is on par with yours."

"Oops!" Non-apologetically, Rem releases my hand. "It's my turn to leave. I'm glad my babysitting duties are over."

I'm such a foolish child! From now on, I won't trust anything he says.

"Clara, don't feel sad. Even when Rem intended to torture you, his ruse has accomplished the impossible."

"I don't think so. Now I distrust him more than ever."

"Rem's trick backfired. He is now comfortable around you."

"I sure hope so."

Rosh grabs some food and sits beside me. She is immobile, looking at the dish with longing.

"Rosh, what's wrong?"

"Porridge was Yuma's favorite food."

"Yuma?"

"Yuma is my daughter,"

My heart twists in a knot. "Rosh, where is Yuma?"

"I don't know. They took her away two years ago, and I haven't heard from her ever since."

"Rosh, who took her?"

"Your people."

According to Rosh, humans had kidnapped Yuma when returning home after an arduous day of labor. The story sounds too farfetched, and I would not believe it if it came from anyone else but Rosh.

Rosh remembers the moment so vividly that she even shivers when she tells me how she tried to get Yuma's attention, but all her efforts were in vain.

It is easy to imagine Rosh's rasping screams when urging Yuma to escape or to feel her paralyzing fear when the men surrounded her daughter. I tear up when Rosh shares how she desperately ran downhill to help Yuma fight the men. However, by the time she arrived at the scene, her daughter had already been abducted.

"My precious girl was seventeen years old."

With a heavy heart, I give Rosh a big hug. We cry inconsolably for a while.

"We'd hoped Yuma would use the blackout to escape, but after all the bombing, I hope she didn't. It'll kill me if I learn that Yuma ended up dead, her body discarded by the road like those of too many others."

"Rosh, don't you worry. I'm sure Yuma is alive. If I ever leave the caves, I'll do everything in my power to bring her back to you."

"Clara, you are a kind soul. Unfortunately, without knowing her whereabouts, rescuing her is impossible."

****

The explosions continue to be part of the

background noise. Even after twelve hours of straight bombing, the Followers' efforts to exterminate the mongrels have not diminished.

What does Rem do when he leaves the caves? Does he wander around the settlement in search of Yuma?

Suddenly, I panic.

What if Mom is risking her life to find me?

I calm down. Mom has to look after three other people and will not put her life on the line. Plus, I wrote her a note, so she knows I am alive and well.

I return to my room to read the report in case there is some useful information to help my hosts rescue Yuma.

Rosh's openness about the mongrels' condition helps me interpret the data, which otherwise, I would have entirely missed. Terms like 'New Heads' or 'Newly Born' have—all of a sudden—taken a terrifying meaning.

Though the report does not mention sexual abuse, it is the only way to explain the massive number of 'Newly Born' kept in captivity.

For the next little while, I read the report with absolute focus, paying attention to all sorts of details. But when the first review sheds no light on Yuma's whereabouts, I throw the document against the rock wall.

The report lands on one of the last pages, exposing some graphs I entirely overlooked. As I bring the document within my reading range, my heart almost bursts out of my chest. The page includes a chart listing the farms with the number of prisoners housed in each of the establishments.

Is Yuma in one of these farms?

There is no mention of the farms' location anywhere in the report. I close the document and put it aside, facing down. As my gaze rests on the back cover, a huge smile appears on my face—there is a list of six geographical locations.

I rush out of the room, searching for Rosh, but the living room is empty.

"Rosh?"

I walk to the kitchen and call her again.

"What do you want?" Rem growls from his bedroom.

"I need to talk to your mom."

"You need to, or you want to?"

"Please, can you call her?"

"What's the rush? Did you break a nail?"

I ignore his attitude. Rem appears to be moody, and I am not interested in a fight.

"Please, tell Rosh I need to talk to her. I might be your prisoner, but I don't have to put up with your temper."

****

The report is a gold mine, coming alive each time I go through its pages.

Lying on the bed, I can almost picture Yuma—a female version of Rem—resting on this same bed after an exhausting day of work.

She was my age when kidnapped. She must have spent lots of time with her brother. I can now appreciate how Rem must resent humans for abducting his little sister.

I suddenly understand his apprehension when I found him injured on my way to the Beacon.

"I would have behaved similarly," I say, fixing my

eyes on the rock.

Forgiveness fills my heart as I remember how he tried to kill me the first time he saw me in the caves.

"I'll be more patient with him from this point forward."

Chapter 7

Rosh knocks on my door half an hour later.

"Clara, were you looking for me?"

"I'm so glad you are back!"

I rush out of the room and into her arms.

Rosh hugs me back, displaying a sincere smile.

"I might know where to find Yuma."

"Dear, what are you talking about?"

"I might know where we are holding her. Well, at least some possible locations."

Although Rem appears to be minding his business, he turns around in a flash. His nostrils flare in anger as he looks at his mom with raised eyebrows. "Mom, how could you tell the girl about my sister?"

"Clara asked."

"Rem, don't blame your mom. Thanks to the information she shared with me, I understood the data in this book. You inadvertently came across the latest report on the mongrel's population."

"Clara, what do you mean?" Rosh holds my arm with intensity.

"The document I took last night is packed with confidential information. I am confident Yuma was taken to one of the farms listed on the report." As I speak, my mind keeps finding new links and possibilities in the reported data. "We could narrow down the search to a few sites if we only select those locations listing new arrivals."

I purposely avoid the term 'head' even though it is used extensively throughout the document.

"If we put our heads together, it might be possible to reduce the search even further."

"I can't believe we had such a valuable document all along." Rosh's gaze remains fixed on the floor, waiting for the information to sink in. She is not ready to allow a spark of hope to ignite in her heart.

Rem, on the other hand, does not trust a word I say and keeps questioning me aggressively about my ulterior motives.

"Clara, you don't need to explain yourself. We are grateful for your thoughtfulness."

"If you give me more information, I might figure things out. The report is very recent and has incredibly detailed charts." I point to a chart and add, "This one in particular. It shows the number of new arrivals and, most importantly, it states their sexes and estimated ages."

"Are you sure?" Rem is skeptical about the veracity of the information and keeps rubbing his chin.

Ignoring his question, I ask, "When did the Followers take Yuma?"

"It's been almost two years."

Now, Rosh is pacing non-stop across the room.

"Rosh, did you say Yuma was seventeen at the time?"

Rosh stops her pacing and nods nervously.

"Let's have a look." As I look down to check on the report, I notice Rem's gaze fixed on the document. I pity him. Being illiterate has put Rem at a significant disadvantage. For the first time in his life, he finds himself in uncharted waters—having to put his trust in a human.

"Yuma should be under the following three categories: *New Arrivals*, *Females*, and *13-19 years old*."

I check the chart thoroughly for those farms meeting these criteria. Once I find them, I say, "Farms 1 and 4 had reported entries fitting these characteristics."

"Dear, I don't understand…"

"If Yuma is in any of these farms, it would be one of these two."

"Are you sure?"

"Absolutely. These people are meticulous with the data."

"This information is useless when we don't have the location of the farms," Rem says, clenching his jaws.

"But we do!"

Rosh looks at me with watery eyes.

I hold her hand in mine and wait until she absorbs the news before offering a triumphant smile.

I point to the specific spot on the back cover. "They included the farms' locations right here. They can't be too far away from the caves."

"But we don't have a GPS. Your people disabled it." Rem growls before throwing the report on the ground.

"I'm pretty sure the Beacon has one," I respond.

"It would be helpful if the humans hadn't reclaimed it already," Rosh says as the flame of hope extinguishes from her eyes.

"Sorry, I didn't know."

"The report is useless," Rem says, kicking the document farther away.

"Rem, be nice. Clara wants to help."

Instead of apologizing, Rem remains dead silent, staring at me with hateful intensity.

An idea pops into my head, and I share it without delay. "The hospital must have one. They need it to pinpoint the location of all emergency calls."

Rem stares at me with a creased forehead. I am waiting for him to snap at me, but a few seconds later, he says, "Brilliant."

Rosh remains silent, slightly trembling. "I don't want to get my hopes up."

Rem walks to Rosh and embraces her with tenderness. "Mom, don't cry. I'll go to the hospital to find the information."

"Are you leaving with these explosions? Isn't it way too dangerous to venture outside?"

"Clara, are you worried about me?"

"Not really. I am worried about your Mom's well-being if something terrible was to happen to you."

"Mom knows I can take care of myself."

"If you are going to the hospital, do you mind asking about my father?"

"Was this your plan all along? Were you seeking ways to get news from your father?"

"Of course not!" I clench my teeth at the absurd insinuation.

"I'll try to remember."

"Of course, he will. Clara, could you teach Rem how to read?"

Rem rolls his eyes but remains silent. He might be interested in learning to read but not from me.

"Rosh, why don't I teach you instead?"

"No, it would be a waste of your time. I'm too old to learn. On the other hand, my son will be grateful if you teach him. Won't you, Rem?"

"There is no need to teach me. My friend is already working on it."

"Your friend might be teaching you stuff, but it certainly isn't reading."

"Whatever my friend teaches me is none of your darn business." Rem's expression becomes stern.

Rosh collapses in the closest chair, releasing a deep sigh.

"I can't believe we had this information all along."

Everybody remains quiet for the next few minutes.

"Clara, I would love to learn how to read. Will you teach me?" His mom's suffering affects Rem more than he cares to admit.

"I'll be happy to help."

Rem meets my gaze for the first time in a while, and I return it without a hint of hesitation. By the time he finally looks away, his animosity toward me has lifted.

"I'll leave right away," Rem tells his mom.

"Take good care of yourself. Clara is right. I won't survive losing you too."

"I'll be extra careful, I promise."

****

Rem is taking longer than usual to return home, and Rosh is starting to worry about his well-being.

"The Council must have tightened security at the hospital. It's probably taking him longer to enter the building," I say, trying to put Rosh at ease.

"Lidia, his friend, will do everything in her power

to ensure his safety."

"I am sure she will. Still, it might take them some time to get close to the GPS and retrieve the information. Are you sure Lidia will risk her job to help him?"

"Lidia is madly in love with Rem."

Rosh tries to appear strong, but the continuous tapping of her foot against the floor tells a different story.

"Should we fix dinner?"

An explosion shakes the caves, knocking us hard to the ground. Rosh is the first one to react to the impact and check herself for injuries. She turns to me and offers a helping hand.

"Come on, Clara. You must get out right away!"

"Out of the caves?"

"Yes, something is not right."

Rosh holds my hand and pulls me to the door. Before leaving the apartment, she grabs a shawl and ties it around my head.

I pray for the mongrels to ignore me. If they realize I am human, they will kill me with the snap of a finger.

The quiet corridor is now full of mongrels hurrying through the tunnels in no defined direction.

"I've never seen so many of us in this part of the tunnels. The bombs must have destroyed a section of the caves." Rosh pokes me forward nervously. Her usual calmness has disappeared.

The continuous bombing acts as a harsh reminder of our present vulnerability. Panic fills the air, and as we move along the tunnel, the mongrels keep bumping into us like headless chickens.

A much closer explosion soon hits the caves. I

manage to rest against the rock just in time to avoid the fall. Rosh, on the other hand, ends up flat on the rugged floor.

"Do you need help?"

"No, I'm good as new," Rosh lies, trying to fake a smile.

"Which way should we go?"

"This way."

Rosh points to the left when all the mongrels are fleeting in the opposite direction.

"Are you certain?"

"There is a secret way out."

Rosh is limping on her left foot, so I follow her close behind in case she needs my assistance.

"Shouldn't we tell the others?"

"No, dear. We all know that if we leave the caves, your people will kill us."

"Then, why are we going to the exit?"

"Honey, it's only for your sake. Your people won't shoot at you."

"I can't leave you in the caves. You'll die."

"I'll die either way, but you don't have to."

A few minutes later, we are traversing another section of the tunnels where the number of mongrels has diminished to a scattered few.

"We are getting closer to the exit."

Rosh is showing clear signs of exhaustion, so I pull her arm to make her stop. "Do you mind if I take a break?"

The explosions have diminished in both frequency and intensity. Hopefully, our leaders believe they have eliminated all remaining insurgent cells.

Rosh is about to respond when the mother of all

explosions hits the ground above us.

The blast is so powerful that it propels me backward, and I bump my head violently against the rock.

Chapter 8

The dim light of the candles has extinguished, and the caves are now in absolute darkness.

"Rosh?"

I try finding the place where Rosh previously stood with both hands on the rock. However, as I hurriedly step forward, I stumble over a crack on the ground and fall hard on my knees.

I am crawling back to the rock for support when I bump against something soft. "Rosh?"

She is having difficulty breathing. Panicking, I trace her body with my hands and soon realize part of the tunnel has collapsed on her.

I rush to remove the rocks, but I freeze when reaching her belly—a giant boulder is on her hip.

"Can you hear me?"

Beads of sweat are rolling down my temples, and some of the salty droplets are getting in my eyes, intensely irritating them.

"You have...to leave. You must...find the exit before somebody finds you."

"I won't leave you." I wipe my eyes with the cuff of my dress and try to remove the rock.

After several failed attempts, Rosh says, "You must go."

The rock has not budged an inch after two minutes of trying. I stand still for a second to catch my breath.

"Rosh, I'll find help."

"Don't you dare…do something stupid!"

I hurry down the hallway in search of a mongrel.

"Clara! Listen!" Rosh's plea becomes less and less audible until it completely disappears.

I rush down the hallway, but several feet later, I must stop to find my bearings. My surroundings are deadly quiet, and as I stand still with my arms extended in front of my chest for protection, they seem to float amidst the dense and dusty air.

The stillness helps me realize Rosh is right. All my efforts to save her would be futile. If mongrels find me, they will kill me before letting me explain Rosh needs help.

Bye, Rosh.

My eyes water as I look back for an instant. I walk slowly through the semi-collapsed tunnel with my arms spread out, sliding my fingers along both sides of the slimy tunnel to find the opening.

As time goes by, and I am still looking for the exit, my arms and legs become tense, and I begin to fear I will soon get paralyzed.

A few steps ahead, I sense a change in the air. Though unsure of its significance, I hurry my pace until I reach an area of the tunnel where the pungent moldy smell of the caves has dispersed.

Being this close to freedom has a bittersweet taste. I can't wait to reunite with my family, but I feel awful about leaving Rosh in such dire condition. Still, I draw comfort from knowing that staying would have changed nothing.

The rubble suddenly moves, and I freeze.

I am about to flee when a mongrel violently grabs

me. I scream in terror, but only groans come out of my mouth.

"What the hell are you doing here? Did you escape?"

"Rem, is it you?" I throw my arms around his neck, holding on to him with desperation. "I'm so glad I found you!"

Rem does not like my proximity and quickly pushes me away.

"Come! Your mom is in distress," I say, darting to where I have left Rosh.

Rem grabs my coat to stop me from walking away.

"What's going on?"

"A big rock fell on her, and I couldn't help her. You need to hurry!"

Rem's face turns white. He releases his hold and sprints ahead.

"Rem, be careful. There is debris everywhere along the tunnel."

"Don't worry. I can see well enough."

When Rem realizes I can't see at all, he holds my hand and pulls me forward.

This time, Rem's touch does not make me flinch. I very much welcome his proximity as it gives me an immediate sense of safety.

We reach Rosh in seconds.

"Mom, can you hear me?"

"Yes…"

Rem hustles to free Rosh, but the boulder is too heavy.

"Let me help."

I try lifting the rock, but its surface is slippery, and my fingers immediately slide off.

"I'll raise the rock, and you remove Mom from under it."

I doubt I am up to the challenge, but I will try my hardest to free her.

Rem takes a deep breath before bending his knees to grab the boulder. Then, he says, "Now!"

I drag Rosh from her shoulders, but something keeps moving under her shirt, hindering my movements.

"Her wings are getting in the way!"

"I can't hold on to the rock for much longer. Please, work around them."

Seer. Please help.

I squat with my feet spread wide. I then step back while pulling Rosh from her shoulders with all my might. Miraculously, she slides a few inches toward me.

"Clara, keep going," Rem says, exhausted.

I repeat the process several times until I succeed at freeing Rosh from the weight of the rock.

Rosh is unresponsive.

"Mom!" Rem slaps her cheeks a few times to wake her up. "She needs medicine right away."

Rem races back home, holding Rosh in his arms.

I follow the sound of his footsteps until it subsides in the distance. I then slowly retrace my steps back to the house, feeling joyful at the fact that Rem is looking after Rosh.

But my mood suddenly changes when three mongrels appear in the distance. I want to cover my head with the headscarf, but I lost it somewhere along the dark tunnel.

"What the…?" One of the mongrels exclaims when

he notices my presence.

"Is she human?" A second one prompts from behind. "She smells like one."

"What are we going to do with you?" The third mongrel grabs me around the waist and lifts me in the air.

Sullu.

With Mrs. Brown's dreadful memories still fresh in my mind, I stop breathing. There is nothing worse than knowing ahead of time what is coming.

The shortest of the mongrels grabs my hands while the gigantic Sullu keeps me suspended in the air.

As I pray to Marten, a sudden surge of power overwhelms me. I use my strength to stamp my foot on the inguinal area of the shortest native.

He instantly releases my hands to bend over and breathe.

I use my nails as claws to scratch Sullu in the face.

Sullu lets go of me to check his bleeding cheek.

Throughout the attack, the third mongrel had remained apart. Now instead of helping his friends, he starts laughing.

I flee while screaming for help.

Unfortunately, the mongrels recover fast and launch themselves after me.

Sullu reaches me first, grabbing me by the neck and choking me. "Fun is over." Suddenly, Sullu exhales a loud groan.

"Get out of the way!" Rem shoves me to the side.

I duck to my right just in time to avoid a punch. I wait with my back pressed against the rock. The healing energy of the stone comes to my aid and settles around my neck. As the tingling sensation intensifies, the pain from the choking dissipates.

Chaos engulfs the tunnel. The sound of punches precedes loud exhaling grunts in what seems a painful continuum.

In terror, I keep away the thought of the group overpowering Rem and sealing my fate once and for all, repeatedly praying for Rem's protection.

The racket eventually diminishes, giving way to rhythmic thumps—someone is taking an awful beating. A few seconds later, all sounds stop.

With my heart thumping inside my chest, I get ready to throw the first punch. *To the count of three. One, Two…*

"Stop. It is me." Rem stops my hands before I manage to complete the move. "I better teach you how to take someone down. We should get going. These thugs won't stay down forever." Rem pokes me from behind, forcing me to trot. "Stay quiet. I'm quite unfit for another round of beating."

When I enter the house, Rosh is awkwardly lying on the ground by the entrance door.

"Mom forced me to leave her when you screamed," Rem says, right away.

However, Rosh is still unconscious.

Rem must have acted on his own accord.

"Thank you."

"You are still in danger. Sullu knows where you live and will be knocking on our door soon enough."

Rem carries Rosh to her bed.

"How can I help? Where is the medicine?"

"I'll get it. Please, stay with Mom. You seem to calm her down."

I stay by the bed, holding Rosh's hand and stroking

her beautiful black hair. I sing one of our soothing psalms, but I stop upon Rem's return.

"Please, don't stop." Rosh has regained consciousness, and she is looking at me pleadingly.

Although I feel uncomfortable with her request, I comply immediately. Thankfully, Rem chooses to remain silent, abstaining from giving his opinion about my singing skills.

Rosh slowly drinks the medication, and once she has swallowed the last drop, Rem tucks her in.

"Mom, you should sleep." Rem then turns to me and adds, "We should leave."

"Will she recover?"

"Of course, but it will take a few hours."

"I'll come back later." I bend down and kiss Rosh on the forehead.

I follow Rem to the living room and sit on the ground with my back resting against the rock.

"Could I get addicted to this medicine?"

"No, your body is being smart, that's all." Rem sits beside me and adds, "Thank you."

"What else could I do? Your mom is wonderful."

Rem is about to talk, but I put my hand on his chest to stop him.

"You don't need to explain why your mom is so amazing. I already know that she inherited this trait from her gobblers' genes."

"I'm becoming way too predictable," Rem forces a chuckle. "Somehow, I'm starting to believe there is goodness in humans too."

"You better believe it. After all, you are mostly human." My back hurts, so I stretch my arms forward to increase the muscles' exposure to the rock.

"Were you headed for the way out?"

Although Rem might get upset with his mom, I admit to the truth. "Your mom didn't want me to perish inside the caves."

Rem rolls his eyes and shakes his head. "I understand why she panicked. The last explosions did extensive damage to the tunnels."

"What's it like outside?"

"I've never witnessed this much chaos. It was quite dangerous going to the hospital, but it was ten times worse coming back home. Things were so bad that I considered seeking refuge inside a building two blocks away from the hospital. Thankfully, I didn't. It was the first structure that blew up."

"It sounds terrifying."

"I wasn't the only one seeking refuge." For a few seconds, Rem shakes his head as if to erase an awful image. "A bomb hit one of us, incinerating him in an instant."

"How dreadful!" A knot is growing in my throat, and I find it difficult to swallow.

"I was fortunate. The bombs missed me every time, including the one that hit the entrance right after I got in. The explosion was violent. I even lost my hearing for a few minutes." Rem touches his left ear and flinches when he puts some pressure on it. "You couldn't have used that passage out. Many boulders are blocking it."

"Are we buried alive?"

"It is too soon to tell. First, I'll have to assess the condition of the other exits."

To avoid thinking about the possibility of dying of asphyxia, I ask Rem if he found any information on the farms' location.

"My friend helped, and I managed to get both." Rem takes out a map from his pocket and unfolds it.

The old paper is wrinkled and dirty; it has been so excessively used that several sections are now unreadable.

"Those two farms are close together."

"Great news, right?"

"This is the best intel we've got since Yuma disappeared." Rem walks to the kitchen and puts the map in one of the drawers. "Your father is recovering well, by the way."

Happiness fills my heart, and I run to Rem and hug him from behind. But the Seer would not condone touching a member of the opposite sex, not even one of the non-human kind.

I let go immediately.

Rem does not react, but he is visibly uncomfortable.

"The doctors have already transferred your dad to the Outpost, where he is receiving your kind of medicine. Silly of them; all they needed to do was wait for the soil to work."

Chapter 9

I try to remain awake in case Rosh needs me but end up falling asleep bent over the kitchen table.

When I wake up several hours later, a much-recovered Rosh is talking heatedly with her son.

Rem has dark circles around his eyes. He must have spent all this time assessing the damage to the caves.

"Rosh, I'm so glad you are feeling better."

"Almost good as new."

"I was terrified! You were lucky Rem returned at the right moment."

"Clara, why didn't you escape?" Rosh stares at me with both hands resting on her hips.

"But…you were dying."

"Come here." Rosh wraps me in a warm embrace. "Thank you."

Rem ignores our show of affection and focuses his attention on the map. He then says, "Mom, do you think this is doable, or does it sound like a suicide mission? Humans have increased security significantly. They shouldn't have bothered. They have already reduced us to a meager few."

"Under the current circumstances, we'll need to travel by night," Rosh says with a permanent smile tattooed on her face. "It will take a couple of days to get there. We'll have to be extra careful, that's all."

"You can't go!" I interject right away. "Please, let me help. You haven't fully healed. Plus, if I were the one to go, there would be no dan—"

"No! You are looking for another opportunity to escape," Rem shuts me down.

What Rem is inferring is absurd, but I remain quiet. He still intimidates me, and I would not dare contradict him.

"Rem, don't be unfair. Clara has the best intentions at heart."

Rem scrutinizes me from head to toe. He even fixes his gaze on mine to learn the truth behind my offer.

The Followers disapprove of people of the opposite sex staring at each other, regardless of the situation. Although I do not look away, I can feel my cheeks burning.

Rosh is still fragile and must hold on to the table to sit down. "Clara is right. I would only slow you down. Besides, Clara could inquire about Yuma without raising suspicion."

"I'm certain of it. Once we learn where they are keeping Yuma, you can plan a rescue operation."

For the next few minutes, Rem walks back and forth across the room. His feet are stepping on the rock with such force that I wonder if he will leave a trail.

"I don't want a human risking her life for us. I don't want to owe Clara another favor."

"Let's exchange favors then."

"Mom, what are you suggesting?"

"When we rescue Yuma, we'll let Clara go," Rosh responds with a smile.

"But this isn't the reason why I wanted to help…"

"Done, but you must be ready to accept the consequences of this decision," Rem says, gazing at Rosh in the eyes.

I am about to voice my objection when someone knocks on the door. Rosh and Rem look at each other before silently signaling me to hide.

I obey the command in a flash, tiptoeing my way to my room.

"Who is it?" Rosh answers in a calm voice.

"Council member, the Council has a message for you," a male mongrel responds, a bit shaky.

"Can't this wait?"

"I am afraid the issue requires your immediate attention."

Rosh invites the messenger inside the house.

"Council member, the Council has received a complaint against your son."

"A complaint against Rem? That's impossible."

"That's what the Council initially thought, but we still must investigate the matter."

"Don't you have more urgent matters at hand? We are presently under fire."

"More reason to address the issue right away. It concerns the human under your custody."

"What about her?" Rem shouts at the poor mongrel.

"The human escaped, and Rem protected her, hurting two of our own."

"Did those bastards mention they were strangling her?"

The messenger remains silent for a few seconds. When he regains the needed courage to finish his task, he says, "The victims asked for the human's head. They argue she could escape again, putting all of us in danger. You must present her to the Council for judgment. If you choose not to comply with the command, the Council will have no choice but to take serious actions against you."

The extent of Rosh's protection and kindness becomes apparent. Because of me, Rosh might be removed from power, or worse.

I can't allow it. I'll give myself up.

"The Council is expecting the human by noon," the messenger says, hurrying to get out of the house.

There is no point in delaying the inevitable. The messenger might as well take me now.

I rush out of the room and to the entrance. I am about to open the door when Rem holds me back. "Please, let me go. You have already done enough for me."

However, Rem does not comply with my request. Instead, he remains in between me and the door.

"You are not leaving."

"Rosh. I appreciate your help, but the end has come," I beg her while trying to move Rem out of the way.

"There is no rush. All I need is some quiet time. Rem, make sure Clara doesn't do anything stupid." Rosh turns around and secludes herself in her room.

"You should let me go."

"I don't think so." Rem sits on the floor with his back against the door. "Mom will explore all possibilities. If there is a way out, she'll find it."

"I don't want to put you in danger."

"You won't. I promise."

Once again, our gazes meet. This time, I connect

with Rem in ways I have never expected. I experience many new sensations at once to the point where I lose track of time and space.

"I found a solution!" Rosh says, entering the room, radiating joy.

"Are you sure?" Rem stands up, shaking his head as if to break our unexpected connection. "What is it?"

"The Council won't touch Clara if the two of you unite."

"What? Mom, have you lost your mind?"

"It makes perfect sense."

"Rosh, what are you suggesting?" I do not understand the implications of the word 'unite' at all.

"The Council's hands will be tied if the two of you are married."

"I won't do it," Rem says, gaping at Rosh in disbelief.

I remain speechless for a minute, wondering how Rosh could come up with such a foolish solution. When I recover my speech, I say, "I won't do it either."

"I'll set it up right away," Rosh says, disregarding our opinions on this crucial matter.

"Mom, aren't you listening?" Rem grabs his mother from her shoulders and gives her a little shake. "Clara won't do it."

"Clara, this would only be a formality for you. I don't understand what the problem is. After all, Rem is my son, and he'll be a respectful partner until it's time for you to go back home."

It is such a horrible idea! Rem shouldn't marry for the sake of saving my life.

My head spins around, and I can't think straight. Appalled by the suggestion, I hurry to say, "We'll never accept."

"I will. But only for Yuma's sake. Once we rescue her, I'll make sure Clara gets home safe."

"I still won't." I dart to the kitchen and grab a knife from the countertop. "See you in Heaven."

I am about to slit my wrist when Rem throws himself on me. We fall hard on the ground, and Rem easily removes the knife from my grip.

"Seriously? Would you rather die than marry me? Ouch!"

"This isn't a joke." Rosh points her index finger at both of us. She then offers her hand to help me get up. "Clara, promise me you won't do anything stupid. I couldn't bear it."

I remain mute. The latest turn of events has devastated my analytical skills, and I can only hope the effects are only temporary.

"Clara, I need an answer. We don't have too much time."

"All right." I keep gazing at the floor while my teenage dreams of marrying my soul mate crumble.

"Good girl! We have less than an hour to get things done," Rosh says, rushing out the door.

A wave of coldness runs through me as my heart breaks into pieces.

Rem collapses on a chair like a sack of potatoes. He remains immobile, with his gaze fixed on the rock.

It's time to grow up. I should be grateful. If things turn out well, I'll return home to my family.

"Rem, sorry."

"Don't be. This arrangement is only temporary." Rem can say it aloud, but he is suffering more than he cares to admit.

"What about your friend?"

"I will explain, and she'll understand."

"Of course, she will. If she knew me, she would understand."

"What do you mean?" Rem turns around with a frown.

"Come on! One look at me, and she'll know the Council forced you into the marriage."

"Ah…I see what you mean." Rem returns his gaze to the rock.

"Don't feel sad. No harm will result from this agreement," I say before heading back to my room to sulk.

My life changes at such speed that it feels like I am free-falling from the sky. Still, there is no point in dreading the marriage when there is no other feasible option.

I shake my head forcefully to get rid of all negative thoughts.

I might be falling, but I haven't hit the ground yet. The arrangement is better than death, and I must focus on the end goal, going back home.

"You should get dressed. The union will take place soon," Rem says from the other side of the door.

I hurry to check the drawers for a cute dress. Regardless of the circumstances, my hosts deserve a clean set of clothes. One garment catches my eye; it is colorful and fancier than the others. I take the outfit out and admire it for a few seconds. I am about to put it back in the drawer when Rosh returns.

"Rensei, the couple will be here shortly," Rosh says before knocking on my door. "Clara, are you ready?"

"One minute, please."

With no time to spare, I wear the dress. Although the garment fits comfortably, it is tight-fitting and against our dress code.

I walk to the group feeling inappropriate. When I finally look up, Rosh's eyes are watery and puffy.

"You look astonishing! I am glad it fits you. Yuma never got to wear it." Rosh dries the corner of her eyes with her fingers. She then introduces me to the visitor.

"Rensei, this is Clara, my future daughter-in-law."

Rensei stares at me with his eyes wide open—Rosh had forgotten to mention the bride was a human when soliciting the ceremony.

My worries about the inappropriateness of my wedding gown banish at the sight of Rem bare-chested. The intricate wooden medallion hanging from his neck acts like a magnet, and I can't look away.

"Good morning." Rensei salutes Rem with a frown.

Rem welcomes Rensei with a quick movement of his head.

"Rem, are you ready to start the ceremony?" Rensei chooses to state his concern this time around.

"Yes, you can go ahead," Rem responds with a cold tone of voice.

"Clara?"

Chapter 10

Time momentarily stands still. The room is dead quiet, and everybody present seems to be holding their breath. I slowly step forward and agree with the tiniest movement of my head.

Rosh exhales a deep sigh. She then stands behind me and whispers, "Repeat what I tell you."

Rensei waits until both of us are facing him to commence the ceremony. He grabs my right hand and places it on Rem's open palm.

"Universe, please embrace the love of this young couple."

Rem holds my wrists and pulls me to him, forcing me to change position. Once I face him, he lets go of my wrists to hold my hands in his.

I remain immobile, with my eyes fixed on the floor. After a minute of silence, I look up to check what is wrong.

"Better," Rem says with a quasi-smile when our gazes meet for the first time. He then adds, "With these hands, I welcome you into my life."

"In your hands, I place my heart," Rosh whispers in my ear.

My legs tremble as I repeat the words.

To my surprise, Rem holds me in his arms and lifts me in the air like a feather. He then sits on a chair Rensei has placed behind him and carefully lays me on his lap.

I am so shocked by his closeness that my shivers stop, and I am left petrified like a statue. The mongrels' ceremonies are nothing like ours, which are solemn and with no touching of any sort.

"Within these arms, I'll keep you safe." Rem tightens his arms around me—a clear sign of affection.

Although I know this is all a pretense for Rensei's sake, my shivers return overwhelmingly.

"Sweet Clara," Rosh consoles me from behind. Soon after, she whispers my next vows.

My words are barely audible when I repeat them. "From now on, we are one soul. Wherever you go, I'll follow."

"Within the warmth of these wings, I'll keep you and promise to be yours forever," Rem proclaims, displaying a beautiful set of jet-black wings.

All I can do is gape at the lustrous feathers that surround me like a cocoon. "They are beautiful."

Rem opens the enclosure and looks at me intensely. Then he says, "Love will flow your way until we turn into ashes."

Rem spreads his wings to their full length before flapping them at an incredible speed to produce the most touching melody.

I sit straight on his lap, marveling at the display of eternal affection. When my eyes flood with tears, I cover them. Without visual distraction, I feel powerful energy striking my heart. Shocked by the phenomenon, I open my eyes.

Rem has already stopped his physical display and is now staring at me with a big frown.

Scared of the surge of emotions I am experiencing

for Rem, I jump from his arms and fall hard on the floor.

Rem remains quiet but extends his hand to help me up.

Rensei looks at us for a few seconds, stunned. He then concludes the ceremony by saying, "The love we witnessed will guide your life until the universe reclaims it."

With watery eyes, Rosh gives me a quick but tender hug. "We must go."

"Right now?"

Rosh repeatedly nods before adding, "Rensei, thank you."

The three of us hurry out the door, leaving Rensei to wonder what the heck is going on.

I am still shaking from the incredibly moving ritual, so I follow Rosh like a five-year-old.

We walk through the tunnels in silence until we reach a large metal door.

"Clara, please remain silent unless they talk to you," Rosh says before knocking on the door. "Council, can we come in?"

"Please, do," a solemn voice responds from inside the room.

A large number of mongrels have gathered for the occasion. As soon as the group notices me, they stare with distrust, rushing to hide some of the documents.

"Council member, are you here to deliver the human?"

"No, Council Leader. I am here to tell you that turning this woman in is impossible."

Her response causes an immediate stir among the Council members. "Are you choosing to defy the

Council's order?"

"Not at all," Rosh says calmly.

"Skrish, we can't comply with the order, as doing so would be against our Natural Law," Rem says, speaking up for the first time. He then grabs my hand and holds it against his chest.

The gesture must have a distinctive meaning among mongrels because all Council members gasp in horror.

"It can't be true," Skrish says, unwilling to accept Rem's words.

"Witness it for yourself," Rem replies in a calm manner.

Skrish approaches us, and without a fair warning, puts his hand on my chest. He then places his other hand on Rem's torso.

After a few seconds, Skrish's mouth drops wide open. He clenches his teeth when he says, "The union is truthful."

Rem releases a soft sigh as soon as Skrish returns to the group to initiate a lengthy discussion.

I look at Rosh, and she seems calm. Still, I spend the next five minutes praying for her knowledge of the Code to be accurate.

The mongrels' discussion eventually concludes, and Skrish breaks the silence.

"This situation is unprecedented. But even when this type of union is unspecified under the Code, Natural Law is clearly against harming a truthful union."

"Then, do we have your blessing?" Rem interjects right away.

"You do."

"Has the Council rescinded the woman's house arrest?" Rosh follows up with hope.

"The human is only allowed to leave the house when accompanied by her new family."

"Such decision is not reflective of the Code's Compassion Law," Rosh refutes the verdict.

"Unfortunately, we are at war with the humans, and warfare rules override all others."

"Understood. What about granting Clara the Pass? She will only use it for protection within the tunnels."

The Council seems appalled by the idea but reconsiders the request for a little while. Skrish approaches a table set by the back wall and takes an object from the top drawer.

When he returns, he ties a leather string around my neck.

I look down and find a wooden medallion that is identical to the one Rem has hanging from his neck.

"If you value your life, never take it off." Skrish's warning resonates in the room.

Rosh bows to the group and leaves the room. Rem follows suit, respectfully bowing to the Council before dragging me out behind him.

Once we are alone in the tunnel, Rosh says, "We were fortunate. The outcome could have gone either way."

"What? Are you telling me my surviving odds were fifty-fifty? You certainly fooled me."

Rosh turns to me, filled with joy. "I'm happy it all turned out well in the end."

Rem is dead silent. When he realizes we are still holding hands, he abruptly lets go of me. Then he says, "I'll go scout for an exit."

Rosh says, "Let's go home."

But without Rem's protection, memories of my recent encounter with the mongrels return. Frightened down to the sole of my shoes, I hold on to Rosh with both hands.

"Dear, there is no need to worry. As long as you carry the Pass, nobody will dare touch you."

"What is the Pass?"

"For us, carrying the medallion is an honor, as the Council only grants it under special circumstances. For you, it's an official defense order. Whoever carries the Pass is under the protection of the Council."

"Why didn't they challenge the fake marriage? More so, what did the man mean by ours being a truthful union?"

"Skrish is a powerful man. Nobody will question his command."

I am about to ask for clarification when several mongrels approach us.

The natives' stance changes into attack mode once they realize I am human.

I immediately duck behind Rosh for protection.

But when the mongrels get close enough to observe the Pass, they abruptly halt to step aside and let us walk by them.

I stop breathing until we are twenty feet away from the crowd.

"You see?" Rosh is as calm as the water inside the bucket.

I nod silently.

"Still, you better stay inside our home unless one of us is with you."

"No problem." *I am not wandering these corridors*

alone—it is a wooden medallion, after all.

"It's been a vexing morning. Why don't you rest for a while?"

Obediently, I return to my room. Within the solitude, all the accumulated feelings burst like fireworks. For the first time since the marriage idea came up, my union's implications dawn on me, and I crumble into pieces. I cover my face with the pillow, to bitterly weep until I am left emotionless.

****

When I wake up from my nap, a few blissful seconds pass before I remember I am not at home with my family. However, I panic as soon as reality hits—I am not only living in the company of mongrels, but I am married to one of them.

Still, it would be unfair to blame Rem. Our union was the only available option, and Rem is dreading the marriage as much as I am.

"Clara, are you awake?" Rosh softly knocks on the door.

"Yes."

"Can you join us? Rem found an exit."

I dress in a hurry and join the duo.

When Rosh sees me, she points at a location on the map. "Your people are poorly patrolling this area."

"We should leave tonight. Are you still willing to continue as planned?" Rem keeps his eyes fixed on the map.

"Of course."

"Then, you must eat well before you leave," Rosh says, walking to the kitchen to fix us dinner.

"Clara, you should get ready. Remember, we'll be out for a few days." Rem holds my arm to stop me from walking away. "Please, grab this bag. Bring the minimum. We will be sprinting for long periods."

Rem does not need to explain himself. The gobblers had chased me before.

When I return, Rosh has already set the table. She has gone out of her way to prepare the most nutritious food she could manage on such short notice.

"First, we will visit Farm 1," Rem says when we finish dinner. He puts his finger on a bend on the Sukku river and adds, "If we want to make it to this point before daylight, we must leave now."

Rem stares at me from head to toe with a deep frown. He already doubts my fitness to tackle such a feat. "Can you handle it?"

My cheeks burn under his scrutiny.

"Clara will manage fine. You'll see," Rosh interjects on my behalf. With a somber look, she adds, "You should head out."

It is hard to depart from Rosh's loving company to face an uncertain future, but it must be done. The only reason why I am still alive is that I promised to help them find Yuma.

Rem is already waiting by the door; he is used to these expeditions and has become quite good at goodbyes.

"Hopefully, I won't slow you down."

Rem's nose flares, but he refrains from complaining about my lack of confidence. He turns to his mom and says, "I'll rescue Yuma. I promise."

"Can I get a hug?"

"Come here." Rosh extends her arms wide, and I take immediate refuge. "Rem, take good care of Clara."

My voice cracks when I say, "I'll never forget your

kindness. Sorry for all the pain we've caused you."

"Honey, don't be silly. None of this is your fault."

I try holding it together, but as soon as Rosh tightens her embrace, I sob quietly.

"Remember, you are part of this family now."

Covering my face with both hands, I hurry out the door.

Rem bends down to tie his shoelaces for the longest time.

I face the rock and wail so much that I keep drying my eyes with my sleeve.

When I regain some self-control, I say, "Thank you. We can leave now."

Chapter 11

Rem and I spend the next ten minutes trotting through tunnels to get to the exit. Even with the Pass hidden under my coat, none of the mongrels have shown signs of aggression. Rem's menacing demeanor is deterrent enough to keep them away.

"We are almost there. It's around the corner," Rem says, breaking the silence.

A boisterous group of mongrels suddenly turns the corner.

I immediately duck behind Rem and grab his coat to make sure he will not disappear.

"Human candy," one of the mongrels says, grabbing my jacket.

"Touch her again, and you'll regret it," Rem interjects, shoving him against the rock.

For the next few seconds, time inside the cave stands still.

Rem assumes a defensive stance and gets ready to strike at the slightest provocation.

As tension builds amongst the group, I decide to intervene before it all goes to Hell. Opening the coat in a hurry, I expose the Pass to the large crowd.

However, everybody keeps looking at Rem, completely ignoring me.

"Excuse me."

Still, nobody listens. The cave becomes eerily

quiet, and all I can hear is the loud flaring of nostrils as they prepare to fight.

"Excuse me!"

This time, the entire group turns around.

When I have everyone's undivided attention, I raise the medallion in front of their noses and dangle it in the air.

One by one, the mongrels step aside until our path is clear. Then, I stroll by them.

Rem follows me without issuing a word. Once we reach the exit, he removes the wooden panel covering it and lets me pass first. He then follows me into the darkness.

"You didn't have to intervene. I had it under control."

"Are you sure? Besides, time was of the essence, and we were wasting lots of it."

Rem clenches his jaws but remains silent. Then he hurries downhill.

The night is pitch black, and it is raining heavily. At least the bombing has stopped, and there are no signs of humans.

When did I start dreading my kind?

I commence the descent, always surveying my surroundings for incoming gobblers. I accelerate my speed to follow Rem tightly, but the task proves challenging since the bombing has devastated the terrain.

Ten minutes later, I feel disheartened. Rem is way ahead, and I will soon lose him.

I speed up my descent but shortly after, I end up stumbling and falling downhill

Alerted by the commotion, Rem turns around,

clenching his fists. He is already rushing back when the shrieking of gobblers shatters the silence.

"They heard you."

The sound becomes stronger as seconds pass. With my heart beating like a drum, I turn around and press my back against his. I comb the area desperately, looking for a place to hide, but there is none.

"Don't move." Rem points at the flock that is approaching from the east.

"They are too many for us."

But when the creatures get close enough to notice Rem, they reduce the speed and circle the area from a safe distance.

"They are youngsters. They fear me."

Time stops while the gobblers weigh their options. Rem and I remain immobile, ready to defend ourselves from an attack.

When the gobblers initiate a strike, Rem emits a terrifying roar. In an instant, the flock flees and disappears in the distance.

"How did you do that?"

"Not a good time to educate you. The youngsters will return with reinforcements."

"I'm ready when you are." Without waiting for a response, I sprint ahead of Rem. If the gobblers return, they will not find me anywhere close.

Rem follows my lead for a while. Eventually, he gets tired of my pace and sprints ahead.

I follow him closely until my legs twitch with exhaustion. Eventually, I must stop to recover my breathing. Then, bent forward, and with my hands resting on my knees, I inhale deeply for over a minute.

However, when I am ready to resume the run, Rem

has disappeared.

****

After more than thirty minutes of chasing a ghost, I fear I have lost Rem forever. By now, my sprinting has turned into a slow trot, and I am in desperate need of respite. Plus, something is poking my left foot, and I can't stand it any longer. I sit on the frozen ground and take off my shoe. A small pebble falls to the ground when I turn it upside down.

Gobblers suddenly screech in the distance. With trembling hands, I hurry to put my shoe back on. Though nothing is amiss, the rumble keeps getting louder with every second that passes. I dart ahead, praying to Marten for refuge.

The large flock that is approaching from the north has already spotted me. Terror spreads through me as the group circles above me, vigorously flapping their enormous wings before leisurely landing a few feet away.

The frightened youngsters have returned with reinforcements. Now, even the smallest one in the group appears full of confidence.

A lump grows in my throat when one of them gets so close that his hairy body almost touches mine.

They take turns shoving me around in a playful attitude until the interaction escalates into violence, leaving no doubt of their end goal.

I pray for my death to be quick.

A massive gobbler suddenly propels me forward, and I am crushed hard to the ground.

Two youngsters hold my arms and press my back against the soil. I frantically kick them, trying to get them off me, but a few others join in the attack and completely restrain me.

The natives are staring at me with hatred, so I keep my eyes fixed on their large foreheads and their peculiar crowns of puffy hair.

"Please, let me go!"

The youngsters keep pinning me down but are having second thoughts about going ahead with the killing.

When my gaze rests on the natives' feet, my stomach clenches. They have four long and thick digits that end in corkscrews like nails—the perfect weapon.

Suddenly, one of the grownups lands on my legs. The gobbler is humongous, and his weight is unbearable.

I shut my eyes, not to look at his terrifying face. An agonizing exhale escapes my mouth each time the gobbler jumps up and down.

However, the pressure stops all of a sudden when an unsettling shriek echoes in the night.

Rem is standing over me—legs spread apart—and the gobbler lies dead a foot away.

The rest of the gobblers are not retreating. The more seasoned males have already recovered from the initial surprise and are closing on Rem.

"Rem, leave. Save yourself. Remember Rosh!"

Our gazes meet for a split second before Rem takes off, grabbing a gobbler in each hand.

A handful of gobblers take off after Rem. Amidst the chaos, the youngsters release me for a moment, and I spring to a standing position to look up in the sky.

The flock of natives is flying too fast, making it impossible to distinguish which one is Rem.

The youngsters soon return their attention to me,

and I hurry to assume a protective posture. With my legs spread apart, and my arms in front of my chest, I get ready to punch whoever dares touch me again.

When the youngsters start closing the gap between us, I bounce back and forth rhythmically.

The youngsters look at each other and erupt in the weirdest of wails.

Are they laughing at me?

My pathetic movements are distracting the youngsters from the attack. But my actions' originality wears off pretty soon, and the group resumes its synchronized approach.

Rem returns when the youngsters are about to seize me. He grabs me in his arms and removes me from danger without even touching the ground.

Rem glides over the terrain until he finds a safe place where to set me down.

"Hide in the rock," He instructs as soon as we touch down.

"Are you leaving me again?"

"I killed the grown-ups. I must now kill the rest, or they will keep hunting us."

Rem's facial expression speaks volumes about his displeasure with what he is about to do. Still, he is determined to kill them to protect me.

The rock is twenty feet wide by nine feet tall and has no visible openings. "Where do you want me to hide?"

But Rem is already gone.

I walk to the rock and soon understand what Rem meant. The rock has a large vertical fissure, which extends from top to bottom. Although it is narrow, I fit perfectly.

Rain pours down on my head from the opening above. However, I remain motionless as the rock itself, waiting for Rem to return.

****

After an hour of stillness, I can't feel my toes. Although the rain has stopped, the wind has picked up, and it is bitterly cold.

I wiggle my toes until blood finds its way back to my extremities. I then move slowly to the edge of the rock to find a more suitable shelter before daylight.

When I am about one foot away from the edge, something moves. With fear gripping my throat, I move one inch at a time. As danger draws near, I freeze and hold my breath.

I soon recognize the familiar cadence of Rem's tired footsteps and quickly exit the fissure.

Rem is in terrible shape. He has gashes all over his body, and blood keeps pouring from a few large wounds.

"Let's go. We must seek refuge before the drones are out."

"Lean on me," I say, hurrying to put my arm around his waist.

Rem must feel terrible because he obeys right away. He points at the nearest hill and says, "There's a cave in there."

"How do you know?"

"I've been there before."

Rem is in no shape to walk uphill, so I put aside my exhaustion and support a considerable portion of his weight.

We shuffle our way up the mountain, occasionally stopping to catch our breaths.

"Sorry," I say during one of the stops.

"What for?" Rem's eyes widen slightly.

"I'm too weak. You wouldn't be in such terrible shape if it weren't for me."

"It's not your fault."

Rem is being kind. But he can't ease the pain I feel each time I look at his precarious condition. When tears blur my vision, I look away. I hold him tight and continue the challenging ascent to the cave.

By the time we reach the entrance, Trappist is already rising.

Rem collapses on the floor as soon as we are safe inside. "Stay close. It will get cold, and we can't start a fire."

"No fire?" My drenched clothes are dripping water on the damp rock.

"It's too big of a risk. The drones will detect the slightest of anomalies."

By the time I sit on the ground, Rem is already asleep. I instantly flash back to the time we first met. Rem's condition is pretty similar to the one he was in on that dreadful night.

The contact with the rock will eventually heal him, but we do not have that kind of time.

Did he bring some soil? Rem seems to be a creature of habit, so he must have some in his pocket.

Hesitantly, I place the tip of my fingers inside his pocket. There is something inside, but I can't reach it. As I try fitting my hand farther in, the movement awakens him.

Rem reacts swiftly, grabbing me by my shoulders and pinning me down against the cold rock. Without regaining full awareness, he lands on top of me, restraining my neck with his forearm.

"It's me, Clara!"

Rem keeps his eyes closed when he frees my neck. "Why is your hand inside my pocket?"

"I was grabbing the powder. What other reason would I have to put my hand in your pockets?"

"The soil is in the other pocket." Rem grins.

Immediately, I remove my fingers and offer my open palm. "Give me the medication."

Without getting off me, Rem removes the small pouch and places it in my hand.

"I must get water," I say, hoping Rem will move, but he does not. "Please, get off me."

"I am good right here." Immediately after, Rem places his head on my chest and goes to sleep.

For the next few minutes, I remain immobile. Rem is sleeping peacefully, and it would be sinful to wake him up. Plus, Rem is too heavy for me to push him away.

Rem's closeness soon stirs new sensations, and my heart rate accelerates to an uncomfortable level.

It takes a single glance at the blood dripping from his back to obliterate those sinful sensations and focus my attention on treating his injuries.

I open the pouch and sprinkle some of the gray powder over the open wound on his forehead. I carefully massage the area until his skin has absorbed all the traces of mineral.

I gently use the same procedure to treat Rem's face, shoulders, and arms.

Rem occasionally reacts with moans, but he never opens his eyes.

Once I treat all the injuries, I unwind for a while.

Chapter 12

Several hours later, I find myself lying on top of Rem and surrounded by black feathers.

When I hurry to get off him, Rem turns to the side, and I end up with my back against his naked torso.

The slow and rhythmic movements of his chest make me uneasy, but I tolerate it. I would rather not wake him after such an ordeal. I remain motionless in the shelter of his arms and the warmth of his beautiful feathers. It takes seconds for my body to mimic his breathing. Like the slow cadence of a tranquil ocean, our chests expand and contract in rhythmic bliss.

****

Rem jerks suddenly; he is having a nightmare.

I remain quiet, waiting for the movements to subside, but the opposite happens. Rem screams in agony.

The shouts are too loud and could put us at risk, so I hurry to shake Rem's shoulders. His shouting persists until I slap him hard on the cheek. Instantly, I pull away to put some distance between us.

"You were having nightmares," I apologize when he opens his eyes.

"Was I?" Rem rubs his cheek momentarily. After using his fingers to comb the unruly strand of hair covering his eyes, he adds, "What did you do to my injuries?"

"I administered the medication topically."

"They are almost invisible." Rem traces the minute scars on his arm.

I hurry to push him away.

"Does my proximity still bother you?" Rem does not let go of me.

"Yes. You barely have any clothes on."

"It didn't seem to bother you last night."

"How do you know? You were deeply asleep."

"Why are you so uncomfortable?" Rem puts both hands around my waist.

"It's not proper, and the Seer wouldn't approve of it."

"Why?"

I do not appreciate where the conversation is heading, as I do not have a good reason to give him.

"It shouldn't bother you. After all, we are united." Rem shows no intention of letting go.

"Not under my faith."

All this time, I have avoided Rem's curious eyes, but he is now grabbing my chin and forcing me to meet his gaze.

"Clara."

Slowly, I look up. At first, the intimacy of the moment feels exceptionally uncomfortable. However, an indescribable sense of peace soon spreads through me. I recognize the emotion right away. I experienced it once during our wedding ceremony.

"Better?"

"Much better."

Soon after, I do the unthinkable—I plant a kiss on his cheek.

"Clara, you are overstepping your boundaries,"

Rem says, arching his eyebrows and sticking his tongue out, pretending to hate it.

Playfully and completely out of character, we engage in a fleeting game: I give Rem pecks on the cheek, and he arches his back and pushes me away. However, our playfulness turns into a different kind of game when Rem, rather than pushing me away, kisses me on the lips.

I am so surprised by his actions that I let myself enjoy his wet and round lips for a brief moment. I soon regain some decorum and sit up rapidly.

"Thank you for looking after me last night." Rem sits up beside me, stretching his arms in all directions.

"I hardly did anything."

"Look. My wounds have almost disappeared."

"Incredible."

I trace the almost unnoticeable scars on his face.

"They looked awful last night."

"Your technique proved to be very effective." Rem fixes his gaze on the ground and adds, "I'm sorry I left you behind."

"It's all right."

"No, it wasn't. I should have known you couldn't keep up. After all, you are human."

"My disadvantage became very apparent last night. Regardless, you came back." Fascinated, I keep tracing the scar on his forehead.

"I must."

"You must. Why?"

"You are my wife." Rem walks away to get some water from his bag.

"We didn't make it to the river's bend, but we are close. If everything goes well tonight, we might reach

Farm 1 before dawn."

"Why don't we fly there?"

"The gobblers would detect us right away. Their tracking ability increases exponentially with airborne objects. Plus, it will be hard to fight them while carrying you."

For Rem, I am more of a liability than an asset. With luck, I will prove useful once we arrive at the farms.

"Are there many gobblers in the area ahead of us?"

"I don't know. Gobblers are nomads. But there are many different tribes in this territory, and some have become quite aggressive."

"Is your kind organized in tribes too?"

"No, the Council is our centralized governing body. But all our progress vanished after the rebellion. Now, all we can do is hide like cockroaches."

"The loss of mongrels is terrible for our planet," I say, feeling awful.

Although it is too early to evaluate mongrels' footprint on Tranquility, there is one undeniable truth: mongrels can be valuable hybrids.

"You might be humans' best legacy."

Rem looks at me with intensity. Once he realizes I am speaking my mind truthfully, he chuckles. "You might be right."

Rem takes some food out of his backpack and gives me half the ration.

Famished, I hurry to take the first bite. The food's gritty consistency forces me to cough it out right away.

Rem laughs aloud and hands me a bottle. "Here, have some water."

I take a sip, but it does not help much to get the

food down my throat.

"Take all the water you need. We are close to the river, and we can refill the bottle later."

I eat the remainder of the ration in silence. Although the texture of the food is quite unappealing, it fills me with energy.

"Is your coat still wet?"

"Just a little."

Rem extends his hand and waits until I give him the coat. He then flies out of the cave to return a few seconds later.

"The coat is drying in a safe spot."

"What happened to your clothes? Aren't you cold?"

"We don't need them. We use clothes to hide our wings from humans."

"Can I touch them?" I shyly point to his feathers.

"No, they aren't toys." But Rem soon extends one wing in my direction. "If you insist."

Very carefully, I touch the small feathers poking out from the end of his wing.

"They are incredibly soft!" The richness of their texture marvels me to no end.

With the tip of my fingers, I keep tracing the rest of the feathers until I reach the largest of the bunch.

"Why is this feather so different from the rest?"

"That one is the most important of them all."

"It is beautiful!"

"It isn't about beauty but about power. We call it the Pathfinder. This feather leads the others during the flight."

"What happens if the Pathfinder falls off?"

"We can lift off, but once airborne, we spin around

and crash to the ground."

"So, you can't fly."

"Correct. It is the method your people use to control us. They cut the Pathfinders right off."

"That's horrible!"

"I couldn't agree with you more."

"The report talks about the energy we harvest from the natives. After seeing the intensity with which you fly, I presume this is where the energy comes from, right?"

"Exactly. But most of the energy is produced at take-off. Unlike us, who use goats' feces as energy, humans have figured out a cheap way to harness our kinetic energy. Your people learned the Ancient Ones…"

"The Ancient Ones?"

"Sorry, I forgot you call them gobblers. The gobblers can't stop rebelling against captivity. It's in their genes."

"So, they keep lifting off?"

"They are an eternal source of energy. Well, not quite. Humans keep them in such horrendous conditions that exhaustion eventually kills them."

"But what about your kind? Did you inherit this trait?"

"A few of us did. However, most of us only comply because you coerce us into co-operating by threatening to kill us or, even worse, to harm our families."

"That's appalling!" I still can't believe we are acting in such a manner.

Our people fled Earth to be free from oppression. But it appears that as soon as we landed on this planet, we found a twisted justification to treat the natives as lesser beings.

"You are right, but your people aren't conflicted about it." Rem's deep resentment is palpable in his tone of voice.

"Considering how the mongrels and gobblers have reacted to me, I must accept your words as truth. Still, I choose to believe that not all humans are bad."

"All I know is that you are different." Rem comes close and holds my hand. He then tenderly caresses my long hair and says, "Hold on tight."

Rem takes me in his arms and flies out of the cave. After a short glide, he lands on a nearby cliff.

Trappist is about to set, decorating the horizon in vibrant orange.

"Stunning!" I have never seen Trappist set from such high ground. "Isn't it dangerous to be outside?"

"Drones stop patrolling at this time of the day."

"Beautiful!" Rem's black hair reflects Trappist's fading rays in unique shades of orange that look like burning coal. A sudden wave of shyness overtakes me.

"Please, don't look away." Rem lifts my chin with his index finger. "Let me take you all in."

We gaze at each other for an unforgettable but futile moment. There is no denying our connection is strengthening, and for a split moment, Rem's ceremonial vows resonate in my mind.

Love will flow your way until we turn into ashes.

Chapter 13

"Do you need to rest?" Rem asks after hours of exhausting trekking.

"Five minutes?" Although the terrain is less irregular than what we traversed yesterday, I am already feeling drained. I point at myself and say, "Human, remember? I can't keep up with your pace. I wish I had your endurance, but I don't."

"Is this a human disadvantage, or is it a Clara thing?"

I laugh at his joke wholeheartedly.

"If we maintain this speed, we'll reach the target earlier than predicted." For once, Rem sounds optimistic.

I am about to respond when the sound of gunshots fills the air.

Humans!

Almost instantly, Rem grabs his left shoulder in pain. Still, he reacts swiftly, pushing me to the ground.

After instructing me to keep quiet, Rem lifts off the ground and disappears into the dark sky.

I stay flat on the ground, fearful for Rem. Although he is tough, he is no match for guns.

When I raise my head to survey the area, darkness is all there is. I am about to rest my head on the ground when a series of discharges shatter the silence. Almost instantly, a crashing sound is followed by an almost unnoticeable shaking of the ground.

Rem!

I rise to my feet to search for Rem. However, I do not know which way to go. I walk in a circle and slowly increase its circumference to cover the entire terrain. But when I find him, I stop dead cold—he is not alone.

I remain hidden while Rem lies on the ground, immobile, and three men in camouflage clothes keep poking him with their guns to figure out if he is dead or alive.

"Do you think the mongrel...was alone?" The youngest man stutters while aiming the gun at the sky. The weapon appears to be burning his hands.

"Let's finish him off and head back to the farm," a gray-haired man answers after kicking Rem in the legs.

The third guard, the biggest one in the group, remains quiet, but he soon puts his gun on Rem's head and gets ready to pull the trigger.

"Help!" I yell in desperation to distract him from shooting.

In unison, the men turn around and point their guns at my head.

The potent headlights momentarily blind me, and I remain still, staring at the light with trembling lips. By the time my eyes adjust to the light, the men have already lowered their weapons.

"Come here. We will protect you." The youngest man seems genuinely concerned about my safety.

But the older men terrify me. Unlike the hateful look in the natives' eyes, these eyes are filled with lust. Still, my mind dismisses the fact as a misunderstanding. After all, these are Followers and should have my best interest at heart.

I walk forward until I am three feet away from the men. Then I say, "I'm so glad you got him. Still, I fear there might be others."

"Don't worry. You are safe with us." The big guy uses his rifle to point at the stars on his uniform. "But why is such a lovely lady roaming this land in the dark?"

"I was heading to Farm 1 when my car broke down," I burst out the first lie that comes to mind. "If you point me in the right direction, I'll be forever grateful."

However, the guards are not interested in my misfortune. The gray-haired man gives me a disgusting glance and says, "There is no rush. Let's first get to know each other."

Rem is immobile, and I can't perceive even the slightest movement on his chest. Still, I can't leave him. Against my gut feeling, I keep moving forward.

"That's nice. Keep coming closer."

The men are thrilled with my co-operation. They throw their rifles over their shoulders, assuming Rem is already dead.

The young man appears uncomfortable with how the other two are behaving but chooses to keep quiet.

"Can you spare some water?"

"Have some of mine." The young man passes me his canister.

"Thank you." But I purposely failed to grab it.

The container rolls on the ground until it stops a foot away from Rem.

As I hurry to retrieve it, my heart sinks to my stomach. There is too much blood splattered around Rem.

When I become blind with tears, I almost step on the canister.

"Let me grab it." The young man offers his help.

"No worries. I'll do it."

This time, when I kneel to grab the canister, Rem moves his thumb.

My heart fills with happiness, and I exhale a deep sigh. However, a violent shove soon serves as a quick reminder of the dangerous men that surround me. Offering no resistance, I fall flat on the ground.

The men hurry to immobilize me against the frozen soil. The presence of evil is palpable in the air. I had hoped Marten's teachings would prevail, but once again, my faith in humanity betrayed me.

I somehow release my hands and punch the big guy in the face. The man lets go of my legs as blood drips from his nose.

Amid the chaos, Rem stops playing dead to smash the gray-haired man against a pointy rock, killing him instantly. He then holds the young guard in the air, twisting his neck with a snap. However, when he turns around to deal with the remaining man, he instantly freezes—the guard is already pointing the gun at him.

"No!" I kick the gun when the guard opens fire.

The bullet brushes Rem's arm.

I yank the gun from the guard, but he instantly knocks me to the ground.

My failed attempt gives Rem enough time to pounce on the guard and smash his head with the water container.

Rem holds my hand to help me up.

"I thought you were dead."

"You shouldn't have come. It was reckless."

"It was amazing, right? I've never done anything quite like it."

"Don't you ever do that again," Rem says, pointing at me with his index finger. "Next time, you run."

"Are you asking me to leave you behind?"

"That's right."

"I could never do such a thing."

"You must. Promise me!"

"Sorry. But I can't." Suddenly, I notice a stream of blood dripping from his shoulder. "You are bleeding."

Rem turns around to show me a second gunshot wound on his back. "I need to rest for a while."

Rem holds me in his arms and takes off. A few minutes later, he lands on a ledge protruding from a cliff.

"Are you sure this is safe?"

The small protrusion barely fits my legs.

"Of course," Rem says, helping me rest my back against the rock.

I hurry to treat his injuries. Each bullet has left an exit wound, and all I need to do is fill them with soil. When I finish the treatment, I say, "There are no gobblers."

"The humans must have scared them away. How are you feeling?"

"I'm fine," I say, but I am freezing. I jam my hands into my armpits to keep warm.

Rem wraps his arm around me, covering me with his wings. "Better?"

Within the coziness of Rem's cocoon, I try to make sense of humans' terrible deeds. In the end, I accept reality. Humans are flawed, and all I can do is prove I am different.

****

When Rem recovers, we continue our journey. But rather than traversing on the surface, Rem leads me to a cave that connects with a deep underground cavern.

Once we are at a safe distance from the entrance, Rem grabs some stuff from his sachet and lights up a torch. He then says, "It has taken the river over hundreds of thousands of years to carve out this passage."

"Is it safe?"

"It should be."

I am not too keen on following Rem. For starters, he does not sound too convincing. Plus, the passage is very narrow, and the ground is damp and slippery. Still, I choose to follow his lead.

After my third stumble, Rem holds my hand and pulls me forward.

"What is that noise?"

The cavern might be empty of gobblers, but it is not quiet.

"All kinds of creatures."

"Should I worry?"

Small heads are popping from all sorts of holes in the rock, their eyes turning a blazing yellow color as they reflect the light of the torch.

"There are lots of them."

"But they are quiet."

"So?"

"It means there are no gobblers around. These creatures dislike them so much that they shriek when they see one."

"What about the mongrels?"

"They don't seem to mind us. Humans, I wasn't

sure what they would do."

I look at Rem in disbelief. "Now you're telling me."

For the next twenty minutes, I follow Rem, holding his hand like a toddler.

As the tunnel's pungent smell gives way to fresh air, I dash to the opening. "Thank you, Seer."

Rem collapses by the hole. "Why do you always say that?"

"What are you talking about?" I sit beside him.

"You always thank your Seer. Why?" Rem looks at me with a frown.

"Because he is our religious leader and overseer of our fate."

"Religious leader?"

"We follow his scriptures. All settlers adhere to his beliefs. Do you believe in a god?"

"A god?"

"God, the creator and ruler of the universe."

Rem considers my question for a while. "Not really. The gobblers believe everyone in this universe is a small piece of the grand puzzle—all equally important in the grand scheme of things. I like this concept."

Thinking of all the atrocities humans had committed in the name of God makes me want to puke. The religious persecution against Followers is only one of the multiple examples of discrimination and violence based on faith.

How many other humans have become planetary wanderers since the Followers left Earth? Would humans behave any better if there were no religions? They would have one less excuse to fight, one less reason to feel superior to those who don't share the same beliefs.

Rem disrupts my philosophical contemplation soon enough. "You did well. Farm 1 is only twenty minutes away. Rest. You have less than an hour to recover."

Even the thought of walking hurts my feet. "What time is it?"

"It's almost dawn. Once the sun is up, the gobblers will be hiding from the drones."

"Should I worry about the drones?"

All settlers are used to the drones as we use them within the complex for various purposes, none of which are life-threatening.

"Drones detect movement and can accurately identify gobblers. They aren't as precise with the mongrels, mostly with those with high human prevalence in their genes."

"Which means…"

"When in doubt, the machines are programmed to take pictures and wait until human operators decide. In your case, they'll soon acknowledge you are one of them and will leave you alone."

"The process seems prone to errors. But what happens if they determine they've found a mongrel?"

"Before the rebellion, humans would capture the young mongrels, leaving the old ones alone. They are now taking no chances, killing us all on the spot."

Now, the thought of walking to the farm scares me to death. For the first time in my life, I am experiencing the fear mongrels face every single day of their existence.

Being human fills me with shame. The Followers have settled on Tranquility and opened Pandora's box.

Does Dad know about these carnages?

The mere thought terrifies me to no end. Desperately, I hope against all the odds that Dad knows nothing. But deep in my heart, I know I am naïve.

I reflect on a talk Dad and I had on the same day I had kicked Owen to defend the old gobbler.

"Clara, what's wrong?"

I had expressed my frustration and rushed to give Dad a detailed recount of Owen's despicable behavior.

"Next time, don't intervene," Dad responded.

"But why?"

"Life isn't as simple as you think. You'll understand once we explain some things to you."

"What do you need to explain? Why can't you tell me now?"

"You'll know once you turn eighteen," Dad had said, concluding the discussion.

Yep, he knows.

Chapter 14

"Everything will be just fine," I repeat Rem's words to keep my negative thoughts under control.

For the past hour, I have kept my eyes on the sky for fear of drones, and my hands hurt from keeping them clenched in fists. I pause momentarily to shake my hands, hoping it will stop the pain. I even wiggle my fingers to stimulate circulation.

Did I miss a turn?

The flat and barren surface is devoid of buildings. The occasional small sand twisters are the only visual distraction. I resume my steady walk, feeling disheartened. But the silhouette of a building soon appears on the horizon.

The initial excitement wears off half an hour later. No matter how fast I walk, the distance to the building seems to remain unaltered. I am about to dart ahead when a drone appears on the skyline.

Knowing humans would not react to it, I keep calm even when the machine reaches a frightening speed. When the drone is about three feet away, it decelerates and hovers above my head.

I feel beads of sweat building up on my upper lip, but I maintain my relaxed walk.

Rather than leave, the drone gets closer, making strange noises.

Is this stupid machine taking pictures?

I glance at the machine and see a four stamped on its bottom.

I'm heading to the wrong Farm.

Large drops of cold sweat are now rolling down my forehead. Still, I pretend to be unaffected by the scrutiny.

Thankfully, the drone soon makes the weirdest of noises and steers away.

When the small flying saucer is out of sight, I drop to the ground to process the fact that I am way off target.

It takes me a few minutes to decide to continue to Farm 4. The authorities already know I am coming. If I do not show up, they will send another drone to check what is wrong.

Without further interruption, I soon reach the farm. However, as I stand three feet away from the seemingly unguarded gate, I am at a loss.

"Good morning." Two guards suddenly appear by the entrance. "Can we help you?"

"Hi, there. I came to collect some information."

My words are a huge gamble. I do not know if people come to the farm to gather the information in the annual report. With my hands clenched in fists, I pray to be right.

"Who sent you? Did you get here on foot?" The suspicious guards check the area for a vehicle.

The rebellion has put everyone on high alert, and I am starting to doubt the guards will let me in.

"Yes. My transport broke down, and I walked out here for almost an hour."

"We need to see some identification first," one of the guards says, extending his hand to me.

But I have no papers to give him, so I say, "My father couldn't make it. He is still in convalescence."

"Madam, what's your name?" The guard is now pointing his gun at me.

"My name is Clara Fitzgerald."

The guard hurries to lower his rifle. He then opens the gate and says, "We didn't know you were Mr. Fitzgerald's daughter. Please, come in."

"Thank you." I try to appear serene, but the thought of my father being a well-known visitor to the farm appalls me.

It could be another Fitzgerald.

I choose to concentrate on my visit's purpose, finding out if we are holding Yuma in this institution.

One of the guards gestures me to follow him.

"You don't need to walk me in," I say with a nervous grin.

"I must punch in the code," the guard says, avoiding my gaze.

I check the building for additional openings, but there are none. The main door is the only way inside the prison.

The guard walks to a sophisticated security panel and punches the password code.

I memorize the long sequence of numbers through the corner of my eye and then repeat it a dozen times to ingrain it in my brain.

The guard directs me to a body scanner and says, "Standard procedure."

"Is this a new scanner?"

"Not really. But this machine can detect the slightest percentage of gobbler's blood."

"Interesting." It seems that my last name has

granted me access to all sorts of information.

As I walk through the three-foot-long machine, the guard instructs me to stop. "Turn to your right and remain still."

I slowly obey his command.

"You are good to go."

The guard takes me to a room full of people, where he stops in front of a smiling middle-aged woman.

"Minnie, please provide Miss Fitzgerald with all the information she needs," the guard says before returning to his duties.

"Good morning!" Minnie hurries to shake my hand. "It's such a pleasure to make your acquaintance."

"The pleasure is mine."

"Is your father recovering well? We heard he's been sick."

My heart sinks into the abysm of certainty. Still, I appear serene when I say, "Absolutely! He just needs to rest for a few more weeks."

"What a huge relief. How can I help you?"

"Dad sent me to collect this year's information."

"This early in the year? It's been less than six months since your father honored us with his visit."

"I know. Due to the uprising, the Council needs updated information."

"That explains it." Satisfied with my answer, Minnie leaves the desk to compile the requested information.

I look around the busy room, wondering if people are wary of my presence, but everyone is minding their business. Not knowing what else to do, I grab a pen from the desk and fiddle with it until Minnie returns, carrying a handful of books.

The books are thick. It will take forever to review them all.

When Minnie notices my panicked face, she says, "Don't worry. I have classified the information by month."

"Unfortunately, I must also review last year's information. The Council found some discrepancies that must be confirmed."

Minnie returns to her desk to fret about the possibility of being responsible for a clerical error, and I sit at an empty desk and bury my nose in the books.

****

After hours of flipping through the pages, I finally find a chart with the number of captured females and their estimated ages. The graph confirms what I had already read in the report; Farm 4 holds two entries meeting our criteria.

I write down both numbers on a small piece of paper before spending the next half hour recording the information I have supposedly come to collect.

"I'm done," I say to Minnie, who is diligently entering data on the computer.

"Got all you needed?"

"Almost everything. All that's left to do is to confirm the sex of two of your entries."

"What's the problem?"

"It's probably a data-entry error. Last year's report mentioned one captured female, and your books are showing two."

Minnie opens her eyes wide.

"Don't worry. I'm almost certain the report is wrong. Still, I must personally verify the entries."

"Do you have their numbers?" Minnie sits back on

her desk to check her database.

"Certainly." I rush to read the numbers aloud.

"The first entry was axed."

"Axed?"

"Terminated," Minnie clarifies for my benefit. "The entry died."

A knot grows in my throat, and I can hardly swallow. I still manage to say, "What about the second entry?"

"It appears to be on the premises. Peter will take you."

The way Minnie talks about the mongrels fills me with anger, and I must stop myself from screaming at her for being so uncaring.

Minnie calls Peter on the phone, urging him to come at once.

Less than a minute later, a young man is standing in front of us.

"Peter, you must take Miss Fitzgerald to confirm one of our entries," Minnie says, hurrying to hand him a paper.

"Right away." Peter turns around and bows to me. "This way, please."

Peter moves around the farm with ease. "I don't recall seeing you at school."

"I'm not from around here. The authorities recruited me from Harmony."

After Peter enters the code for another third time, I say, "Is the entry too far? I am glad the facility is well-protected."

"Security is paramount within these walls. Unlike the other farms, which had jailbreaks during the blackout, nobody escaped from Farm 4. We have a huge backup generator."

"Very reassuring."

But, for once, I am hopeful. Peter has been using the same code to open all doors.

"Way over the top. We need to memorize a new password each day."

"What?"

"As I said, nobody makes it out of here alive."

"How do you manage to do such a thing? It sounds complicated."

"The password is changed at sunrise. We have a pretty well-oiled communication system to pass the new code around."

I pray for Yuma not to be here. Nothing could be worse than knowing where she is and not being able to get her out.

Chapter 15

"The entry you are looking for is in the next wing. Why do you need to see her?" Unlike Minnie, Peter refers to the mongrel with respect.

"I found a small disparity in the report, and it needs further verification."

"Beware of the smell."

"What smell?"

The first draft of pungent air hits me, and I instantly gag.

Peter grins at my strong reaction.

The odor is unbearable—a mix of decomposing feces, urine, and blood. I lift the collar of my dress and bury my nose under it to reduce my exposure to the supersaturated air.

I hate covering my nose when we are the monsters forcing the mongrels to live under these dire conditions. But unless I do it, the pungent smell will force me out of the room without completing the task.

"Is this your first time?"

"How can you do this job?" My hands curl into fists, and I must stop myself from punching Peter in the face.

"My parents died a few years ago, and now it's up to me to take care of my two younger sisters."

"Can you at least do something to help them?"

"I do the only thing in my power. I'm kind to

them." Peter's beautiful gray eyes denote a deep affliction.

Peter waits until I regain some self-control to lead the way.

A stabbing pain spreads in my chest when I see the room. The pungent smell fits it like a glove. A staggering number of metal cages are distributed along a central corridor and are packed with emaciated mongrels. Their blood is splattered all over the room, making it look like one of those medieval dungeons I have seen in my history books.

"She is not too far away," Peter says a few feet later. He points in both directions and adds, "We keep the females to our right and the males to our left."

"Seriously?" My eyes twitch with anger. "There is no point in stating the obvious."

"You would be surprised at the number of guards who can't tell them apart. It's quite shocking."

"You are kidding me, right?"

"Unfortunately, no."

Most of the mongrels are in a standing position. As I walk by them, some are moaning in pain while others are suffering in silence. The few who are lying on the soiled concrete floor look already dead.

Peter recoils after every moan. "This group has just finished its shift. They've been working eight hours straight."

The old mongrels scream in fear and move to the opposite extreme of the cages when they see us. However, the youngsters seem to acknowledge that the guard is Peter and remain undisturbed.

"Are they supposed to sleep inside these cages?" The mongrels are fragile because they are isolated from the rock.

Peter points to his right. "Entry 4523." He then positions himself in front of the mongrels, obstructing my view.

"You can trust me. I mean no harm." Grabbing his arm with a sense of urgency, I add, "I must confirm it's her."

With a movement of his eyes, Peter signals the presence of a security camera. It is registering our every move.

By the time Peter walks away, the females inside the cage have already moved to the rear.

"I'm not going to hurt you. Do you mind coming closer?"

None of the mongrels obey.

I step forward to take a better look. The natives are facing the back wall, and all I see are their lacerated wings. "Can you help?"

"Only if you ax her."

"Excuse me? Do you want me to kill her?"

"Relax! That's not what I meant." Peter takes a few steps backward. "If you tell Minnie Yuma is dead, she'll believe you."

My heart skips a beat. "What did you call her? Praise the Seer! Yuma, you are alive!"

"Promise me," Peter says, gazing at me with intensity.

I immediately write her death down in my notebook.

"Done!" I then look at the females and add, "Yuma, please step forward."

Peter nods his head, giving Yuma the go-ahead to comply with my request.

My eyes water as one of the females approaches.

Yuma's eyes are a beautiful light-blue color. Even under these appalling conditions, her beauty stands out.

"I'm so glad I found you!"

"Do I know you?" Yuma stops two feet away.

"May I talk to her in private?"

Peter looks at Yuma, waiting for her consent to step aside.

Instead, Yuma says, "Peter won't talk."

I drop the pen on the floor and kneel in front of the cage to grab it. "Rem is coming for you."

Without waiting for a response, I walk away.

Peter follows me in silence until we exit the room. He then asks, "Who are you?"

"Someone who cares about Yuma."

"How can I help?" Peter is ready to get on board.

"It's better if you don't get involved."

"What's the plan?"

"I have no idea. But we'll figure something out by tonight."

"Tonight?"

"Yep, before you change the security code again."

As we return to the office, Peter finds a silent way to point out the security cameras' locations. This knowledge will prove invaluable during our rescue mission.

"Safe trip back home," Peter says, vowing to me when we are back in the office.

I shake Peter's hand firmly, hoping he will read gratitude in my gesture.

"Were you able to confirm the data?" Minnie probes as soon as I enter the office.

"I did. The data was correct, but the timing was

Susana Aclan

terrible. I found it deceased. Can you imagine? It was still a bit warm."

I emphasize the word 'it' to make Minnie believe I share her views on the mongrels. It works.

"Do you want me to ax it?

"Most certainly. You want to keep your immaculate record-keeping."

At the sound of the word 'immaculate' being used to describe her work, Minnie forgets all about the mongrel's death and engages in a self-praising monologue.

I am about to leave when Minnie says, "Do you need transportation? They told me you arrived on foot."

"It won't be necessary. After spending all this time among those animals, I'm in desperate need of fresh air."

According to the map, the complex is an hour-walk away. Minnie has no reason to doubt my words. After all, walking is Tranquility's primary means of transportation.

"I know what you mean. Those creatures are repulsive."

I refrain from screaming back at her. My efforts would be pointless. Minnie has no empathy for the natives.

"Until the next time." I extend my hand to her, and she energetically shakes it.

"Lovely to meet you!"

I remain silent.

"Please, send my regards to your father!" Minnie adds as I walk away.

Still, I do not respond.

I find my way out of the building, discreetly

128

checking for security cameras. Once I am outside, the guards hurry to open the gate.

Without stopping to say goodbye, I anxiously exit the compound.

As I traverse the vast emptiness in search of Rem, I take deep breaths—my lame attempt to get rid of malevolence.

However, as soon as I check the time, chills run down my spine. Completing the mission has taken much longer than I anticipated. With less than an hour of daylight to spare, I hustle to the prearranged meeting point.

The news of Yuma being alive will fill my hosts with joy. Still, anguish has taken hold of my heart, repelling happiness like oil and water. My childhood beliefs have collapsed to the ground like a house of cards, and I painfully surrender to reality. My repressed emotions eventually overflow, and I inconsolably cry.

I continue my journey unaltered until the sound of a drone reaches me from a distance. I hurry to dry my cheeks before it passes me by. But the machine slows down and circles above my head.

Not again. Why aren't you leaving me alone?

The authorities can't allow something terrible to happen to Mr. Fitzgerald's daughter.

Upset with the disruption, I stop my walk to face the camera. I then force a big smile while shooing the drone away until it returns to the farm.

Trappist is about to set, and with the distraction, I lost my bearings.

The drones will soon stop surveying the area, and it will be a matter of minutes until the gobblers find me. I suppress a shiver and race ahead.

****

By the time darkness fills the space around me, I collapse with exhaustion. A few seconds later, I try standing, but my legs keep twitching with fatigue. I am about to crawl my way to the nearest rock when the ground shakes—someone landed behind me.

My heart leaps to my throat, and I can't move. On my hands and knees, I keep staring in the opposite direction.

"You are roaming way past Farm 1."

"Rem?" Relief swells through me, and I instantly relax.

I am about to express my happiness when Rem signals me to remain quiet. He grabs me by the waist and flies me to a nearby cave.

"I am so happy you found me."

"Are you sure? It looked like you were fleeing."

"Me? No! I got lost and ended up in Farm 4."

Rem's forehead creases, and his eyes narrow until they almost disappear. "I thought you were not coming back."

"Why wouldn't I? You knew the guards wouldn't hurt me." I play dumb.

It is only natural for Rem to distrust me. No human has ever stuck around to honor the end of a bargain.

I can't take offense at his reservations. "Yuma is alive. I saw her."

Rem stops blinking for a minute.

With a lump growing in my throat, I hold his hand.

In response, Rem hugs me tight. Trembling in my arms, he says, "How is she?"

"We must get her out tonight. I memorized the security code, but they'll change it tomorrow morning."

I say nothing about his sister's emaciated condition. Instead, I spend the next half hour describing the farm's security protocol and equipment.

Rem listens attentively, stopping me whenever he needs further clarification. When the flow of information stops coming, he asks, "How did you manage to remember all this?"

"I have a great memorizing system. Do you think it's enough to get in?"

The corners of Rem's mouth turn up. "It's much more than I expected."

Rem's enthusiasm is energizing.

"When are we leaving?"

"I appreciate all you've done, but you aren't coming."

"What do you mean?"

"It's way too dangerous."

"You need me," I say, grabbing Rem's arm.

"You have already done enough. I'll take it from here."

"You won't manage without the code."

"You'll give it to me."

"No, I won't. And you won't succeed without it." I tighten my grip around his arm to transmit a sense of urgency. "Please, let me help. Yuma can't spend another day on the farm."

Our gazes interlock for the next little while. Rem flinches as if he has witnessed Hell itself.

"They won't harm me. I'm sure of it."

Rem lifts an eyebrow and glares at me.

My family name will protect me better than a shield, but I can't tell him. Now, more than ever, my identity must remain a secret.

Chapter 16

"We'll fly from here," Rem says, breaking the silence after an hour of trekking.

"What about the gobblers?"

"We're too close to the farm. They won't make an appearance." Rem lifts off without further discussion.

In less than five minutes, he lands a hundred feet away from the gate. He leaves me in the dark to disable the guards. He has sworn he will not harm them, but I doubt he will keep his promise.

A few minutes later, the gate opens, and Rem greets me.

The two guards are tied up by the entrance door, unharmed.

Rem has been deactivating security equipment since Yuma was kidnapped. He speeds ahead and disables the entrance security camera in seconds. He then gives me the go-ahead to punch in the security code.

I hurriedly enter the long sequence of numbers, but the door does not open.

"I thought you knew the passcode," Rem says after my second—equally unsuccessful—attempt.

I take a deep breath and vigorously shake my arms before punching in the numbers for the third time. Luckily, the door opens wide.

The hall is empty, and the corridor leading to

Minnie's office is dark. Still, I am confident there are plenty of guards protecting the facility.

We walk into the building through a small gap between the body scanner and the wall to avoid detection. As we head straight to where the prisoners are caged, I keep pointing at the security cameras for Rem to disable. Our pace is slow but keeps us safe, at least until the guards decide to check what is wrong with the security system.

I am about to draw Rem's attention to yet another camera when he shushes me. Someone is approaching at a swift pace.

As Rem gets ready to fight, I punch the security code on a nearby door. The door opens right away, revealing a storage chamber. I signal Rem to follow me inside.

As a response, Rem grabs me from behind and whooshes me inside the small room.

The place is full of empty containers, and there is hardly any room to stand.

I stay in Rem's arms, waiting for danger to pass. My head rests on Rem's chest. As the footsteps get close, I concentrate on his heart's rhythmic beating, and pretty soon, it is the only sound I hear. Eventually, the footsteps fade away, and we resume our methodic approach.

The moment we stop by the door, which separates Rem from his beloved sister, I place my hand on his chest. "Brace yourself. The conditions inside are despicable."

Rem quietly waits for me to remove my hand and to open the door. When he sniffs the revolting stench coming from the room, he bends over to throw up.

When I notice the silence, my face turns white. I have forgotten the most crucial piece of information.

"What's wrong?"

"Yuma isn't here."

"Where is she?" Rem asks, covering his nose not to puke again.

"She is working." I timidly point to the back door.

Rem swiftly carries me to the back of the room, avoiding all cameras. He then puts me down to enter the code himself.

The metal door instantly unlocks, but I hesitate to open it. After checking that there is no other possible exit, I open it just enough to peek through it cautiously.

It is another empty hallway.

I fit through the small gap and say, "I'll go first."

The scent of Evil.

The mongrels' blood is smeared all over the floor, the walls, and even the ceiling. Several thick brownish trails of blood lead to multitudes of doors.

The bloody scene transfigures Rem with anguish, and he opens the closest door in desperation. His face goes pale at the magnitude of the discovery—all rooms host dozens of mongrels.

Rem slams the door shut and rests his hand against the filthy wall.

"I must free them all."

I agree with Rem wholeheartedly, but freeing everyone would require a significant change of plans.

"Why don't we focus on rescuing Yuma? Once we find her, she might give us valuable insight into this operation."

Rem takes a few seconds to respond. "You are right. Let's stick to the original plan."

He isn't going to drop it.

After disabling another half dozen cameras, we arrive at a large metal door. The screams coming from the other side are ear-piercing, and Rem's face deforms in pain.

Ashamed of the atrocities that are taking place on my beloved Tranquility, I hug him. Rem accepts my affection, and I remain in his arms, feeling the intensity of his tremors.

When Rem moves away, he seems more steadfast than ever. "Stay here. I'm going in."

"Your idea is suicidal. I'll do it. The humans won't hurt me."

Although Rem is intrigued about what I am not telling him, he chooses to trust me. "Be very careful."

"Of course." Slowly, I punch the security code. However, when the door opens, I am so scared that I can't step forward.

"You have done more than enough." Rem lifts my chin with his index finger to make me meet his gaze. "Now, it's my turn."

The thought of Rem ending like the rest of them gives me the courage to proceed. I cup Rem's face in between my hands and kiss him on the cheek.

Rem hugs me with equal desperation.

When he breaks the embrace, I move away and say, "I've got this. You must stay hidden until I return."

I open the door, squeeze into a small gap, and hide behind a big wooden box.

The squealing of the prisoners is unbearable. I use my hands to cover my ears, but the sound cuts through my fingers like knives.

Like in the hallway, the floor is splatted in blood.

Some of the stains are an old-brownish color. Others are fresh and vibrant red—a gory palette of endless pain.

When I poke my head from behind my hiding spot, the size of the room shocks me.

Not too far away, a guard is violently forcing a group of mongrels to lift off the ground. The guard's shouting and the slashing of his long whip are echoed throughout the room by other equally aggressive guards.

As a result, hundreds of prisoners are lifting off the ground only to crash a few seconds later. This chaotic movement of mongrels creates a visual illusion when the cables connecting them to the colossal turbine intertwine with each other in a fluid mesh of horror.

How am I supposed to find Yuma amidst this chaos?

White coveralls hang from the nearby wall. Most are tainted, but a few are immaculately white.

I rush to grab a clean pair but soon reconsider my choice. The guards' coveralls are almost solid red. I take the dirtiest one in the lot and put it on.

The smell from the cloth is so overpowering that I pause to overcome my urge to vomit. When the impulse subsides, I grab a helmet from a shelf a foot away. I am about to walk away when I come across a barrel full of bloody whips.

After taking a deep breath, I grab one; it is indispensable to complete my outfit. I walk along the periphery of the room, remaining as far away from the other humans as possible.

The guards keep the females at the back of the room segregated from the males. This single fact will simplify my task, but I still need to walk through the entire male population to get to them.

I am not too far from the turbine when a gigantic guard starts walking in my direction. I instantly turn the other way to avoid his scrutiny.

When the guard is ten feet away, he breaks into a trot. I get ready for a confrontation, but the man stops a foot away to strong-arm a collapsed prisoner into working.

I use the distraction and hurry to the back of the room, halting by the turbine. The entire area is covered in a pinkish mist, and even when I step back to avoid it, the thick fog showers me in red droplets.

Bursting with revulsion, I keep moving ahead. This time I concentrate on counting the number of steps it takes to reach the back of the room.

Thirty-five.

Thankfully, by the time I reach the first female, the mist has diffused.

The female is badly hurt, and there is a pool of blood underneath her feet. The few others that surround her are about to collapse too.

The number of guards on this side of the room has diminished, mostly because the females pose no threat. Still, if I want to keep the guards away, I must keep up the appearance. Against my strong urge to ease the mongrel's suffering, I remain unmoved and even do the unthinkable—flick the whip to force the female to keep working.

The mongrel obeys my command, but she hardly manages to lift off the ground before violently crashing on the floor.

I hate this place.

With my stomach twisted into a painful ball, I continue my search for Yuma.

There she is!

Yuma is standing two rows away. Although blood covers her entire body, she seems to be in much better shape than the rest of the females and keeps lifting off without intimidation.

I accelerate my pace without disrupting my occasional flogging. By the time I am standing beside Yuma, she is already recovering from yet another crash landing.

"I'm here to get you out."

The subtle change in Yuma's breathing indicates she heard me. I keep walking until I reach the last prisoner in her row before turning around.

"What's the plan?" Yuma is tying her worn-out shoes.

"We weren't expecting to find you working. Do you have any suggestions?"

Yuma raises her head for the first time. She is not impressed with my lack of preparation. A few seconds later, she says, "Bathroom break."

"Are you even allowed?" The smell of urine is so strong that I have assumed the opposite was the case.

"Only under extreme circumstances. Just keep walking."

I walk to the other end of the row. When I turn around, Yuma is groaning on the ground.

I am hustling my way back to her when a guard offers an unwelcome intervention.

I search for ideas to get rid of him, but I am drawing a blank. I am about to walk by them when I see his face. "Peter?"

Chapter 17

"Could you be a bit less conspicuous? I spotted you as soon as you entered the room."

"Sorry, I'm doing my best. I thought you didn't work tonight."

"I volunteered to cover for a sick guard."

"Well done! Though I'd rather keep you out of this mess."

"Don't mind me. There are times in life when we need to act on our principles regardless of the consequences."

Yuma looks at Peter with her mouth wide open.

Finding another human willing to take part in our rescue operation fills me with happiness. "What do we do next?"

Without responding, Peter unplugs the connectors from Yuma's silicone harness. Though a straightforward task, I am glad he is taking it over as it speeds up the rescue mission.

"Keep walking, or the guards will know something is amiss. Go wait for us by the door," Peter says, his gaze fixed on the floor.

The environment is so loud that I miss most of his words. "Excuse me?"

"Go!" Peter points to his right with a quick movement of his head.

Two guards are standing nearby. I walk away in a

flash. After witnessing how compassionately he unplugged the cables from Yuma's back, I trust Peter will do whatever it takes to keep her safe.

I am halfway to the door when a guard yells, "You, come here!"

I slowly obey once I realize he is talking to me.

"Hurry. I don't have all day!"

"Yes, Sir. How can I help you?"

The guard is kicking a poor old mongrel who is lying on a pool of blood.

"Take this piece of shit to the Recycling Room."

The Recycling Room?

The native is about to die, and the guard wants me to dispose of him. I can almost visualize the disgusting place—a dark and damp room filled with piles of rotten natives.

Over my dead body.

"Right away," I say, moving forward to grab the native.

"Are you new? I don't remember seeing you before," the guard asks with suspicion.

"Absolutely. They just transferred me from Farm 1."

"No wonder they did." The guard stares me down before turning around to harass other exhausted prisoners.

I lash the whip on the ground by the mongrel's feet to force him to stand up.

The poor native can hardly move, but he still obeys.

The old mongrel stumbles his way to the door, collapsing ten feet later.

Seer, please keep him alive.

I kneel and hold the native's head in between my hands. He is in excruciating pain and gasping for breath. The second time I pray, I commend his soul to Marten, hoping death will meet him soon.

"Sir, can you hear me?"

The mongrel opens his eyes, confused. No human has ever addressed him with such respect.

"I'll help you." I hurry to hold him in my arms.

The mongrel is skin and bones, and I carry him with ease. This small act of kindness would raise eyebrows, but nobody is paying attention.

When I am by the door, I look back to check on Yuma and Peter; they are still at the back of the room.

I rush out of the room, hoping to find Rem. However, the corridor is full of dead guards, and Rem is missing.

Did they capture him? Should I hide?

My heartbeats instantly accelerate.

"Go…" Even in his dire condition, the old mongrel has noticed my uneasiness.

"No. First, I'll find you a place to rest in peace."

Flinching at every noise, I search for a quiet place where to set him down. However, all the doors I open lead to rooms packed with other suffering natives.

By the seventh door, my arms are exhausted, and the mongrel is about to slip to the ground. I hustle to punch the security code but enter the wrong sequence of numbers. I hold on to the native with extra care until I manage to key in the numbers again. This time, the door instantly unlocks.

It is a storage room.

I kick some cleaning containers from one of the corners to make room for the native. "No one will find you."

"You are…too kind."

"Sorry. I wish I could offer you more than this."

"This is perfect. But could I…bother you with one last request? Can you tell my family…I love them?"

"I will be honored. What's your name?"

The poor mongrel can hardly find the strength to continue. "My name is…Rushmar."

"Rushmar," I repeat, but the mongrel is already unconscious. "Goodbye."

My heart hurts at the thought of leaving the native alone to die. Still, I hasten out of the storage room to find Rem.

The sound of a struggle instantly forces me to forget about Rushmar, mostly when realizing that the noise source is Rem strangling Peter.

"Stop! Peter is helping us."

Yuma is standing by the two, spaced out. When she sees me coming, her mind seems to click to what is happening around her, and she starts urging Rem to release Peter.

But Rem is not listening, and Peter's face is rapidly turning a purplish-bluish color.

I kick Rem in the shins to get his attention. It takes several powerful kicks to get him to turn his head in my direction.

"Let Peter go! He is a friend."

This time, my words cut through Rem's rage-induced trance, and he instantly releases him.

Peter collapses on the floor to catch his breath.

"Are you all right?"

"I'll survive," Peter says, rubbing his neck with a grimace.

"Thank you!" Yuma embraces Rem for the first time in two years. She is ecstatic about seeing her brother and the promise of imminent freedom.

As Rem hugs her sister tight, he gazes at me with gratitude.

I look away to give them some well-deserved privacy.

"We must leave. Other guards will arrive soon," Peter says while surveying the hallway for danger.

Rem issues some sort of an apology before going back to ignoring him. Then he turns to me and says, "Clara, you need to get Yuma out."

"What about you?"

"I must do something first."

"But we won't manage without you." Even if we could escape the premises, the two of us would not survive the gobblers without Rem's protection.

Peter holds Yuma's hand and says, "I can get us a transport."

Instantly, Rem gets ready to pounce on him.

Yuma places Peter's hand against her chest in a gesture I recognize right away.

Rem looks composed, but his eyes are filled with rage. He is already regretting sparing Peter's life.

"Why don't you come with us?" Yuma asks, clearly terrorized at the thought of her brother staying behind.

"I must get everybody out."

"You won't manage it alone. I'll help," Yuma says, releasing Peter's hand and walking to Rem.

"No. You are exhausted." Rem looks at Peter and adds, "Please, take them home."

"Peter, you can go with Yuma. I'm staying with

Rem."

Rem pulls me aside. Once we are ten feet away from his sister, he says, "You have completed your part of the deal. You are free to return home."

"Do you think this is about the deal?" My blood boils with anger. "Helping the prisoners has nothing to do with the deal or with you for that matter. It's about principles and how I choose to live my life."

Rem frowns at me for an instant. He then grabs my hand and says, "Stay close."

Pulling me back to where Yuma and Peter are waiting, he adds, "I entrust you with my sister."

"I'll take Yuma home. She will be safe with me," Peter says, meeting Rem's gaze.

"Before you go, any suggestions on how to break pandemonium loose?"

"I have an idea."

We follow Peter to the end of the corridor and into the last room to the right.

Peter grabs a large container of turbine fluid and hands it to Rem together with a lighter. "You will have to destroy the generator. It will bring mayhem."

"Where is this generator?" Rem asks, grabbing the container.

"Outside, by the back door on the Misty Room." Peter points to the room where we found Yuma.

"Misty Room?" I am outraged by the name.

"I know. They make it sound too dreamy—"

"How many guards are in there?" Rem interrupts.

"A handful," Peter responds before I can talk.

"One of them is enormous," I instantly burst out.

"That's Samuel. He is the worst of the bunch."

"I have a plan." Rem walks to Yuma and carefully

wipes some of her fresh blood with his fingers to spread it over his face, arms, and torso. Rem turns to me, creasing his forehead. "Will this work?"

I hurry to spread more of Yuma's blood randomly over his body.

Yuma gapes at the sight of Rem accepting my help. I would have thought it impossible a few days back. However, there is no denying our relationship has transformed since the so-called Union.

"Done," I say, once I cover Rem's neck in blood.

"Let's go." Rem turns around to talk to Yuma. "Go straight home and stay with Mom until I return."

Rem stares at Peter, giving him the "If something happens to my sister, I'll kill you" kind of look.

Peter ignores the threat and calmly turns around to lead Yuma to the exit.

"Wait!" I trot to Peter, undoing the knot on the leather thread holding the Pass. "This will keep you safe inside the caves."

Aware of the significance of the Pass, Yuma makes a sudden backward movement. She is about to talk when Peter pokes her from behind to keep her moving forward. She obeys without delay.

Chapter 18

We are standing outside the Misty Room, ready to go inside. We have gone over the plan twice, and Rem has already put the lighter in his pocket.

Rem sets the fluid container by the door.

"I'll come back for it later. Are you ready?" He then puts his hands behind his back to pretend they are tied up.

"Stay calm regardless of what you see," I say before punching the passcode.

"I can handle dire situations."

"I know you can."

Once the door opens, I push Rem toward danger.

After the first few steps, I put my hand on his shoulders. "You are way too straight to look real. Also, pretend you can't walk properly."

Rem responds with a quick nod.

Though Rem walks in front of me without making any abrupt movement, the sudden tensing of his back indicates he is appalled by the scene.

The first time I lash the whip on the floor by his feet, he stops momentarily. However, by the next time the whip hits the floor, he is already expecting it, and he does not even flinch.

Samuel is on the other side of the room, focusing his attention on a collapsed prisoner. There are no guards directly ahead of us.

Sticking to the plan, I search for a healthy prisoner. However, as we walk by the rows of males, I realize none of them meets the necessary criteria—fit enough to unplug the energy connectors.

I am almost at the last row of males when I spot a possible candidate, a short female working non-stop in the upcoming row. But when I get close enough to see her, I hesitate to get her involved. She is an incredibly young mongrel.

She is a new slave. Her back has no slashes, and her wings are barely bleeding. Like Yuma earlier, she does not need prompting to take off.

When I reach her, I look around to ensure that no one is looking. Then I whisper, "Stop."

Rem's eyes snap to the left, which is where the last row of males is. His forehead creases when he sees a poor old mongrel who has already collapsed on the ground.

When Rem turns his gaze at me, I signal him to check his right. Before he has the chance to argue, I say, "She is our only hope. There is no one else."

Not happy with my choice, Rem turns his attention to the males. But the next three mongrels in line can hardly lift off the ground, and the fourth and last is already unconscious on the floor.

Resigned, Rem fixes his gaze on the female. Then he gives me an almost imperceptible nod.

The girl has stopped working to look at us. Based on how she stares at me in the eyes, today must be her first night on the farm. None of the other prisoners would dare look at the guards with such curiosity.

"This could be your last night in this terrible place," Rem says, gazing tenderly at the little girl.

"We'll get you out," I say when the young girl looks at Rem with her forehead creased.

The mongrel's face lights up, and she hurries to grab my hands.

I let go of her hand in a hurry. "Sorry. But you need to pretend, can you do that?"

The little girl nods energetically.

"Is there anybody else who could unhook these cables?"

"My mom," the girl says, pointing at a female two rows away. After she is sure I have seen her, she turns in the opposite direction and points to a young entry working by the back door. "My sister."

A flicker of hope lights up in my heart. With luck, this family's story will have a happy ending.

The only guard guarding this section is busy verbally abusing a prisoner who has succumbed in her pool of blood. Still, I stand in between the guard and Rem to obstruct the view before giving him the go-ahead.

Rem hurries to unplug the connectors from the girl's back. "What's your name?"

"Ramesh."

"Ramesh, unplug your mom and sister. As soon as chaos breaks, unplug the others."

The girl nods in agreement but remains immobile like a statue.

"Go!"

Ramesh gets down on her hands and knees and crawls her way to her mom. The pink mist engulfs her soon after, and it blocks us from seeing if she succeeds at unplugging her mom's connectors.

Regardless, Rem moves along to our plan's next

step: deal with the guard before he realizes something is amiss.

The guard's verbal abuse has now escalated to violent kicks. He is so focused on inflicting pain that he is utterly unaware of Rem's approach.

Rem strikes the guard at such high speed that he falls to the ground and hits his head on the concrete. Then he punches him in the face. "Don't worry. The guard is not dead."

At this point, does it matter? If the guard remains unconscious, he'll perish once the place burns down. On the other hand, if he wakes up, the prisoners will kill him—either way, terrifying deaths.

Rem grabs the guard by the shoulders and takes him to the back wall, where he drops him against one of the corners.

I am walking my way up to where Rem is standing when Samuel sees me. "What's going on down there?"

His voice sends instant chills down my spine. "Where is John?"

"He went to the washroom."

Samuel clenches his jaws and says, "John never leaves his post without letting me know first."

Samuel is now staring at me with distrust. He knows something is wrong. He darts to me, blowing his whistle to alert the other three guards who are standing closer to me.

Like watchdogs, the guards obey Samuel's command, launching themselves in my direction.

Although I am unprepared to defend myself against four guards, I wait with my arms at my chest and my hands curled in fists. As I stand still with sweat rolling down my temples, I recall the youngsters' laughter.

I look pathetic.

The closest guard keeps getting closer.

I look away to avoid his fist hitting my face.

When the man is three feet away, Rem flies above our heads and violently drags him away.

I can't even look up to see how Rem disposes of the guard. I have to get ready for the next guard in the line of attack.

The fact that the guard is a woman puts me off momentarily. However, I soon react and prepare to punch her.

The woman is charging toward me with a crystal-clear goal—my annihilation. When she is close enough, she lashes her whip hoping to hit me. However, she is still a bit far, and the whip hits the floor three feet away.

Rem is flying back to help, but he will not make it before the woman does.

I have dropped my whip at my feet. I bend over to grab it when an excruciating pain breaks on my back. This time, the guard's aim is perfect.

I stand up straight and wait for the next flogging. I am so focused that I see her movements in slow motion.

When the guard cracks the whip one more time, I grab its thong and yank it from her hand. The pull is so strong the leather string burns my palm. Still, the thick handle comes flying from the guard's grip, hitting me hard on the shin.

The guard quickly adjusts her strategy, approaching me with her fists, ready to fight. When she strikes, I duck fast enough to avoid her first blow and her subsequent uppercut.

I am still holding the guard's whip in my hand, so I shorten the grip on the thong until my hand is one foot away from the handle. I throw it in the air like a lasso.

The maneuver catches the woman off guard, hitting her head with the heavy handle.

The guard wrestles with me to yank the whip from my hand, but I am determined to keep it. After a short exchange of punches, I kick her in the stomach until she ends up flat on the ground. A few seconds later, I shut my eyes and kick her in the head with all my might.

The third guard is gone. Rem must have dealt with him while I was fighting the woman.

However, Samuel is still charging toward me and will soon knock me down. When he is about four feet away, his stern expression changes to one of anticipation, and a smirk appears on his face. He is already savoring my imminent obliteration. As Samuel is about to reach me, his face transforms into one of disbelief before disappearing from view.

When I look up, Rem is hauling him around the room as if he were a mouse.

Samuel keeps flapping his arms to release himself from Rem's hold.

"I'll kill you all. Useless beasts!" Samuel screams empty threats. He is so used to being in power that he can't accept that he is in a very vulnerable position.

Suddenly, Rem smashes Samuel against the wall. I am about to cheer for him when I remember how appalled I was when witnessing Sullu do the same to Mrs. Brown.

Seer, I have lost my faith. I can feel it in my bones! Are you even real? Or are you a tale intended to make us feel special?

Rem drops Samuel from high in the air.

Samuel lies motionless on the ground, blood

pouring from his twisted head.

"Oops. I might have enjoyed killing this one." Rem lands beside me. He holds my hand to trace the wound left by the leather strap. "Does it hurt?"

"It's nothing."

Now that the guards have been disabled, the mongrels stop working to stare at us in disbelief.

"Look. The girl has untied almost all the females." Rem's shoulders drop to a relaxed position as he smiles for the first time.

"What now?"

"Now, we unleash pandemonium."

Chapter 19

"Move everyone out of the room before the explosion." Rem has the container in his hand and is about to blow up the generator. "I'll give you five minutes. Promise me you'll leave the room before."

"I promise."

"No matter what." Rem makes sure I meet his gaze this time around.

"Absolutely!" I am trusting my survival instinct to take care of that request.

Rem takes off, landing by the back door and rushing outside.

When Rem disappears, I sweep my hand across my forehead to wipe the sweat and get ready to complete the task. However, the females are resting on the ground instead of freeing the male prisoners.

Gritting my teeth, I dart to the back, cracking my whip. I hate threatening the natives, but I will do whatever it takes to get everyone out of danger.

The prisoners hurry to their feet and hustle to the front, helping others along the way. My forceful intervention speeds up the evacuation process. Almost half the room is empty by the two-minute mark, and everyone is gathering by the door.

When there are less than twenty seconds left of the countdown, I realize I will not leave the room in time.

I am about to dash to the front when a female trots

to the back wall. I command her to turn around, but she continues her steady trot unaltered. Defying an arsenal of fears, I chase after her. I catch up to her and pull from her arm to guide her to safety.

The female is disoriented and resists with incredible strength.

"You must go back!"

The female still shows no sign of comprehension.

I close my eyes and punch her in the face.

The mongrel falls to the ground but still insists on fighting me off.

With just seconds to spare, I grab her feet and drag her to the front. I have managed to advance ten feet when the female screams in distress.

Her agonizing shrieks attract several prisoners' attention, who react very negatively to a guard dragging an elder by the feet. The rescue mission is about to turn into a slaughter.

Just as the group is about to seize me, the explosion blows everyone off their feet.

The momentary darkness recedes as the fire spreads, unleashing chaos.

For an entire minute, I stay on the floor, recovering from the blast.

The front door remains closed, and everyone is still gathered inside the burning room.

"Get out of the room!" But my words are lost amidst the madness.

Ramesh is standing by the door with her family.

I wave at her until she meets my gaze and then signal her to open the door.

Ramesh interprets my request right away. But even after she opens the door, none of the prisoners dare step out for fear of the guards.

With smoke thickening, unless the mongrels soon evacuate the room, they will all perish.

I keep flicking the whip until a handful of prisoners poke their heads into the corridor. When no guards confront them, the rest follow suit in a stampede.

The fire has reached the turbine and is causing all kinds of explosions as the electrical system catches on fire. Soon, a dark cloud of acrid smoke spreads across every inch of the Misty Room.

The old female remains on the ground twenty feet away. At the sight of the flames, she extends her arms to me. She then follows me to the exit without reservation. However, her lungs have filled with smoke, and she must stop every other step to cough it out.

I am ten feet from the crowd when she stops again. This time, I remove my overall and tie it around her face to limit her exposure to smoke.

"How are you holding on?" Rem lands beside me.

I am about to respond when I suffer from a coughing spell.

"You don't look well. I'll get you out."

"No…" Pointing at the female, I add, "Please, take care of her first."

Rem gazes at me with intensity. He then grabs the female in his arms, and they immediately take off.

Rem maneuvers around the fire and exits the room through a big hole in the roof.

A few mongrels attempt to emulate Rem's exit, but without their Pathfinders, they collapse on the ground soon after.

I line up at the door, waiting for my turn to exit. My cough is getting worse, and I am now having difficulty breathing. A week ago, I would have prayed to the Seer for help. Today, even when I try to verbalize my old prayers, the words stop short of exiting my mouth. As I stand amidst such a chaotic scene, framed by slavery and torture somehow justified in his name, I feel ashamed to be one of his Followers.

"Your turn," Rem says, bringing me back from my confusion.

When Rem is about to grab me, I point at the jammed entrance and urge him to help the others. This time, Rem insists on securing my safety first, which forces me to shove him out of the way.

Rem laughs at my stubbornness and flies us to the front wall, but rather than landing by the jammed door, he touches down on the opposite end of the wall and starts punching a new opening.

Rem has lost his mind.

I have underestimated his strength. In a few minutes, there is an even larger hole in the wall.

Immediately after, Rem redirects the prisoners to this new exit and even carries some of them out.

"What should we do now?" I tug Rem's arm to get his full attention.

All of the mongrels are still inside the dark hallway. Within this restricted space, the prisoners will perish within minutes. I point to an exit sign at the opposite end of the corridor. "Should we check it out?"

Rem immediately disappears from my sight.

I am nauseous and suffering from a massive headache. Still, I follow Rem to the sign, tripping over collapsed mongrels.

Rem's frustration is palpable when he says, "I opened the door, but none of the prisoners want to leave. They just stare at me, confused."

"It must be the smoke inhalation." I flick the whip, purposely hitting a few mongrels. "Everybody out!"

I am hopeful the prisoners will regress to what is familiar to them and will unquestionably follow my commands. I turn to Rem and say, "You might want to help those who can't walk."

I stumble along the hallway, continuously cracking the whip. By the time I exit the building, dozens of confused mongrels are breathing down my neck.

The big cement courtyard is empty. All the guards have vanished from their posts along the prison's periphery.

As I stretch my arms to the sky to fill my lungs with fresh air, the mongrels continue to gather around me.

The light of transports speeding away becomes visible to the north of the farm. "Are those the guards?"

"They must be. Destroying the generator has rendered them powerless and very vulnerable," Rem says, coughing heavily.

"I can't believe they aren't fighting back."

"All locks are power activated. The guards know it's impossible to control this large number of mongrels without electricity. But our advantage is only temporary. They will return in larger numbers once the sun is up and the drones are active."

The confused mongrels—rather than escaping—are collapsing on the ground.

Rem breathes deeply and jumps into action. "You are free. You must seek refuge before dawn!"

The exhausted prisoners remain motionless, and some of them even lie on the concrete.

"Go!" This time, Rem issues a threatening roar.

It works. The prisoners start to disperse to the surrounding areas.

"Help the wounded!"

The mongrels continue to diminish in number until only a handful of mongrels remain in the yard.

"The others haven't come out yet." A thick layer of soot and sweat covers Rem's entire body.

"Shouldn't their cages be unlocked?"

"I'll go check. The prisoners might be unable to open the doors from the inside," Rem says, putting his hands on my shoulders to stop me. "Clara, stay here and make sure the rest of the prisoners leave the yard."

For once, I do as I am told. I am coughing out smoke, and in this condition, I would be of no help.

The remaining mongrels leave without me having to use the whip.

When I look toward the building, my face turns pale. The fire has already expanded to several other sections.

"Rushmar!" I cover my face with my sleeve and rush inside the building.

Dark smoke fills the hallway.

I hold my breath and stumble in the dark to the storage room. Although the air has become uncomfortably hot, the flames have not reached it yet.

I open the door, but the doorknob burns my hand. I grab my skirt and wrap it around my hand.

The cloth is thick enough to shield me from the heat.

I find Rushmar and kneel beside him. "Rushmar, can you hear me?"

There is no response.

I brush his face with my fingers. His skin is much colder than mine.

I place my ear against his chest to listen to his heart—there is no sound. A wave of remorse overwhelms me, and I kiss him goodbye.

"Rushmar, safe journey back home."

I am about to find my way out of the building when dozens of mongrels stumble into the corridor.

"Run to the exit. Hurry!" I keep pointing to the sign, which is now almost covered by smoke.

Some mongrels follow my instructions right away, but others remain immobile, staring at me with hatred.

I want to use the whip to coerce them to obey, but I lost it. Fear suddenly hits me like thunder. These mongrels have not seen me free the others. For them, I am one of the guards.

With my back to the wall, I search for Rem, but he is nowhere close.

The situation escalates in the blink of an eye when one of the prisoners screams, "Let's get her."

"I'm not a guard!"

I instinctively reach for the Pass but soon remember I have given it away to Peter.

By now, a group of six males has gathered around me. When I try to flee to the exit, I trip on a collapsed mongrel and fall to the ground.

Almost instantly, the mob attacks.

"You must leave, or you will die!"

But these mongrels do not care about their fates. They are willing to risk their lives to erase me from Tranquility.

As the group's excitement grows, others join in. Some of my attackers must be first-generation mongrels because their toenails are very much like those I have seen on the gobblers.

I fight them back, even when their kicks hurt like stabbings. When the pain is too intense, I assume a fetal position and pray for a miracle.

As seconds pass and I keep bearing the lacerations' pain, I acknowledge it is time to brace myself for an excruciating death. Almost instantly, my mind searches for a moving image to carry me to the afterlife.

My brain surprises me with a memory of Rem's beautiful eyes, and I try to lose myself in them.

"Touch her again, and you'll die!"

Am I dreaming?

I do not know. I lost track of time the moment the angry mob began kicking me non-stop. I want to open my eyes, but they are swollen shut. My pain is too acute, and I can't move even when the aggression subsides.

Rem turns to the mongrels and orders, "Go help the others!"

Immediately after, he grabs me in his arms and carries me out of the building.

When fresh air hits my face, I inhale profoundly, but the ache in my chest is too intense. My limp body hangs from Rem's arms, and I remain in the same position even when he lifts off the ground.

"Rem. You must...help..."

But Rem does not respond.

My face is pressed against Rem's chest, and all I hear is his irregular heartbeat.

Is Rem crying? Am I already dead?

****

I immediately recognize the inside of the

reconfiguring machine. Although ten years have passed since the last time I saw one, I remember every little detail.

My hands are tied, and I can't move them. Still, I do not panic. The nurses had done the same when I was a child. The potent lights, the loud vibrations, and even the weird shape of the screws are now too familiar. Although way back then, only my leg hurt, every inch of my body keeps painfully throbbing this time around.

Where is Rem?

"Hello!" But the noise makes it impossible to hear what is going on outside the machine.

Suddenly, I notice something round in my hand. *The panic button!*

I press down on it right away.

Instantly, a female voice says, "Thank the Seer! It took way too long for you to wake up."

"Please, get me out."

"The treatment is almost over. Can you wait for a few more minutes?"

I stop pressing the button to signal my agreement. But the noisy and sterile tube makes minutes turn into hours.

When was the last time I saw Rem? All I can recall is Rem entering the burning building. *Did Rem die?*

Suddenly, I remember the terrible beating, and I shiver from head to toe. It explains the need for a reconfiguring machine.

But how did I end up in the hospital?

As soon as my mind catches up with reality, my face transforms with sadness. I had completed my part of the deal, and Rem returned the favor by taking me home.

With a lump growing in my throat, I press down on the panic button without realizing it.

"Darling, the session is over," the nurse says almost instantly, rushing to get me out of the machine. "How are you?"

I am overwhelmed by sorrow and not listening to her.

"Honey, please let go." She carefully removes the panic button from my hand.

"Where am I?"

"You are on board the Outpost Hospital." The friendly nurse holds my hand in a very nurturing way. "You are so fortunate to be alive."

"Am I in space?"

"Yes, those monsters left you at the brink of death. The doctors transferred you here without delay."

"How long have I been unconscious?"

"Almost two weeks have passed since your arrival. The good news is you are on the mend."

"Is my father still here?"

"Your father? Honey, they found you outside the hospital without identification. What's your name?"

"My name is Clara. Clara Fitzgerald."

"Fitzgerald? Are you Anthony's daughter?" The nurse sounds flabbergasted. "Your father was our patient until last week. Imagine! The two of you under the same roof, and we were never the wiser."

"So, is Dad fully recovered?"

"Good as new."

Though I swallow back tears, my eyes soon betray me.

"Sweet Clara."

But the good news does nothing to reduce the

stabbing pain in my chest. The ache is so intense that I must check if a knife is sticking out of my body.

"I'll contact your parents and tell them you are here," the nurse says when my weeping becomes too intense, and I gasp for air.

The kind nurse holds my hand until the sea of sorrow recedes. While drying my tears with a tissue, she says, "Honey, you are safe. Those monsters won't harm you again."

Those monsters?

"Have you visited the farms?"

"Honey, which farms are you talking about?"

If I tell her about the farms, the nurse will believe I am delirious. "Just ignore me."

The nurse takes me back to my room and says, "Honey, call me if you need anything."

As soon as the nurse disappears, I search around the room for soil to ease my pain. However, there are no rocks—we are floating in space. Disheartened, I remain in bed, my gaze fixed on the ceiling.

The recent struggles have taught me that life is as unpredictable as Tranquility's weather. A brief break from the life of pretense within the walls of the complex has been enough to reveal Tranquility's appalling dark side. All of a sudden, Rushmar's face comes to mind, and my heart bleeds in agony. His passing, like those of so many others, is an irreparable loss for our planet.

A surge of electrifying energy unexpectedly runs through me, and I soon become aware of my life's purpose. *I must shine the light on Tranquility.*

Chapter 20

The mongrels' rebellion has become nothing but a historical event the Followers will tell and retell for years to come. The dark side of my beloved Tranquility endures, unaltered by the brief but violent events of those few dreadful weeks.

My escape from Hell, on the other hand, is taking longer than I would have ever imagined. Hell was not my imprisonment at the hands of the mongrels the night of the rebellion or the terrible beating I endured from Farm 4 prisoners. Hell is learning to live without Rem.

I was unaware of how deeply I had fallen for the beautiful mongrel until he disappeared forever. My heart aches for Rem, and I wish I could be with him. However, Rem has left for good, and he made it clear by abandoning me at the hospital.

My sorrow is as deep as the first day, but it has become part of me, like a constant throbbing that mimics each of my heartbeats. Each day, I must fight the urge to die to try to change the status quo.

I started searching for confidential information as soon as I came back home from the hospital. I hit the jackpot when I came across secret files hidden inside a locked metal cabinet. The cabinet was in the storage room, concealed behind many old cans crowded along five sets of shelves. I had missed the cabinet during my first two searches, but success comes to those who persist, and I finally discovered it when combing the house for yet a third time. After that, it was a matter of opening the combination lock. After trying hundreds of random numbers, I entered the most obvious ones, our family's birthdates. Ironically, the safety gave way when I punched in mine.

The cabinet held documents dating back to the first settlement's time, a historical depiction of the Followers' colonialist behavior. It took weeks of clandestine visits until I finished the agonizing activity. Now, I possess such a good grip on Tranquility's state of affairs that it will be difficult to fool me again.

However, the knowledge came at a price, as since reading these files, I have been carrying a burden. But the worst blow came from learning that Mom is also aware of the deception. She is not only a passive witness to the atrocities but one with a more influential role in the decision-making of our colony. Mom is a Council member.

****

With fear trickling down my spine, I dart into darkness. Once I am out in the open, a stranger grabs me from behind—I have made a terrible mistake.

The attacker covers my mouth with his large hand to stop me from screaming. The man's strength is overpowering, and even when I fight him, he whisks me inside an adjacent room with ease.

Terrorized, I resist, but my lame kicks make no dent in the man's ability to restrain me. Even the chest pain that has been my constant companion since Rem abandoned me at the hospital disappears.

"Stay still," the man commands, placing his back against the door for extra protection.

It can't be.

Once danger subsides, my captor removes his hand from my mouth but keeps holding me tight against his muscular body.

Is it him?

Immobile within his embrace, I sense the current of energy radiating from my captor and striking my heart. Even when my mind still doubts his identity, my heart has already recognized him.

What if I am wrong?

I wait for several seconds until I harness the courage to speak his name. "Rem?"

I am craving Rem with such desperation that I turn around to face him when no denial comes my way.

Rem stays still, waiting for me to make the first move.

"I thought I would never see you again!" I break down at the sight of his handsome face.

Rem shushes me, but the strength of his embrace speaks of a similar longing.

Within the warmth of his hug, my breathing and pulse soon accelerate—a clear sign of my body succumbing to our contact. But I am not the only one feeling ultra-sensitive; Rem trembles ever so slightly each time I caress his neck.

My devotion to Rem is absolute, and when he lifts my chin and devours my lips, Marten's disapproval does not enter my brain. The proximity of his naked torso makes my body ache with desire, finding it difficult to breathe.

My physical reaction becomes even more erratic when Rem surrounds me with his wings, sealing me inside his loving cocoon. Our connection is so powerful that I tremble uncontrollably. My sensorial inputs are too overwhelming, keeping my brain in a fog-like condition.

Rem carries me to a nearby bed, where he continues to profess his endless love. I am about to surrender to him in body and soul when I hear, *ring...ring...ring.*

No!

The beeping of the alarm instantly awakens me. No matter how much I try to fall back to sleep in Rem's warm embrace, it is impossible.

Broken-hearted, I bawl in bed. Like so many other times, anguish grips my heart in a fist. The squeeze continues until there is no more life left to give.

****

Life at home has become unbearable. Regaining a sense of belonging has proved challenging, mainly when I second-guess every word my parents say, even those expressing love.

Is it possible to be so monstrous and so loving at the same time? I have gone mad. How can I miss my days in captivity?

I wish I could run away, hide in one of the transports that visit the other colonies. But two strings keep me prisoner in this land, each one connecting me to one of my little brothers. Without my influence, they might end up like my parents.

My life is a pretense. I am back at school and conducting myself like the old Clara, always on par with everybody's expectations. I do not like living this lie. However, there is some relief in knowing my conformity to the Seer's doctrines is a façade. Deep inside, I am as committed as ever to bring about change to this planet.

I had confronted my parents about what is happening in Tranquility but found it to be a moot point. There is an unwritten code prohibiting disclosure of anything of importance to Followers under the age of eighteen.

I have patiently waited for the magic date to arrive, and as of midnight tonight, the wait will be over.

Tick-tock…tick-tock.

The wait fills me with anxiety. During the past few days, my parents' behavior has been very irritable and out of character. They are not looking forward to the imminent discussion, but they will have no excuse to put it off from midnight onward.

My parents' stand on the ongoing abuse of the natives remains uncertain, as they have resolutely refused to address any of my questions. In the end, their sentiments on the matter are irrelevant as they are still an integral part of this machinery of torture and deceit. My only hope is to never become like them.

****

Midnight has passed, and there is still no sign of my parents. I can hear their footsteps, pacing back and forth in the living room, and their occasional indecipherable whispers.

Earlier tonight, my parents failed to convince me to go to sleep. They know the news will horrify me and must be afraid of losing my respect.

Suddenly, I am startled by noises.

They are coming.

"Clara, are you awake?" Mom knocks on my door.

In silence, I exit the room and stride to the living room, my parents following me a few steps behind.

Trembling with anticipation, I sit on the edge of the couch and wait for them to settle down on the opposing sofa.

"Coming of age carries huge responsibilities," Mom stutters, avoiding my gaze.

My father, who is sitting beside Mom, observes in silence, his right hand tensed on the sofa armrest. Their body language is making me uncomfortable.

"Growing up doesn't scare me," I burst out resolute. I am not the one who has hidden behind pretenses.

"I was your…"

It is almost laughable witnessing how such eloquent people can hardly articulate three words together.

I wouldn't want to be in their shoes.

Eventually, Mom accepts the inevitability of the moment and talks without further hesitation.

"I was your age when Grannie told me about my duties within the colony. Now, it's your turn to assume equal responsibilities. Starting tomorrow, you won't be returning to school."

"Excuse me?"

This speech is nothing like the one I expected to hear. My back muscles are tensing along my spine like a feline ready to pounce on prey. I have never felt this level of outrage in my whole life. Going to school is my only solace, and the only thing anchoring me down to the edge of sanity.

"I still have a year left to complete my studies. All my schoolmates are staying, and so am I."

"You are different. Being a Fitzgerald comes with enormous responsibilities. We wish we could spare you this legacy, particularly after all you have suffered in the hands of those monsters. Still, the colony has its strict rules which we must follow for its survival," Dad says, tapping his foot repeatedly on the dense carpet.

"Tomorrow, you'll begin training at the Council Academy," Mom states emphatically.

My head is about to explode. However, I pretend to be levelheaded when I say, "I'm not cooperating unless you tell me everything."

In truth, I am not planning to comply at all. I rest against the comfortable backrest and wait for my parents to talk.

My parents look at each other hesitantly, but they eventually comply with my request.

During the next two hours, they talk without interruption, reminding me of my history lectures. Like every lecture on the planet, they start by describing the terrible hardships the settlers endured when they first arrived. Mom even has the nerve to insist on how the Followers survived the hostile environment by making alliances with the natives. Same old garbage the school has fed me for years.

It is mind-blowing how my parents choose to ignore talking about mongrels. Nonetheless, my education suffers no blow, as each time they speak about the natives, the Followers' brush has distorted reality. By the time my parents blame the gobblers for the rape of our women, hence, the mongrels' hideous existence, I am already expecting it.

At times, their speech is dull, and my thoughts wander off to how different my reaction would have been without my short exposure to the natives' lives. I would have unquestionably followed my parents' guidance. I would have had no reason to distrust them.

When their discourse is over, I propel myself from the couch. I stand tall a few inches across from them before confronting them.

"I know about the Farms."

My parents look at me, bewildered.

"You've wasted my time feeding me propaganda. After I insisted on the truth for so long, I had hoped you would at least admit to your involvement in these atrocities. But I stand corrected."

My parents remain dumbfounded and unsure of how to respond. Suddenly, the air in the room is so thick I could cut it with a knife.

"Dear, what farms are you talking about?" Dad knows nothing about my visit to the farm and attempts to get out of an uncomfortable situation by playing the dumb card.

"Don't bother denying it. I read your report."

Dad gapes in horror as his sweet baby girl exposes his lie. In shock and unable to articulate an answer, he gazes at Mom, hoping she will make his discomfort disappear.

"Your dad obeys orders," Mom says, intervening in his defense. She is nervously fiddling with her ring. "Honey, compiling those reports is his job."

"Mom, don't even go there. I know you are a prominent member of the Council, and as such, responsible for everything that happens in Tranquility."

Mom trembles while struggling to find something to say.

"I found your secret cabinet. It's time for you to say something truthful, for once in your life."

Chapter 21

My parents were generous with the information but clarified only a few of my questions. They had always accepted the data at face value, never questioning their elders even when the story did not add up.

My parents confessed that Tranquility has nine energy farms in operation. Though there are others in the neighboring colonies, collecting their data was never part of Dad's job. The Council has no interest in meddling in each colony's self-reliant energy supply.

According to Mom, the establishment of energy farms began when a few Followers settled a clandestine operation in Amity, using gobblers they captured in Tranquility. The Council caught wind of the farm and its real purpose just at the time when Tranquility's settlers were suffering from an energy crisis. Misguided by desperation, rather than punish the culprits, the Council replicated the operation, justifying torture as the only way to preserve the Seer's word.

Once the Followers realized the natives' energy potential, it was a matter of time before greed overpowered humanity. As the human population expanded, the short-term power plant became indispensable for our survival, and one institution spiraled down into multiple, very profitable establishments. Later on, the settlers figured out the gobblers' energy production paled in comparison to that of the mongrels. The difference was so staggering that, over time, the number of mongrel farms surpassed gobblers' two-fold.

Still, the historical background has not offered any insight into how to eliminate torture without jeopardizing our survival.

Guided by a fierce determination to eliminate inequalities once and for all, I agreed to attend the Council Academy.

But to attend classes, I had to move to the Council grounds first. The move turned out to be a blessing in disguise, as it keeps me away from my parents. Although Mom regularly attends Council meetings, we never cross paths. All our interactions with the Council are through its delegate, an old ogre called Grant.

But life in the Academy is challenging. Ever since my arrival, the students from all over the colonies have avoided me like the plague. It took me a week to learn an invaluable lesson—not all settlements are equally important. Although all teenagers come from the colonies' elite, I am the only student whose parent is a Council member. As such, everybody dislikes me and stays away. But most importantly, the elite's offspring have attended the Academy for nearly three months, and I am struggling to catch up.

Though extremely busy, most days I am disappointed. There is much new information, but most of it is lies. Thankfully, all the confidential documents I reviewed at home have helped me discern truth from falsehood.

The teachers are like clones, dressed in the same dull and ultra-conservative fashion expected of the Followers. Like in my old school, each class begins and ends with a prayer. Now I parrot words that felt meaningful a few months back. The most unbearable course is religion, and I hate spending hours reading Marten's doctrines. As I pay close attention to his teachings, I find them not insightful but vengeful and condemnatory, particularly of those Marten considered nonbelievers. The most demoralizing aspect of attending this course is witnessing the students absorb every word of the gospel without the slightest sign of analytical process going through their brains. But I can't blame them. I was just like them before the rebellion.

I have learned not to voice my opinions as the teachers will refute them as blasphemy. Cameron, the oldest student in the class, is the only one who occasionally questions the teachers. However, it never ends well for him. He gets extra readings to steer him back into unquestionable submission to the scriptures.

Science remains my favorite subject. Due to its intrinsic nature, science is one of the few courses where the teachers can't deviate too much from the truth.

"Do you care to work on the project together?" Cameron catches up to me as I am leaving history class.

I do not want to work with Cameron, but this is a group assignment, and I have no other available option. "I guess…"

"Should we meet after dinner?" Cameron asks excitedly.

"I will be in the library, as always," I say and hustle down the hallway to my next class.

****

It is late at night, and Cameron is a no-show.

I'm going to kill him. What a waste of time! I could

174

have finished the project already.

I am about to leave when Cameron saunters in. "Thank the Seer. You are still here."

No apologies?

I have no patience for lazy people. But what upsets me the most is that Cameron is not carrying a single book. I rush to my feet and grab my belongings.

"I'll do the assignment and let you also get credit for it," I say, stomping out of the library.

****

I enter the classroom and hand in the project without waiting for Cameron. His irresponsible behavior still makes my blood boil, as I had to work until past midnight to finish it.

I survey the room and find Cameron chatting with a group of girls by the back wall.

How can those girls like him?

I choose a seat as far away from Cameron as possible. However, right before the class starts, he takes the vacant chair beside me.

"You don't need to bother. I already handed in the project," I say, hoping he will sit somewhere else.

"I saw you."

I want to get away, but my chair is touching the wall already. I am about to leave the classroom when the teacher introduces his lecture.

"Good morning. Today I will show you our energy-producing farms."

It is the first time a teacher mentions the farms, and I am intrigued about what he will say. I rest my back on the chair, determined to ignore Cameron.

As soon as the teacher starts his presentation, I gag in disgust. Although he shares several photos, all images show sparkling clean establishments. The authorities had taken the pictures before the farms became operational. Not surprisingly, he abstains from showing pictures of the appalling sleeping quarters and their inhumane cages.

The teacher presents some of the graphs from Dad's report but without any descriptive language. I patiently wait for images of bloody natives, but they never come. The slideshow is absurd and almost laughable.

Although the kind of garbage the Council teaches our future leaders is outrageous, I was half expecting it, which triggers no emotional response. However, my mental state suffers a sharp turn when a photo of the Misty Room appears on the screen.

I am immediately thrown back to the dreadful night of the escape, and I shiver from head to toe. For a moment, I can sense the droplets of the pinkish mist setting on my skin and its sickening smell filling my nostrils. I even cover my ears to avoid listening to the prisoners' agonizing screams after crash-landing on the floor.

Thankfully, a sudden movement of my chair returns me to the present. I look at Cameron and find his gaze fixed on the teacher. But when I glance at the floor, I see his foot resting against my chair.

I keep staring at Cameron to figure out if he kicked the chair on purpose, but not once does he meet my gaze.

The fake show-and-tell concludes a few minutes later. When the teacher offers to answer our questions, I do not hesitate to speak up.

"Do you have pictures of the farms in operation? It

isn't clear how we harvest energy."

"Clara has an excellent point. You've omitted to mention what our source of energy is," Cameron adds in his easygoing way.

But when I look at Cameron, his laid-back demeanor has disappeared. Now Cameron is looking at the teacher with an unusual intensity.

The teacher's nervousness becomes apparent. Still, he plays it cool and resorts to what all Followers do best, lie.

"There is no need. With the Seer's blessing, we'll visit one of the farms next week."

"Bullshit," Cameron whispers in my ear. "That will never happen."

Although I agree with Cameron, I remain quiet. This kid could be in it with the teacher and could be playing a part to weed out untrustworthy Followers.

"We'll visit Farm 4. This farm was recently rebuilt after being destroyed by an accidental fire."

The teacher will show us the sparkly-clean institution before it becomes operational again.

"Accidental fire, my ass…" Cameron says, moving his chair closer to mine so that nobody will hear what he has to say. "They don't want anyone to learn the truth. Farm 4 was destroyed during the largest breach in the history of Tranquility."

"How do you know?" Cameron has captured my full attention. This information is not common knowledge.

"I have my sources. The mongrels must have been terrified, don't you think?"

Cameron meets my gaze with confidence. There is no doubt that he trusts the integrity of his information.

"How would I know?"

For the remainder of the lecture, I avoid looking at Cameron. As soon as the bell rings, I hurry out of the classroom.

****

Since my recovery, I have been faking not having memories of my time among the mongrels. It was easy to pretend once the doctor confused my unwillingness to reveal their whereabouts with temporary memory loss.

"Temporary amnesia is normal in cases of psychological trauma. It would be best not to pressure Clara into remembering such terrifying events. With time and the Seer's blessing, her memories will return." The doctor's diagnosis was an absolute blessing, and it allowed me to keep the caves safe.

The only other human who knows about my active involvement in Farm 4's destruction is Peter, who will never talk.

I shouldn't worry about Cameron. He knows nothing.

Nonetheless, I have done my best to avoid him, and at times, it has taken tons of creativity. For whatever reason, Cameron obsesses about me. A few hours ago, I was studying in the library when Cameron arrived and walked straight to me. Fortunately, Lucy, the librarian, intercepted him midway to inquire about some overdue books. I took advantage of the momentary distraction and left the room through the back door.

However, after witnessing Cameron's determination, I fear he will eventually find a way to talk to me.

****

Thank the Seer!

A wave of relief washes over me at the thought of putting space between me and my stalker.

I have not thought about our religious leader in a while, but today, he is my savior. The Academy has granted a three-day break to celebrate his birthday, and I am going home and away from Cameron. I will use the time to strategize a solid plan of evasion.

It has been a long day of lectures, and I feel exhausted. Trappist is setting, and the colorful display brings back memories of the time I saw it set from high ground. Remembering the way Rem looked at me at that time causes a stabbing pain in my chest.

Darkness rapidly gains ground over the compound, and the temperature drastically drops to uncomfortable levels. The constant rattling of my teeth eventually brings me back to the present.

I wait for the transport by the gate. A bunch of unruly and excitable students has assembled a few feet away, and I am looking forward to some quiet time inside the bus.

When the transport arrives, it finds me jumping in one spot to keep warm. As soon as the door opens, I rush to the last row of seats and sit by the window.

The girls cluster together at the front to get a closer look at the young driver. Some boys sit close to them, but others spread around the vehicle to mind their own business.

I set my bag on the seat beside me. Plenty of empty seats are still available for latecomers. Given how everyone has avoided me, I am confident no one will dare claim it.

As the transport is about to depart, I close my eyes

and let go of my worries. My mind soon travels back to my brothers and how excited they must be about my imminent arrival. Unfortunately, a sudden movement of my seat pulls me from my thoughts.

"Did I wake you?" Cameron is sitting beside me, his back resting against the seat and squeezing my bag.

"There are plenty of empty seats. Why don't you sit somewhere else?" I turn my head and gaze at the window. The transport is already in motion, and the Council grounds are fading already.

"I'd rather keep you company."

"I'd rather be alone," I reply, uncommonly rude.

But Cameron ignores me.

"Do you mind?" I point at my backpack, hoping Cameron will move to another seat.

But all Cameron does is move out of the way to let me grab the bag.

I violently snatch the bag from behind him and place it on my lap.

"Clara, your name is quite popular these days," Cameron speaks enthusiastically, oblivious to my bad mood.

"What do you mean? Nobody I know bears my name." I immediately close my eyes.

For the first time in a while, I pray to Marten for Cameron to leave me alone. But the Seer ignores my plea—surely retribution for the cold shoulder I have been giving him lately.

"Your name is trending within the mongrel population."

I keep my eyes shut. However, Cameron has sensed my uneasiness, and he is soon back at it.

"The mongrels are praising this Clara girl. They

say she was instrumental during their successful escape from Farm 4," Cameron says, poking my shoulder with his pencil until I gaze at him. "Impressive, right? Unfortunately, Clara died at the hands of the same group she saved—or so they say. They now hail her as one of their most beloved martyrs."

"It's a myth." Cold sweat drips down my spine, and I must fight the urge to flee.

"Yep, you're probably right."

"Are you going back home?" I hurry to change the subject.

"No, there isn't enough time to go back to Serenity. I'll stay with my cousin, Owen. You know him, right?"

"Unfortunately, I do."

"Yep, Owen can sometimes be an ass." Cameron laughs while fidgeting with his fingers.

"Owen is an ass all the time."

Cameron chuckles wholeheartedly. "You're right. Honestly, I'm planning to stay away from him as much as possible. I'm not at all like Owen, in case you are wondering."

"I wasn't. But I must admit I've already noticed some similarities."

"You're killing me!" Cameron clutches his chest. "If you ever stop avoiding me, you'll soon realize my cousin and I are nothing alike. But by the way, why are you always evading me? Did I ever offend you?"

Cameron gazes at me with intensity. Luckily, I look out the window and see we are about to reach my house.

"Excuse me. I'm getting off," I say, standing in a flash. As I walk past him, I add, "Enjoy the break."

Chapter 22

"Your brothers were heartbroken. They act all tough, but they dearly miss you when you are away."

"Do they? Really?" Although the boys barely left my side during these last few days, they have made a point of keeping their emotions under wraps.

"They talk about you all the time." Mom is helping me pack my tiny bag. "I only wish you didn't have to go back to school this soon."

"I wish I didn't have to go at all."

These days, I have hoped to understand the dichotomy of my parents. On the one hand, the devotion to their children is absolute. However, on the other hand, they are unaffected by the misery of others. I might never understand their behavior, let alone forgive them.

"I could drive you tomorrow."

"No, thank you. I'm already a pariah. I'll take the transport, like everybody else."

"Do you want me to pack you a snack?"

"Sure, thank you." I am not at all hungry, but my brothers have already left for school, and I would rather be alone than in Mom's company.

I sit on the bed to ruminate on my life, which is full of contradictions. Attending the Academy has proven useless, and it has been delightful not to look over my shoulder for fear of Cameron's approach. Still, my body urges me to return.

I put my head between my hands and close my eyes. As my thoughts swirl around, I soon realize a simple explanation for my contradictory behavior, Rem. The Academy's hectic pace keeps my mind busy, while the break has provided ample free time for my mind to fill with memories of him.

The time apart has not lessened the pain, and I still spend most nights lying in bed, unable to sleep. These past few days, Rem's omnipresence has felt very real. Yesterday morning when I was outside playing hide-and-seek with my brothers, I could feel his pull so vividly that I stopped dead in my tracks to search my surroundings. However, it ended up being a figment of my imagination. But what was real indeed was the physical pain caused by the disappointment.

Sadly, the yearning is a small part of the problem. I mostly worry about him. The thought of him spending his days trapped inside those caves makes me anxious, especially when this is the best-case scenario.

Suddenly, an old memory of sweet old Rushmar resurfaces. As I remember his fragile condition, anguish overcomes me. The sense of grief soon morphs into one of guilt as I have not yet fulfilled my promise.

"Clara, your transport is here."

With memories of Rushmar still lingering in my mind, I grab my bag and stroll to the entrance.

Mom waits by the door to give me a quick hug before I get inside the transport.

Welcome to Lonely Land.

The students stare at me as I move to the back, but none of them speaks to me.

Cameron is sitting beside a cute girl at the very

back of the transport.

Relieved, I choose a seat midway and sit by the window, placing my belongings on the vacant seat. Next, I concentrate on finding a way to pass Rushmar's message along.

However, the noisy surroundings handicap my capacity to explore options, and frustration builds up until it overflows into agitation. I am about to shake my arms, hoping to release some of these negative vibes when my seat moves.

Not again!

"I am so glad the break is over. Do you mind?"

When I open my eyes, Cameron is already moving my bag to the floor. "Yes, I do."

"I almost died of boredom. It sounds hard to believe, but I was looking forward to school."

Why doesn't he leave me alone? Is he trying to find out if I am a mongrel sympathizer?

"Was Owen intolerable?" I start a trivial conversation.

"It was absolute torture. How can he be such a pompous ass?"

"Not having Owen around is the only good outcome of leaving school," I say, faking a chuckle.

"I hear you. Owen is such a racist pig."

"In that case, how did you spend your time?"

"Figuring out what's going on in Tranquility."

So much for small chitchat. I'd better stick to not talking to Cameron ever. I grab my head and pretend to have a headache. I then say, "I should rest for a while."

Cameron remains quiet for the remainder of the journey. Nevertheless, every time I check him out through the corner of my eye, his demeanor is intense.

What the heck? He isn't going to let it go.
****

Last week, my social life had a sudden change when Lidia, the most popular student, was ostracized for no apparent reason. Soon after, when she found herself without her entourage, Lidia sought my company. I readily welcomed her as Cameron seemed to dislike her with intensity.

Lidia has been a godsend. Since she became my friend, Cameron has failed to find the opportunity to talk to me in confidence. Each time he tried, Lidia interrupted him mid-sentence, changing the topic to one of her liking. Lidia's performance has been short of exemplary to the point where I have changed my solitary ways to ensure I never go out without her.

Unfortunately, my luck ends when Cameron intercepts me on my way to the library.

"Sorry, did I scare you?"

I am about to walk around Cameron when he changes position to impede my progress.

"What do you want?" I kick the ground with my foot, blaming myself for letting my guard down.

"Lidia isn't the right friend for you. She is immature, plus haven't you seen the photos?"

"Which photos are you talking about?"

"Why don't you ask Lidia about them? They are the reason why everybody stays away from her."

What could be so terrible to cause such commotion? Knowing the Followers, it's nothing of importance.

"I like her—end of story. I don't care about what's in those photos, but it's evident everyone else can be judgmental."

The next time Cameron obstructs my way, I use my bag to shove him aside. Cameron falls to the ground like a sack of grain.

"Sorry, but don't you ever block my path again."

"Don't bother apologizing. I know you don't mean it." Cameron is already standing up and brushing the dust off his clothes. "I was protecting you. I thought you might want to keep a low profile. Keep hanging out with her, and you will attract unnecessary attention."

I turn around and walk to Cameron, pointing my index finger at his face. "I don't need protection, let alone coming from you. Stay away!"

I march to the main building with my hands sweating and my heart beating irregularly.

"Hi, Lidia."

By the time I manage to fake a smile, Lidia has already noticed something is wrong.

She says, "You are a bit late. What happened?"

"It's nothing. Should we go find a table?"

Lidia nods and drags her feet behind me.

I sit at an empty table, and Lidia chooses the chair beside me.

After five minutes of uninterrupted silence, I say, "Lidia, what's going on?"

"I knew you would eventually find out."

"What are you talking about?"

Lidia's gaze snaps to the floor before she shyly says, "Who told you about the pictures?"

"It doesn't matter. All you need to know is I don't care."

"You must see them. Being around me might smear your name," Lidia says, grabbing her bag.

Lidia's hands are shaking while she moves things

around her bag.

"Lidia, stop. I already told you that I don't care."

"Hold on," Lidia says, searching her bag until she finds what she is after.

"Why do you have your phone?" Students are forbidden from keeping any type of communication device.

"That's not the point." Lidia keeps her gaze on the phone for the next several seconds, searching for the pictures.

"Nothing you can show me will change the way I feel about you."

Lidia hands me her device and says, "Here. Take a look."

My heart sinks to my stomach, and my hands shake so vigorously that the device falls to the floor.

Witnessing Lidia's passionate kiss shocks me to the core. Unlike others who judge Lidia for her improper behavior, my reaction has to do with the guy's identity—Rem.

"I knew it would change everything…" Lidia says before she starts crying.

Why didn't I clue in on the fact that she was Rem's Lidia?

As soon as I notice that my eyes are watering, I escape to my room. Once inside, I throw myself on the bed and cover my head with the pillow.

How dare Rem kiss her so passionately? He is my husband!

****

The photo is undeniable proof they still are a thing. But the real shock came from learning Rem did not abandon me because I was human. He left me because he did not want me.

What was I expecting?

Lidia was Rem's girlfriend before I appeared in his life, and he never pretended not to care about her.

Ashamed of my outburst, I wash my face and get ready to leave, hoping nobody will notice I have been crying.

I find Lidia where I left her. When she sees me, she hurries to dry her cheeks with her coat.

"Lidia, I'm so sorry I reacted in such a lousy way. Will you forgive me?"

Surprised by my apology, Lidia steps forward and hugs me. "I should have told you earlier about the whole incident."

"Do you want to talk about it?"

For the next little while, I appear undisturbed while Lidia shares her love story. Lidia had met Rem while volunteering at the hospital a few years back. Soon after, she was already madly in love with him. Her volunteering turned into a part-time job that allowed her to meet Rem without her parents' prying eyes.

The way Lidia describes Rem is a carbon copy of how I would respond if somebody would ever ask about him. We are two teenagers blown away by a ravishing mongrel. But Lidia and I are not comparable. Rem has chosen to remain by her side instead of mine.

"Don't worry. People will forget about this impropriety soon enough," I say with an edge of jealousy in my voice.

However, Lidia's sadness has nothing to do with the fact that everybody is staying away from her for breaking Marten's rule. She does not care much about other people's opinions.

"Then, why are you so sad? Is the guy hurt?" I must control myself not to appear too concerned about Rem's well-being.

"No. My boyfriend left me…" Lidia is too sad to give me an explanation.

The news instantly comforts me. I remain quiet, hoping Lidia will not notice my mood swing.

"We had not seen each other for the longest of times. My boyfriend works in the colonies and travels all the time." Lidia lies to my face. "When he came back to the hospital during the break, I was over the moon. Unfortunately, all he wanted was to say goodbye."

Lidia cries so inconsolably that her breathing becomes distraught at times.

My selfish heart rejoices over the news. Still, I feel the obligation to cheer Lidia. "Don't worry. Your boyfriend will soon reconsider."

But Lidia cries with increased desperation.

After everything Rem witnessed on the farm, there is no wonder he feels the need to sever all his ties to humans. But Rem will return to Lidia once hatred lessens in his heart. Lidia had helped him find Yuma, and Rem will always be grateful for it.

"You need to give him some space, but he'll reconsider. You'll see."

"No, he won't," Lidia says, her gaze fixed on the ground. Eventually, she gains self-control to add, "He married somebody else."

I gape in disbelief. Rem had used me as an excuse to dispose of Lidia permanently. Yet again, our union has proven useful.

"I'm so glad we talked. Thank you for sticking

around even when it might affect the way others treat you," Lidia says, issuing a loud sigh.

I chuckle aloud. "Don't worry. The only person who talks to me is Cameron, and I much rather prefer that he stays away."

"I hated not being honest with you. Now I'm much happier."

I remain quiet. Honesty might make Lidia happy, but not reciprocating upsets me tremendously. However, Lidia would gain nothing from learning that I am Rem's wife; the news would only increase her suffering. Still, I regain some peace of mind when remembering our union was a mere formality meant to save Yuma.

"I was running out of things to say," Lidia says, oblivious to my tribulations. "I was filling the time with senseless chatter to stop you from ever mentioning those silly photos. Honestly, how did you put up with me? I drove myself crazy."

Lidia's confession makes me laugh.

"But how did the authorities find out about the photos?"

"It happened on the way back from the break. I was so sad that I grabbed my device to look at my boyfriend one last time. Unfortunately, I wasn't careful enough, and one of the girls saw it. The rest is history."

"Senseless rules. I don't get what's the big deal about a kiss."

Chapter 23

Tonight, I am pulling an all-nighter. I have four exams this week, and two of them are tomorrow morning.

I am about to head out to the library when I am distracted by a noise outside my window, and I get the eerie feeling someone is watching me.

Heart racing, I run to the bathroom and hide behind the door.

After five minutes, I harness the courage to tiptoe to the window and check.

Nothing!

I am putting on my coat when something or someone scratches on the window.

I lean against the wall, away from prying eyes. I search for something to use as a weapon, but there is nothing. I take off my right boot and walk to the window, pointing the heel toward imminent danger.

Boot in hand, I leap in front of the window.

There is nothing amiss.

No one. Nothing.

No sound.

No danger.

I survey my surroundings for intruders, but the yard is empty; no one is hiding behind anything.

I look up to the sky, searching for natives, but the aerial defense system lights are still on.

I grab my bag and head out the door.

My senses on alert, I dart to the main building. When I am about ten feet from the library, Cameron appears from behind a column.

"What are you doing? I swear, if it was you who was peeking through my window, I'll kill you."

"No! Are you insane? I heard noises and came out to check."

Cameron stares at me as if appalled by the insinuation. "Earlier today, you mentioned you were coming to the library, and I was making sure you were all right."

"Thank you…I guess. But you don't have to worry. I can take care of myself."

"I don't doubt it for one second," Cameron responds with his characteristic smirk. "Still, doing it makes me feel better."

Suddenly, Cameron springs to alert, using his body to protect me against an invisible danger. "Did you hear that? I swear, something's going on."

I scan the yard from behind Cameron's shoulders. "We better go inside. I've been uneasy all night."

The man guarding the door lets us in. I settle down in my usual spot, a cozy nook by the fireplace.

"Do you mind if I join you? The place is empty, and it's giving me the creeps." Cameron looks nothing but relaxed; he must be offering his company for my sake.

I gesture for him to take the vacant seat across from mine.

Cameron gets comfortable on the chair and quietly concentrates on his studies for some time.

"This is bullshit." Cameron rises to his feet and

approaches the fire to throw his book into the amber flames.

"What are you doing?" I try grabbing the book, but it is too late; half the pages have already caught fire. "Why did you do such a stupid thing?"

"I enrolled in the Academy to learn the truth about our colonies, but the information in this library is worthless."

I agree with Cameron wholeheartedly, but I still do not trust him.

"What are you talking about?"

"Clara, you don't need to pretend. I'm quite aware of who you are."

Cold sweat rolls down my temples, and I can't stop fiddling with my pen. "Seriously, what do you mean?"

"Faking ignorance doesn't suit you. I can read you like a book." Cameron comes close and whispers in my ear. "After all, you are a living legend."

Cameron appears to know my true identity and my active involvement in illegal activities.

"Regardless, I have reliable sources. You should be proud of what you've done. I wish I had the guts to do something similar."

"You are funny. Hearsay doesn't make it true."

"Someone saw you that night."

"It's impossible."

"Quite possible."

"I heard there were no witnesses." *Cameron is making this up to get me to confess my involvement.*

"No humans survived, but hundreds of mongrels lived to tell the tale. You are an inspiration to them, mostly to one very impressionable young girl."

"Ramesh?" My blood boils as I imagine the worst.

"What have you done to her?"

"Chill. I adore her. I'll be forever grateful for what you've done for her and her family."

"How do you know them?"

"Our planet is a bit more open-minded than yours. Although back in the day we imported mongrels from Tranquility to be used as prisoners, our current delegates are more progressive and have integrated them into our community. Ramesh's parents are our servants. Somehow, all the females were picked up on their way home and taken back to Tranquility. By the time my family realized where they were, the farm had already burned down. It took some time, but I found the three of them unharmed, hiding in a nearby cave."

"I'm so glad they are in good health."

"Luckily, they survived to tell the tale, and it's all because of you."

Cameron speaks with such reverence, I fear he might worship me. "Ramesh was the bravest. We couldn't have done it without her."

"Yep. Ramesh is an amazing young girl, and she is obsessed with you."

"Ramesh shouldn't be. I did nothing out of the ordinary."

"Ramesh and her sister described the farm in detail. The Followers' atrocities sounded too farfetched, and I didn't want to accept them as real. Still, the slashes on her mom's back were living proof and irrefutable. It took her some time to recover, but because of you, the damage was reparable."

"Then, you are nothing like your cousin."

"Not at all. The first time I heard about this bad-ass chick who fought against inequality, I was thrilled.

Your actions have inspired mongrels and humans alike. There is an underground movement whose members are dying to meet you."

"Underground movement?"

"It is a young and disorganized organization, struggling to grow in numbers. They are upset with the ruling oligarchy and want to overtake the Council at all costs. Are you interested?"

I remain quiet for a moment, struggling to process the bombshell Cameron has dropped. "Not sure. It sounds like bickering from an angry mob. I fear the rebels will not address all inequalities, just their own."

"To tell you the truth, I was hesitant to join them too. That is why I'm studying at the Academy. I want to find a solution to our complex situation."

I stand and give Cameron a spontaneous hug.

"Wow! I should have talked to you much earlier." Cameron seems moved by my emotional display. "Thank you for freeing them. Ramesh and her family are part of my family, and I love them dearly."

When my mind catches up to my actions, I rush to break the embrace.

"Don't sweat it. I was thrilled when I realized who you were, and I almost hugged you there and then," Cameron chuckles shyly. "But I realized a powerful kick to my privates would have met my display of affection."

"Smart man." I let out a sincere laugh. Next, I extend my pinky to him and say, "Swear with me that we'll do everything in our power to eliminate inequalities."

Cameron grabs my pinky in his and says, "I swear. But don't be afraid when you learn how deep the spread of injustice is. You won't believe it's possible."

****

The school continues to be a farce, but I tolerate it because I am making progress through other means. During class, I restrain myself from reacting to teachers' lies, as I doubt they even know what is happening in Tranquility. The teachers are not part of the Council, hence, not privy to any of their secret information. I pity them. Sometimes, I even smile at them, making them believe I agree with their teachings.

Lidia turned out to be a captivating person once pretenses were off. I like hanging out with her, and we are slowly allowing ourselves to talk about more serious matters. I now understand why Rem fell for her.

My busy schedule helps numb my longing for Rem, but there are still some moments when I sense him close, mostly at night. I am quite aware that this sensation is not real. However, the thought of Rem looking over me helps me navigate those frightening moments when I feel something terrible is about to happen.

Cameron has become very protective. Every night, he waits for me by my door to walk together to the library, where we share tons of information. The rocky relationship we initially had has already evolved into a friendship, and I now trust him with my life.

I have opened up about my experience in the hands of the mongrels. However, I left out all my interactions with Rem and Rosh, as they are too painful to share and irrelevant to our common cause.

Tonight, the library is full of students preparing for exams. I am sitting on my favorite couch in the library, and Cameron has just shared tons of evidence he has been collecting since he was a boy.

"How did you get all this information?" I whisper to avoid being heard.

"Ramesh's parents treasure me as one of their own, which has granted me complete access to the lives and challenges of the mongrels in the colonies."

"I hope to get the chance to meet them. They sound very loving."

"I hope you do. The entire family is mourning you, and they'll be happy to learn you are alive. Even Ramesh's grandad was inconsolably crying when the rumor of your death reached them."

The memories of sweet old Rushmar suddenly come back to me, and a lump grows in my throat. I instantly turn my head to the wall to avoid being seen.

Cameron hurries to my side, standing in front of me to cover me from the rest of the students. "Clara, what's wrong?"

But I can't speak. My breath stutters every time I take a deep breath.

Cameron turns his head around to ensure no one is watching. He then breaks the rules and comforts me by patting my head. "I'm always here if you ever want to talk about it."

Cameron continues to stand still, blocking me from everyone's view, until my weeping subsides.

"Thank you. I feel much better now."

Cameron returns to his seat but keeps looking at me intensely.

"I promise, I'm fine."

"Let's stop until tomorrow." Cameron is still not convinced. "Come on. I'll walk you to your room."

I follow him in silence. Thankfully, as soon as I

step foot outside the library, the fresh air calms me down.

"I met a sweet old man on the farm. His name was Rushmar," I confide in Cameron once we stop outside my room. "I promised him that I would send a message to his family, but I still don't know how."

"You could write them a letter."

"A letter? But I don't know where they live."

"Don't worry. I'll pass it along to my contacts. They'll help," Cameron says with a big smile.

"Are you sure?"

"Yes. I'm confident somebody knows Rushmar. The mongrels are a tight group and know one another pretty well. If you write it tonight, I'll deliver it tomorrow."

****

I spent the night putting into writing how much Rushmar touched my soul and how his last thoughts had been for his family. Now, although it is still dark outside, I get ready to deliver the letter.

I open the door, and the chilly air makes me gasp. I breathe deeply, waiting for the air to relax me, but the eerie calmness has the opposite effect. For a minute, I stand still outside my room, deciding if I should go or wait until daylight.

Eventually, I run to Cameron's room, which is on the opposite side of the complex. My heart races with every shadow, and every noise startles me to death.

With trembling hands, I hurry to slide the letter underneath his door.

Once back in my bed, I try to sleep, but my mind refuses to shut down. Cameron's source had told him a rebels' attack was imminent, and I feel depressed. The two of us still lack sufficient in-depth knowledge of the rebels' reasons behind their rebellion to develop a tantalizing non-violent option that would change their minds.

Should I warn Mom?

But if I do, Mom will advise the Council, which will result in the rebels' mass extermination.

I won't tell her. If I fail, I'll make sure she knows in advance so that she can protect the boys.

When it is time to go to class, I blame the lack of sleep for my uneasiness. But it is tough to pretend everything is fine. The clock is ticking, and I must find a solution in a hurry. Violence, like a virus, is about to spread all over our cluster of colonies.

Chapter 24

I had the awkward feeling something terrible was about to happen all day long. I could even feel it in my bones earlier this afternoon.

I am absorbed in my thoughts when the noises outside my window return. At first, I discard them as a fabrication of my fragile mental state.

The noise could be Cameron waiting by the door to accompany me to the library.

I am about to open the door when the scratching gets louder. It is coming from the glass. Almost instantly, there is a pull on the window—somebody is trying to break into my room.

Praying for the window to hold, I hide by the door.

The locking mechanism soon disengages, and the window slams open. A trespasser enters my room almost instantly.

In a panic, I run out the door and hide behind a giant column.

Heavy fog covers most of the complex, preventing me from seeing danger.

I am relieved Cameron is nowhere close. If something terrible happens to me, he will still be around to find a solution to this madness.

The intruder exits my room, shouting all sorts of profanities. He stops a few steps away, hoping to locate me somewhere in his proximity. After surveying the area to no avail, he contacts someone on his radio. With a trembling voice, he says, "I lost the target."

The man on the other end reacts aggressively, yelling so loud the intruder must hold the radio away from his ear.

"Yes, Sir! I will find her," the intruder says, running to the main building.

I hide inside one of the adjacent vacant rooms to figure out what to do next, but I am too terrified and can't concentrate.

I am pushing a couch against the door when Cameron knocks on my door, several feet away.

"Clara, are you all right?"

I remain quiet, unwilling to involve him in my predicament. After several failed attempts, Cameron stops and hurries to the main building.

I am about to seek refuge inside the guarded library when a massive explosion shakes the ground.

Fire breaks out in the main building immediately after.

I freeze when I realize the fire is close to the Council's sleeping quarters.

Mom!

Just a few hours ago, Mom told me she was staying for the night. Her Council meeting was postponed, and she wanted to know if we could dine together. I declined her invitation, offering to meet for breakfast instead. Now, as I think the worst, regret fills my heart.

"Clara? Are you in there?" Cameron is back, kicking my door relentlessly.

"Cameron? Please, stop making so much racket!" I signal him to approach me.

"Were you hiding here all along? I feared you were

in trouble."

"You mean, dead? What's going on?"

"The revolution has begun. We must go. You aren't safe."

"I figured that much when somebody burst into my room."

"Who? When? If that's the case, they'll be back soon. We need to hurry."

"But why do they want me so desperately?"

"Come on. You are like royalty. The rebels can't afford to leave you alive."

The rebels want to eliminate all successors.

"Don't you think you should have warned me ahead of time?"

"It was just a hunch, and I didn't want to scare you unnecessarily."

Cold sweat drips down my back as I think about my siblings.

"What about you?"

"I'm low on the totem pole. I won't be their immediate target. Let's go!"

"But I can't. I must find Mom. She is spending the night in the complex."

Cameron's face reveals terror. He keeps staring at me without uttering a word.

"Cameron, what is it?"

But Cameron does not dare to respond.

"Cameron! You must tell me."

"I was on my way to the library when the explosion hit. The bomb has severely damaged the main building, and it's filling with smoke pretty fast. It will be a challenge to find your mom."

I race to the main building. Although our

relationship might be strained, I love Mom dearly, and there is nothing I would not do to keep her from harm's way.

Cameron follows me a few steps behind.

A second and more powerful explosion strikes. The blast is too violent and throws me off my feet, propelling me backward.

I lie on the ground, confused. My body hurts, and my ears ring so much I can't think.

Cameron recovers first and comes to my aid. "You must hide. You are way too exposed."

I follow Cameron's lead and take cover behind a giant statue of Marten.

The scene becomes even more chaotic when bewildered survivors pour out of surrounding buildings and into the courtyard.

I am about to guide them toward safety when the rebels open fire. One by one, the survivors collapse a few feet away.

In desperation, I poke my head from behind my cover to find the shooters.

Cameron grabs me by the shoulders and squeezes me against the statue before shielding me with his body.

"Don't you dare move!"

Cameron's willingness to risk his life to save mine jolts me to the core. "I won't move. Please, don't expose yourself on my behalf."

"You can check from behind me," Cameron orders without breaking the shield. He has suddenly become a much more assertive individual.

On my tiptoes, I survey the area from over Cameron's shoulders.

"Found one! Thirty feet away, on the gymnasium

roof." I keep looking and find a second shooter perched on top of a transport by the main building entrance. "Second one to our right, a few feet away from the crowd."

"I see them," Cameron confirms a few seconds later.

"What are we going to do? They are killing everyone!"

The students keep stepping outside the building and into the gunmen's shooting range.

"Don't come out!" I warn the survivors, but my screams are lost in the chaos.

My heart bursts with anguish at the sight of Lidia.

"Lidia, no! Stay inside!" I scream at the top of my lungs, but she is disoriented.

When Lidia spots us, she races out of the building with a bright smile of recognition.

But a bullet hits Lidia midway.

I almost faint while watching how Lidia's momentum carries her to collapse a foot away.

I rush to move her out of the snipers' shooting range, but a second bullet strikes her abdomen. Blood gushes from her wound at an alarming rate.

Now safe from the shooter, Lidia is already unconscious.

I hold her tight in my arms while desperately trying to dig up some of the frozen soil with my nails.

"She is hardly breathing!" I wail as I pour the few dirt traces that have stuck to my nails on Lidia's wound.

"Commend her to the Seer." Cameron already knows Lidia's injuries are fatal.

I lower my head to Lidia's ear and say, "He came for you."

This lie will ease her passing much more than the Seer would.

"Who?" Lidia asks with difficulty.

"Rem. He went looking for you. Just wait. He'll be back soon."

Lidia's gaze regains some luminosity as she receives a small infusion of life. "Really?"

"He was crazy worried about you. You must rest until he comes back."

Lidia absorbs every word I feed her, and when her time to meet the Creator comes, she is in a complete state of bliss.

"Look!" Cameron is pointing at a gun sticking out of Lidia's coat. "Where did she get it?"

But I am not listening to him. My weeping is out of control, and the torrent of tears has already drenched my coat.

Cameron has no time to get emotional. He grabs the gun and shoots at the rebel, who is balancing on top of the transport.

The man falls to the ground like a sack of potatoes.

By the time Cameron points the pistol at the shooter perched on the roof, the rebel has already hidden behind a thick wall and is unreachable.

I am about to warn Cameron about attempting any risky maneuver when he leaps forward, pointing the gun at the sniper.

"Don't!" My heart burst with anxiety when I fail to stop Cameron.

The sniper has quick reflexes and shoots Cameron in the leg first.

Cameron falls to the ground in agony, blood pouring down his leg and onto the frozen soil. Although he attempts to seek shelter, his leg is already uncooperative.

I grab Cameron's uninjured leg to pull him to safety, but Cameron is way too heavy to be dragged in a hurry. All I can do is get the shooter's attention before Cameron dies.

I vault from behind the column, exposing myself completely. I cover my eyes with my hand right before the rebel fires his gun. Immobile, I wait for death to claim me, but no pain follows the sound.

I look through my fingers with one eye. The laser light has disappeared, and the shooter is hanging—head down—from the gymnasium ledge.

"Are you insane?" Cameron says, holding the smoking gun in his shaky hands. When he confirms the rebel is not moving, he puts the gun down and lies flat on the asphalt.

For a brief second, absolute stillness takes hold of the Council grounds.

As I hurry to take stock of the situation, I look at Lidia. She is lying a foot away from Cameron; her face still holds the remnants of a smile.

"You must go. More rebels will arrive soon," Cameron says with a trembling voice. His main concern continues to be my safety, even after losing so much blood that he is about to pass out.

"I'm not leaving you," I say, holding his hand. Cameron will not survive without immediate treatment.

I remove one of my shoelaces and wrap it above the wound to stop the bleeding.

The lace is strong and keeps a tight grip on Cameron's leg.

I use the gun as a hammer and bang the ground

until some chunks of soil become loose. After collecting enough dirt, I treat Cameron's injury.

I have just finished filling his wound to the rim when another explosion shakes the complex.

With a hand movement, Cameron urges me to leave.

Ignoring Cameron's nagging, I search for a place to move him. I am about to give up when I spot a large rainwater barrel by the entrance door.

The barrel is full of liquid. The water surface is frozen but gives way as soon as I smash it with the gun.

I knock it down with my foot to empty it to the last drop.

"Somehow, you must fit inside it," I say to Cameron apologetically.

Cameron looks at me, baffled. When he realizes that I will not leave him until he complies with my request, he painfully squeezes in.

"I'm sorry, but I must roll the barrel back in place to avoid suspicion."

Cameron bravely tolerates the pain, only emitting a groan when the barrel violently crashes against the wall.

It takes me a while to position the barrel in its original position. When I succeed, Cameron says, "Clara, take…the gun."

"You keep it. I won't use it anyway. Please, rest until I come back."

Cameron looks terrible, and I hate leaving him behind, but I must find Mom. Forcing all worries about Cameron's health out of my head, I cautiously approach the entrance to peek inside the lobby.

Students lie dead on the white marble floor. To

enter the building, I will have to step on them. In horror, I search for another way in, but no option is at hand.

Engulfed in a grief stupor, I take a few tentative steps forward. As my feet sink into the warm mass of beings, I cover my mouth to stifle a scream. I continue with my unsteady walk, stopping at times to avoid falling on my classmates.

When the carpet of bodies transitions into one of rubble, I am already facing the Praying Room. Just this morning, we all gathered here for our daily prayers. As I now stand above the ruins and amidst a ring of menacing flames, life feels surreal.

My recent brush with danger during the mongrels' rebellion had left a deep dent in my courage, and I can't stop dreading the perils that lie ahead.

All sorts of hazardous debris cover the floor. After a few seconds of indecision, I slowly take a step on the hard and uneven surface. When an image of Mom pops in my head, I overcome fear and pick my way to the other end of the room.

How am I going to find Mom? Fire and rubble are everywhere. Even if I am lucky enough to see the needle in the haystack, Mom is probably dead.

Chapter 25

The ruins are anything but quiet. The yellowish blazes emit all sorts of eerie sounds as they swiftly claim terrain and ignite all the flammable material in their path.

My wailing leaves two white patches across my smoked-stained cheeks. My nose is clogged, making breathing almost impossible.

Mom's last words return to me. "I'll meet you downstairs for breakfast."

She is on the second floor.

Unfortunately, the main stairs have collapsed. I am making my way to the small stairs at the back of the building when screams from survivors filter through the scorching noise.

Is Mom one of these help seekers?

Hope stirs in my heart. But unless I find Mom within the next five minutes, the harmful fumes will kill her.

I walk with my arms spread out to counterbalance my path's irregularities with the sporadic sound of gunfire keeping me company. My thin thread of hope disappears as I realize the rebels are combing the wreckage and killing the ailing survivors.

The revolt is not about control but total extermination.

With my heart squeezed into a knot, I stumble

through the rubble and arrive at the exit sign without injuring myself any further.

The fact that the blasts spared this section of the building, leaving the stairs intact and adequately lit, is not coincidental. The rebels needed an easy way to access the second floor.

I hurry up the stairs, stopping by the door to look through a small opening.

The scene is comparable to the one on the floor below, fire and smoke filling every cranny. However, the gunshots sound much closer, which can only mean that the rebels are near.

I must use all my strength to fight back fear and step into the room.

There is debris everywhere. The probability of my feet getting stuck in this trap-infested obstacle course is high, and every step I take becomes a gamble.

When I get close to the sleeping quarters, I panic even more. Dense blackish smoke fills the air and does not allow me to see where I am stepping.

After a few minutes, I gaze back and sigh, disheartened. My progress has been minimal. Hearing Mom's voice would help me locate her, but she must have already figured out gunshots met all the other requests for help.

If Mom is alive, she is quiet as a mouse.

I cover both my mouth and nose with the sleeve of my sweater to filter the smoke. Still, my throat itches, and I might not have another choice but to cough the smoke out.

Somehow, I arrive at the sleeping quarters without detection. But I have no reason to rejoice; the blasts have devastated this section of the floor.

The eerie silence of the ruins is disturbing. Even the flames are quiet as if in silent mourning.

Did the rebels comb through this area already?

Disregarding negative thoughts, I focus my attention on locating beds. Mom sounded exhausted when we talked, and she must have been sleeping when the explosions hit.

After I hustle through the first couple of rooms, I collapse in despair. The detonations have pulverized the beds.

My attempt to stop crying provokes a coughing spell instead. I bury my face on my long skirt until the coughing subsides. I then listen for signs of rebels approaching, but my surroundings remain quiet.

I am about to resume the search when the rubble moves. As I locate the source, a man's hand sticks out from under the debris.

I am kneeling to grab the hand when the man groans.

"Grant? Is that you?"

"Clara?" Grant holds on to my hand in desperation.

With my free hand, I remove the debris from his face.

"Run…Save yourself. I'm already half dead."

A large section of the ceiling is covering Grant. It will be impossible to free him.

"Just go!"

"Have you seen Mom?"

Grant releases my hand and points toward the adjacent room. As he exhales a final grunt, his hand lies motionless on the rubble, waiting for the flame of life to extinguish entirely.

With no time left to ponder on the fragility of life, I

crawl my way to the next room, where I find the bed buried in debris. I throw myself on the ground and dig the rubble with both hands.

"Mom. Are you all right?" Without any acknowledgment coming my way, my digging becomes frantic. "Mom!"

"Sweetheart…is it you?" Mom's voice is coming from the opposite end of the room.

A wave of relief runs through me with the force of a tsunami.

"Mom! Where are you?"

"Shush. They'll hear you," Mom says in a softer tone.

I find Mom trapped inside the shattered bathroom and partially covered in bricks.

"What's going on? Did the mongrels attack again?"

"No. Followers are to blame for these atrocities," I say while I hurry to remove the bricks.

"Followers? It can't be true. Are you certain?"

"Definitely."

But I soon discover all my efforts have been in vain. A thick and long metal rod is sticking out from her shin. "Are you in pain?"

"Don't worry about it. Do you think you'll be able to remove it?"

I grab the rod with both hands. I spread my legs wide to pull the rod as hard as possible. "It's not moving."

The metal rod is screwed to the floor.

My initial delight at finding Mom alive has faded, and I tremble with agitation. Still, I keep pulling on the rod until Mom screams in terror.

"Clara, run!"

I turn around and find myself a foot away from a massive mongrel. "This isn't possible."

Mom reacts swiftly, grabbing a big piece of brick and throwing it at the mongrel. The projectile's trajectory is precise and hits the native in the middle of the forehead.

"Mom, don't you dare hurt my husband!"

Rem rubs his forehead with the back of his hand.

"Is it you?" I throw myself in Rem's arms, unable to distinguish if he is real or a smoke-induced hallucination.

Rem hugs me back, and for a fleeting moment, the constant throbbing pain in my heart disappears, and a sense of peace fills me.

Remembering my dear friend, I whisper, "Lidia is dead."

"I know." Rem tenses in rage. The news of Lidia's violent passing shakes him.

"I told Lidia you had come. She was happy when she passed," I whisper in his ear. As a response, Rem inhales deeply.

"Your husband?" Mom interrupts all of a sudden. "Clara, are you mad? He is a mongrel!"

"Momma, I'm quite aware Rem is part native."

Mom looks at me in horror. "How could you do such a thing? He is a hideous creature."

I disregard Mom's comment and ask, "Rem, are you all right?"

However, Rem remains quiet, and his gaze is fixed on the horizon as if he is listening for noises.

After a couple of seconds, Rem breaks the embrace and walks to Mom. "There is no time to argue. The humans are coming."

"Don't touch me!" Mom says when Rem grabs the rod.

Rem ignores Mom and yanks the rod out of her leg.

Mom tolerates the excruciating pain in absolute silence. Once the metal is out, she loses consciousness.

"Mom. You need to wake up," I say, slapping Mom on the cheeks a few times.

Mom is disoriented, and a few seconds pass before she can interact again.

"I can't feel my leg."

"Rem, you'll have to carry her out."

"That's out of the question! Clara, get out before they kill you," Mom pleads.

"Please, go! They won't hurt me." I flat-out lie to stop any further discussion.

Rem knows he will not manage to return for me before the rebels show up. Still, he accepts my decision and grabs Mom in his arms.

"No! Please, take Clara." Mom keeps pushing Rem even when the rebels are fast approaching.

"Mom, trust me."

My assertiveness shocks Mom, and Rem uses the distraction to carry her to a big hole in the wall.

When the rebels enter Mom's room, she puts her arms around Rem's neck, surrendering to her fate.

Stiff as a statue, Rem takes off, and both disappear from view.

There is no place to hide in the bathroom, but there is a hole leading to the next room.

I hurry to squeeze through the opening, but as I am about to cross to the other side, rebels enter this other room, too, blocking all my escape routes. Petrified, I stand still with one leg in each room, waiting for the gunshot.

Milliseconds later, a bullet brushes my arm. As I wait for the rebels to deliver the fatal shot, someone orders, "Don't shoot!"

Almost instantly, the same person orders me to turn around and face him.

I comply without delay, and one of the rebels grabs my arm and pulls me back into the same spot where Mom lay a few seconds ago.

Several masked rebels surround me, and my heart beats so fast that its tempo seems to engulf the entire room. In a trance, I keep my stare fixed on the hole through which Rem left for fear of his return.

But Rem is way too smart to expose himself. He will lay low—keep a close eye on me—until he feels he has the upper hand in a surprise attack.

"What do you want from me?"

Two of the rebels grab me by my arms and hold me down, while a third one places a device a few inches away from my head.

From the corner of my eye, I peek at the gadget. There is a picture of me on the screen.

"Jackpot!" The man says, lowering the device. Speaking to the radio, he adds, "We found the target. What do you want us to do with her?"

I wait for the execution order, but nobody shoots.

The rebel hands me a mask and says, "Put it on."

Without wasting time, I grab the mask and take several deep breaths of compressed air. A minute later, we are marching out of the room and to the stairs.

The reduced visibility does not seem to bother the rebels. The screams of survivors have stopped, and the only sound that remains—other than the noisy flames—

is that of boots parading along the smoke-filled floor.

The tightness of the group diminishes as the exit sign increases in size. Some of the rebels are now pointing their guns to the floor.

"Stop!" The leader of the pack instructs all of a sudden. "On alert!"

The rebels offer their backs to me to survey the surroundings with their powerful lights.

Rem?

But unlike the rebels, I search for him up on the ceiling.

Oh, no!

Rem is holding on to a massive chandelier right above our heads.

However, the rebels are expecting a human counterattack and not the intervention of one of our planet's flying species.

Every time the lights hit the area around the chandelier, Rem remains frozen like a statue, avoiding detection.

When there are no more noises, the leader orders the group to keep moving. When the rebels resume their march to the staircase, their formation regains its original rigidity, and they keep pointing their guns at an invisible enemy with clenched hands.

The group arrives at the exit and adjusts its formation to the width of the stairs. The rebels relax as soon as the door closes behind them. The fact that there are no openings along the way seems to give them a false sense of security.

The stairs are free of smoke, and some rebels take their masks off, revealing a mixed bag of humans. Unlike the Council members, who are mostly white, the rebels represent a vast diversity of races. Both sexes are present in equal numbers, their ages ranging from the young to the occasional septuagenarian.

They all march in silence except for the rebel up front, who keeps communicating with another group.

"Is the transport waiting?"

"We are already by the door."

"Great. We'll deliver the package in less than one minute."

I keep my mask on as it is helping me to remain calm. I follow the rebels without objection while my mind fires possible escape scenarios for when we exit the building.

"We are about to exit the building," the man up front communicates to the outside group.

However, this time there is no answer.

The leader signals everyone to halt. His command catches me by surprise, and I stumble on the stairs and into the woman walking ahead of me.

I am about to talk, but the woman hurries to shush me. The lack of a response from the rebels waiting outside is putting everyone on edge.

"I repeat, we are about to step out."

The radio remains silent. Immediately, the leader signals the group to be on guard.

Rem! My heart leaps with certainty.

When the rebels open the door to peek through the gap, several bodies lie scattered on the ground; some are still shaking in agony.

The one in command orders four rebels out. A couple of seconds after, they all scream in distress until only silence remains.

Panic echoes in the faces of all remaining

insurgents. They did not expect to find themselves in a life-or-death situation. Some turn around to look up the stairs, wondering if they should go back to the burning floor.

Their leader seems overwhelmed by the situation and orders a more significant number of rebels out. This time, their disposal is swifter as gunshots welcome them as soon as they exit the door.

The rebels keep staring at each other, dreading to be the next to be called to confront death. Their faces are whiter than paper when they recite Marten's prayers.

"What do you know about this attack?" The leader barks at me from a few steps below. "Who were you talking to upstairs?"

"I wasn't talking. I was praying."

"It looks like your prayers have been answered. Tell me, whom did we miss?"

"I don't know. I was searching for Mom when you found me. It must be the guards; there are several guarding the perimeter of the Academy."

"How many in total?"

How should I know?

Still, I think of a reasonable number to appease him. "One dozen."

The number does not trigger any response, which means I am not too far off from his calculation.

"Something is wrong." The leader rubs his chin forcefully. "They must have known we were coming."

The man is not thinking straight. If the Council knew about the rebellion, they would have been better prepared. He is about to address me again when the upstairs door slams closed and the emergency lights go off.

Brilliant! I rejoice at Rem's cleverness.

The leader slams the door open with a kick and says, "Get out!"

Like the students did a short while ago, the rebels stumble outside the building in a state of confusion. As they fearfully stand on the road, they are no match for the shooter firing from the rooftop or Rem's supple movements.

The rebels push me from behind, and I stumble down the stairs and end up unprotected amidst a violent fire exchange.

Immediately after, their leader grabs me from behind. Although the man is shaking badly, he still manages to stick his gun to my head and yell, "Freeze, or she dies!"

Chapter 26

The rebel has figured out that the counteroffensive includes a mongrel. He is now betting on my celebrity status to keep the few survivors alive.

The gun burns my temple, rendering me speechless.

The frantic shooting stops, and Rem lands on the nearest rooftop to figure out what to do next.

As I look up, I catch a glimpse of the shooter's head.

Mom?

"You! Open the transport door!" the leader yells at one of the two survivors.

The woman opens the door but not before firing a few rounds toward Rem.

I gasp in terror as the bullets miss Rem by a hair.

"Hold your fire! Our fight isn't with the natives," the man in charge commands while pushing me inside the transport. When I resist, he adds, "Move or the mongrel dies."

The rebel knows Rem's well-being is vital to me.

My throat tightens, and I jump inside the vehicle.

With a swift movement of the gun, the rebel signals the two remaining insurgents to step inside the transport. Next, with a voice shrill with terror, he says, "I won't kill the girl if you stay still."

Once the leader gets in the transport, the vehicle

220

speeds away.

With the air defense against natives still active, Rem will be unable to follow us by air.

Nonetheless, I sigh, relieved; both Mom and Rem are unharmed. Plus, death does not seem to be part of my immediate future.

As soon as the rebels feel safe, they blindfold me with a thick cloth. They then tie my hands behind my back and tighten a thick rope around my ankles.

I remain immobile out of sheer exhaustion. After seeing Rem, the uncertainty of my future does not scare me any longer. Although our reunion was under duress, it has given me an infusion of energy.

Were my last words for Lidia truthful? Was Rem looking for her?

Rem would have helped me either way, maybe more so after learning how violently Lidia had died.

Nevertheless, I choose to celebrate the fact that he is alive and well.

****

After a long trip, the transport stops, and the rebels order me out.

"Be careful. There is a big gap," an unknown man instructs while grabbing my arm to help me out.

Once outside, I quietly wait for the man to issue further instructions.

"There is no reason to keep your eyes covered," He says, untying the cloth from my eyes.

When I open my eyes, a young man is standing a foot away. His light-green eyes, which contrast dramatically against his dark skin, are looking at me inquisitively.

I take a step back to put some space between us but

lose my footing.

The young man hurries to grab my arm, stopping me from falling to the ground.

"Hopefully, this won't turn into a habit."

Surprisingly, I find myself chuckling at his joke. In these stressful circumstances, his sense of humor is refreshing.

The three rebels who kidnapped me have already dispersed among the crowd.

"My name is Frederick, but everybody calls me Fred."

"Clara," I reply, even when it is evident he already knows who I am.

Fred remains still, looking at me from head to toe.

"You are smaller than I expected."

"Were you expecting a giant?"

"Something like that." Fred chuckles.

The mystical Clara must be incredibly almighty to achieve the seemingly impossible. "Disappointing, right? After all, I'm a common girl."

Fred does not answer right away. He keeps gazing at me as if trying to figure out how I survived such a brutal beating at the hands of the natives. "You might be somewhat different, but certainly not common."

A sudden wave of shyness invades me, and I glance away, pretending to be looking at my surroundings. Trappist has risen, and its rays are hitting the neighboring mountains' peaks, giving life to the barren terrain.

"We are in a very secluded area," Fred states the obvious.

Disheartened, I remain quiet.

"Can I trust you won't attempt to escape?"

I hurry to nod in agreement.

Fred grabs his pocketknife and cuts my binds with a swift movement of the blade. Then he points toward a partially concealed metal door set in the nearby escarpment.

"Come on, that's the refuge."

Fred keeps looking up, pointing his gun at an invisible enemy.

"It isn't safe now that drones aren't patrolling the area."

"Fred, why didn't you kill me?"

"We thought you'd be a good bargaining chip."

"But you smashed Tranquility's leadership at its core. There is no one to bargain with."

Fred is referring to my so-called influence over the mongrels, but he chooses to remain quiet.

The door has a distinctive native carving on its surface. Noticing my admiration, Fred says, "We call it the Hatch. We found it not too far from here."

The Hatch looks like a miniature version of the doors I have seen inside the caves.

"It has proven impenetrable," Fred says while we wait for someone to open it.

When an older woman lets us in, I must crouch to enter my new prison.

"Bigger than you expected, right? It took some time to excavate this refuge. However, everything is possible when a large group of people works together to achieve a common goal."

Although the sheer size of the excavation is impressive, the cave's safety is my main concern. Nature has tested the mongrels' caves' stability for millions of years, but this excavation is recent. Still, the high probability of the mountain collapsing on the refuge does not seem to bother anyone.

The rebels have divided the ample space into sections. The area located immediately to my left is their meeting/dining room, and it is presently full of exhausted rebels. The rebels who brought me in are resting quietly by some injured insurgents who seem to be waiting for treatment.

Fred leads me across the refuge, and as I follow him, I can feel the heavy weight of the insurgents' stares. Afraid for my life, I hurry my pace and stay close to Fred.

The meeting room soon gives way to the sleeping quarters, which continues to the back wall. Fred stops by the rocky wall and points to one of the cots. "You can rest for a while."

"I don't want to take anybody's bed. I won't be able to sleep, anyway."

"Don't worry. It's my resting place. I will have no trouble finding another one." Fred looks somber as his gaze lingers on the beds of his fallen comrades. Pointing to one of the nearby cots, he adds, "I might take Lucas's. Unfortunately, our leader didn't make it back."

When Fred turns to leave, I hurry behind him.

"Clara, trust me. No harm will come to you."

Fred's babysitting duties are over. Anxious, I hurry to the bed and press my back against the rock.

Bless Tranquility.

My planet's energy pours into me almost instantly. I remain immobile, arms wrapped around my legs, waiting for the rock to ease my angst.

Tranquility's complexity keeps surprising me, and

I almost chuckle aloud at how dull my life was a few months back. I had anticipated the rebels would execute a violent coup to cripple the Council. However, I had never envisioned such a degree of brutality.

The Hatch keeps giving way to rebels regrouping after the attack. The tired crowd remains by the dining area except for the woman cooking breakfast by a rudimentary kitchen set to the Hatch's right.

When everybody is back from the battlefront, the four dozen rebels regroup for a meeting. The mood of the group is somber while they dedicate the initial moments to honor their dead. When one of their squadron leaders stands up and addresses the crowd, the rebels cheer up.

After the man speaks a few introductory phrases, a humming sound overtakes the refuge. Even when I put extra effort into listening, the noise muffles most of the words.

The annoying noise is coming from the Hatch. An enormous fan set above the entrance is feeding fresh air into the confined quarters. As my gaze rests on what is under the fan, I almost leap out of the cot.

Impossible!

All sorts of guns are leaning against the wall. They are accessible to everyone. Suddenly, the possibility of escaping this prison takes root.

All I have to do is grab one.

I can hardly control my excitement. But acting on impulse would be suicidal. The crowd would notice me before I even get close to the weapons. Still, they pose such a magnetic attraction that I can't stop looking at them.

I lie down on the bed. If someone catches me

looking at the guns, they will kill me.

Suddenly, the fan stops humming, allowing me to focus my attention on the spoken words. Though I have missed the context of the conversation, the term 'Beacon' reaches me loud and clear.

Is the Beacon under their control? No rebellion can succeed without severing all communications.

After the mongrels' uprising, the Council had boosted the Beacon's security. Unless the rebels secured help from within, their chances of overpowering the guards are slim.

Where else did they attack? Did they target Council members' residences?

I choose not to worry about the safety of my family until I gather additional information. Chaos has taught me that fear will diminish my mental capacity, and I need to be at the top of my game to figure a way to escape.

****

I wake up to find an older adult sitting on the cot beside mine. He is pointing his gun at my head.

What time is it? Where is everybody else?

As soon as I stand, the man follows suit.

"Do you want to eat?" The man moves a few steps away, keeping his gun aimed at me.

"Yes, please."

The man approaches me and pokes me with the gun until I walk forward. With the tip of his weapon, he directs me to the kitchen. He reaches for a big pot set on the counter and serves me a spoonful of fried potatoes. He points to a nearby table and says, "Sit."

Once I comply, the man sets the plate and a spoon on the table.

"Eat."

I am about to show him my gratitude when he walks to the end of the table to continue his guarding duties from afar. He must have heard all sorts of tales about me, and now he fears me.

I grab the spoon and devour the food.

The man has long and deep wrinkles that make him look old. His thinning hair and crooked back talk about a life plagued with hardship.

"Please, what time is it?"

"The sun is about to set," the older man says after checking his watch.

I articulate a silent thank you. I then ask, "Where are the others?"

The man creases his forehead but emits no sound.

"Can I use the washroom?"

"No!"

Startled by his strong response, I wait for an explanation, but none comes my way. I look around the ample space for a restroom, but there are no doors other than the Hatch.

Having an outhouse would explain his firm opposition to my idea.

I'll have to wait until the others return.

I hand-signal a request to return to the cot. The man allows it with an awkward nod.

Suddenly, somebody bangs on the metallic door.

"Thank the Seer!" The man hurries to the Hatch and unlocks it in a flash.

A group of exhausted rebels fills the refuge in seconds. As they drag their feet to the dining tables, they look at me to confirm I am still inside. Some of the insurgents even exchange articles once they see me.

Were they betting on me killing the guard?

I spot only two of the rebels who brought me here. I keep my gaze fixed on the door, waiting for the woman, but Fred is the last one in before they lock the door for the night.

Did she die?

I count the rebels. There are seven less than this morning.

"Clara, how are you feeling?" Fred stops by my cot soon after. He can hardly walk.

"Could I use the outhouse?"

"Certainly," Fred says, signaling me to follow him.

"It takes some getting used to, but we won't live under these dire circumstances for too much longer."

Fred stops by the door to grab a shotgun.

As the crisp air hits my nose, I breathe deeply.

The night is dark and scary, and Fred looks a bit on edge.

"The outhouse is about ten feet to your left. Can you see it?"

The tiny structure is set against the rock. The door is held firmly shut by a wooden pole.

"This way, we know there is no danger inside."

Fred removes the pole and hands me a small flashlight.

The latrine consists of a small hole in the ground. The smell coming from the hole is revolting, forcing me to hold my breath the entire time.

When I exit the outhouse, Fred is pointing his gun at the sky.

"I heard a shriek. We should head back."

Although I have not heard it, I hurry behind Fred.

Once we are back inside the refuge, Fred says, "We

had some horrible experiences at night. We don't venture out unless strictly necessary."

I am about to return to my cot when Fred invites me to join him for dinner.

"Thanks, but I already ate."

"Please?"

I follow Fred closely while he walks among the crowd looking for a place to sit.

Fred walks to a table with two free chairs. By the time I join him at the table, everybody has stopped talking.

"Clara will spend a few days with us," Fred says when noticing the group's discomfort. "Please remember we don't have a beef with her. Clara will prove helpful in the days to come, so act friendly, or at a minimum, be polite."

"But she is one of them! She should be dead." A rough-looking man stares me down with hatred.

"There is no point in keeping her alive!" A few others voice their support for the angry man.

"Lucas's views and actions were radical." Fred stops for a second to allow others to object to his words. When nobody interjects, he continues. "I was always very vocal about my disagreement with his narrow views and methods. Still, for whatever reason, you have entrusted me to replace him as your leader. In such a capacity, my commitment to the cause remains intact, but Lucas's lethal methods no longer stand. If any of you rejects my leadership, now is the time to speak up."

Some rebels gaze at each other as if wondering if they have what it takes to take over the leadership role. After a tense few minutes of silent consideration, everyone goes back to eating.

Fred signals me to sit beside him.

"You don't need to worry about a thing."

I disagree with Fred's assessment but obey without delay.

The discussion has served a purpose; highlight my vulnerability. Now I know most rebels wish me dead and will seek the smallest provocation to cut my life short.

Chapter 27

I am tossing in bed, the hatred of the rebels weighing heavily on my fragile mental health. Several hours have passed since the lights went off, and everybody is placidly resting. The sudden eruption of snores is the only disturbance to the quietness of the refuge.

No matter how hard I try to sleep, rest evades me. I am in the middle of a self-pity monologue when noises startle me. The sounds resemble nails scratching on metal, and they are coming from the Hatch.

I initially ignore them. It is not the first time my mind plays silly tricks on me. However, my theory crumbles when the noises intensify and the rebels wake up. Within the next few seconds, chaos engulfs the refuge as the people hurry to grab weapons and stand guard by the door. Soon, the scratches escalate to violent blows.

As memories of my dealings with gobblers resurface, my heartbeat rapidly accelerates, and I begin to hyperventilate.

The insurgents stand by the Hatch, assuming a seemingly well-rehearsed defensive stance. As I glance around the room, I notice some of the rebels have not left their beds, even when fully awakened.

"The Hatch has proven impenetrable," Fred's words return to me. *This isn't the first time the gobblers have tried to break in.*

The disturbance ends as suddenly as it started. Guns in hand, the rebels wait for Fred to allow them to break ranks.

As darkness resumes, I remain alert, waiting for the next break-in attempt, which never comes.

****

I am now a pariah in a sea of people. The group has agreed to keep me alive but has insisted on excluding me from their daily activities.

I have explored several escape options, but none of them proves viable. I am allowed to wander around but always under watchful eyes. Each time I approach the weapons, someone cuts me off and signals me to head back to my cot.

The possibility of escaping while visiting the outhouse has also proven impossible. A group of rebels always accompanies me. They would be more than happy to pull the trigger at the slightest provocation.

Nobody expects me to join their prayers, which take place by the Hatch twice daily, without exception. Although opposed to the Council's ruling, these rugged-looking people are fervent Followers, living their lives under Marten's restrictive rules.

In contrast to Rosh, who had opened up about their condition, these people do not wish to instruct me on their challenges. Fred is the only person who interacts with me, hence my sole source of information, and he has only shared a few things here and there.

"All of us have been struggling for years to live decently within our society," Fred says, sitting across from me at the dinner table.

"Is that right?"

"You probably haven't heard much about dissension here in Tranquility because the Council has succeeded at repressing dissidents. But the outcries in the remaining colonies have been much more numerous and—in some instances—produced many violent uproars."

When I stay quiet, Fred says, "Our founders planted the seed of resentment in the early days of colonization. For starters, they only allowed non-white Followers to settle in the colonies when they realized none of the white people wanted to perform the most dangerous jobs."

His accusations are horrendous, but there is a ring of truth to them. I can't name more than one non-white classmate in the Academy.

"My ancestors were lured to settle in Amity with a promise of a life of equality that never materialized."

****

Since that talk, I have been ruminating on the topic of inequality. I have accepted that I am part of the problem. I never cared enough to notice that other settlers did not share my reality.

It has been two weeks since my arrival, and I am bored out of my wits. So much so, I am contemplating heading for the guns to force the rebels to kill me. Even the novelty of the gobblers' break-in attempts has worn off.

Unlike the first few days, night has become my ally. Dreams allow me to escape this confinement, and without physical boundaries, I travel vast distances.

Fred was instrumental in making this happen. On my third night of captivity, he exchanged cots with the man sleeping beside me. He must have heard me tossing and turning all night long and decided it was time to intervene. Although I was uncertain it would make a difference, his presence acts as a buffer and allows me to rest.

Though I thought it impossible, the rebels' resentment worsens with each day in captivity. All their difficulties on the battlefield instantly translate into hatred toward me. Their disgust has become as palpable as the rain. They show it in different ways, like how they look down on me when we cross paths or how they avoid stepping foot near me.

Whenever Fred is away, they feed me the scraps. As a result, I have been progressively losing weight, and my stomach is in constant pain. Still, it is hard to blame them when they barely have enough food to feed themselves.

Each day, a different group of rebels leaves the refuge for hours on end. Some return; others are never to be seen again. Their numbers keep diminishing, and each night there are more vacant beds. I have been trying to gather intelligence, but they discuss nothing of importance in my hearing range, keeping me in an information vacuum.

I fully appreciate the extent of Rosh's kindness. Still, I try not to reminisce about her because every time I do, Rem's memories always tag along, making my captivity ever more painful.

After all these weeks, I am still clueless about the role I play in the rebellion. All I know is there is a role—otherwise—I would be dead.

Fred is my sole protector and my only solace. Every day, he spends time with me no matter what. His visits keep me sane, and I crave his arrival like the desert waits for the rain.

But today, solitude is hitting me harder than usual, and I am on the verge of tearing up.

"I appreciate your patience. Unfortunately, unfolding events are delaying our progress concerning your release."

The news hit me like a hammer, but there is no point in asking Fred to share details.

Fred looks at me with sympathy. "Sorry, I didn't notice you were so unhappy."

As soon as those words exit his mouth, I get an overwhelming urge to cry, and even when I try hard not to, I can't stop it.

"It's time for you to go to the outhouse," Fred says, grabbing my arm to pull me to a standing position.

Although I find his reaction odd, I still follow him to the entrance, almost dragging my feet.

The rebels are gathering by the dining tables. With a bit of luck, none of them will notice my pathetic display.

Fred grabs a gun and opens the Hatch. I am in such a hurry to get out of the refuge that I almost fall to the ground. I look up to the beautiful clear sky, embracing the fleeting distraction.

"Feeling better?"

"A bit. Thank you."

"I heard about the time you spent with the mongrels, and I hate to be the one subjecting you to yet another captivity."

I keep quiet. My eyes fixed on the ground.

"I only hope we are treating you better."

"That isn't true." This time, I speak up. Silence would tacitly indicate an agreement with his statement when the opposite is the truth. "Some of them were kind and loving, and I dearly miss them."

Fred gazes at me inquisitively. When I choose to remain quiet, he says, "I'm so sorry. What can I do to make your stay a bit more tolerable?"

Nothing!

Still, I take the time to consider the question.

"I would like to help with the chores. It'll make the time pass faster."

"Are you sure? I explicitly asked others not to bother you with work. I didn't want you to think we treated you as a slave."

"Everybody else contributes to the chores. I really wouldn't mind it."

"I could arrange it. I'll team you up with Rose."

"Rose?"

"Rose is our cook, and she is lovely. I'm sure she won't mind..." Fred looks up, pointing his gun to the sky.

The distant sound of a drone reaches me, but I can't locate it either.

"Run!" Fred hurries me back to the Hatch, hoping to seek refuge before the drone spots us.

With a sense of urgency, Fred knocks on the metal door unceasingly. However, nobody opens.

When the sound of the drone increases in strength, Fred shields me with his body while keeping aim at an invisible threat.

The Hatch finally opens, and we duck inside. As I glance at the sky for the last time, I notice an object reflected in Trappist's rays.

Mom, is that you?

"A drone missed us by a hair. I thought we had

disabled them all," Fred says to the group gathered around the dining area. Immediately after, they start a heated discussion.

I return to my usual spot, feeling a bit optimistic.

****

The mood inside the refuge is somber. Unlike a few days ago, when the rebels seemed to have the upper hand, I can now read uncertainty in their eyes. The insurgents never expected to live in such confined quarters for such an extended period, and a few of them are already showing signs of cabin fever.

Whatever is going on outside these walls is hindering the rebels' progress. It might have to do with the fact that drones have resumed flights and are now targeting the insurgents and significantly decreasing their numbers.

I can't speculate on why some rebels disappear only to return—unharmed—later on.

Witnessing their struggle has revived my hopes of living in a more evenhanded society. Once the rebels reach their breaking point, they could be willing to agree to anything to get the hell out of this hole.

In the meantime, I keep myself busy. Fred made good on his promise and arranged for me to work with Rose. Although Rose did not like the imposition, she soon warmed up to my presence to the point where she now welcomes my daily company.

After rotating their cook daily, the rebels unanimously agreed Rose was, by far, the best one. A few insurgents nominated her as their official cook, and the motion passed without opposition. Rose welcomed her new non-violent role with open arms as she seems to hate violence and recoils every time she holds a gun.

This morning, Rose looks exhausted. Her voice has an edge of nervousness.

"Did you wake up last night?"

"Of course. The gobblers are getting bolder."

For the first time since my arrival, all sorts of terrifying vocalizations served as background to the gobblers pounding and scratching of the metallic door. The attempt to open the Hatch had been more vicious than ever, and everybody was up by the door, armed and ready.

"Do you think the Hatch will hold?" Rose keeps looking at the entrance even when it is the middle of the day.

"I think so. The metal is thick as this rock." I knock on the rock by the stove. I then add, "The only way to get through it would be with the use of explosives."

"Explosives?"

I immediately regret my words. Explosives would open the hatch and bury us alive. "But you shouldn't worry. I'm certain the natives don't have any."

****

People are fearful and only exit the refuge for short explorations.

Rose is growing apprehensive to the point where she snaps at me for no apparent reason. For days, I have tried to pull information out of her, but she refuses to talk.

"Rose, there is barely any milk left. What do you want me to feed them instead?"

When I arrived, the food was on par with that served at the Academy. Now, both the quantity and quality have diminished, and Rose struggles to provide decent meals.

"The scouts haven't acquired any provisions. I fear that what we have won't last a week."

Clarity suddenly hits, and I realize that the best indicator of the health of the revolution has always been right in front of my nose. All I needed to do was pay attention to the food.

People are fearful and only exit the refuge for a short exploration.

The door suddenly opens to let a group of rebels inside. Fred hurries to one of the cots carrying an injured woman. The nurse immediately joins him to provide her with emergency care.

The woman's injuries must be extensive. Each time the nurse touches her, she cries in agony. Fred remains by her side until the nurse injects her with some powerful painkillers. Once the medication kicks in, he joins the rest of the rebels for a long and intense discussion.

As always, they keep their voices low. After the meeting is adjourned, Fred gazes at me with his brows drawn together.

"Damn it!" Rose returns to the kitchen to violently rearrange the frying pans.

"What's wrong?"

"Some of the Council members who were unaccounted for have now reappeared." Rose continues her dinner preparation in absolute silence.

I point to the poor woman who is breathing with extreme difficulty.

"Will she recover?"

"Probably not. We don't have the right equipment to treat her," Rose says between her teeth, her jaw muscles twitching visibly.

"Did you use soil?"

Rose's mouth drops so wide she could swallow an entire sack of grain. She has not heard about Tranquility's healing properties.

I search for Fred among the crowd and signal him to come.

"I wouldn't bother you if it wasn't important."

"Clara, you never bother me." Even when exhausted, Fred behaves like a gentleman.

"It's about her." I turn around and point to the injured woman. "I might be able to help."

"Who, Lisa? Thank you, but you can't."

"What's wrong with her?"

"A drone shot her. The nurse removed the bullets, but the internal damage is way too extensive."

"Have you tried using soil?"

"Soil? What do you mean?" Fred looks as clueless as Rose did before.

"I know it sounds crazy. Still, there is no harm in trying. All I need is a cup."

"A cup of soil?"

"Tranquility has healing powers. The natives use it all the time. It worked on me, trust me."

"I trust you. I'll get it right away."

I grab a cup of water and wait for Fred to return.

Lisa is in critical condition and will not drink the solution. I will have to apply the treatment topically.

I leave the cup of water on the floor to grab the soil from Fred's hand. Pinching the powder between my fingers, I treat each wound with utmost care.

Lisa moans in pain, primarily when I treat her worst injuries. I can feel the rebels' hateful stare fixed on me, but I manage to ignore them and finish the job.

"She won't show signs of recovery for the next few hours."

"Thank you. You are exceedingly kind," Fred says aloud, trying to stop the others from staring in disgust.

In silence, I return to my culinary duties while the rebels pray to Marten for Lisa's swift recovery.

****

"Water, please," Lisa whispers.

"Are you all right?" One of the rebels rushes to attend to her, exhilarated.

"Not too bad," Lisa says, unaware of her precarious condition.

"It's a miracle! Praise the Seer," the rebels say, refusing to give me any credit for Lisa's incredible recovery.

A few minutes later, Fred approaches me.

"Clara, thank you. Lisa's recovery is unbelievable."

Lisa is already sitting up in bed, eating a few bites of food.

Fred sits on his cot and stays quiet, his feet nervously tapping on the floor.

I can tell Fred has something to say, so I wait for him to break the silence.

"We are negotiating your release."

"What?" An infusion of hope enters my body, and I almost leap with happiness.

"We are taking too many losses, and a possibility has presented itself."

The Council must have had a contingency plan in case of an attack.

"Is the Council still functional?"

"No, but they have regrouped with help from the

241

strangest of sources, causing us a big setback. I'm afraid you won't be heading home yet."

Fred appears uneasy with the terms of my release and keeps speaking in an encrypted manner.

My excitement grows at the thought of being released to the mongrels.

"Who are you negotiating with?"

"The gobblers."

Chapter 28

I can't breathe. Images of the gobblers' lethal toenails keep popping in my head, and I become nauseous.

"They approached us with an offer we couldn't refuse." Fred sounds ashamed of the decision.

"You can't be serious."

"They offered to help us fight the coalition with only one condition."

"Me?" It sounds too far-fetched. There is no reason why the gobblers would want me.

"As you already know, the ferocity of their nightly incursions has increased these past few weeks. I have recently learned that the reason is their desire to capture you. Now, after so many failed attempts, they have decided to negotiate for your release. There seem to be no limits to what they will do to get hold of you."

"I don't get it. The natives hate humans."

"You killed the leader's eldest son, and he's looking for retribution."

I am thunderstruck by the lie.

He must have been one of the youngsters Rem killed on the way to the farm.

"Can you just kill me?" I raise my hands in prayer. "There are no boundaries to the atrocities the gobblers must have planned for my arrival."

"This isn't what I wanted." Fred looks away to

avoid my gaze. He paces back and forth in the minute space in between our cots.

"We voted, and the majority chose to accept the offer."

The rebels' decision does not surprise me. Their hostility has grown deeper since the food scarcity crisis worsened.

"I hope their help proves worthy of my agony."

****

The last few days have gone by in a daze. I have remained in bed, only leaving to go to the outhouse. My sorrow is indescribable, and as I lie down and weep, I place both my palms on the rock for support.

I have refused food and water ever since Fred gave me the news.

What would be the point of eating? They have already delivered my death sentence. I'm a breathing corpse.

The approaching change of hands feels like having a large rock hanging around my neck and dragging me to an abyss from where I will never resurface.

Rose approaches me with a plate in her hand.

"Clara, good morning."

I remain quiet with my gaze fixed on the rock.

"Darling, you need to eat." Rose sits beside me, her fingers clenching the plate.

"Thank you, but I can't."

"I miss you in the kitchen." Rose sets the plate on the bed to hold my hands.

Rose had tried to convince me to help with the meals, but I had categorically refused.

"Sorry, but I don't have the strength."

"I don't blame you. I'll leave you alone. Please, eat

a few bites." Rose bends down to whisper in my ear, "I voted no." Then Rose pats my head with tenderness.

Choking back tears, I grab her hand and hold it for a little while—my way of thanking her for her kindness.

Tranquility has become chaotic to the extreme and impossible to predict. My childish dream of solving our deep-rooted problems is unobtainable, and this realization troubles me more than my fate. Worst of all, I seem to be the catalyst for all violent conflicts taking place on this planet. I bawl uncontrollably.

Rose remains by my side, holding my hand until I have no more tears to spare.

****

The rebels have been upbeat since they confirmed the deal with the gobblers. They are chatty and lighthearted, even when there is hardly any food to eat. Undoubtedly, they have already figured out how to take advantage of the sheer number of gobblers in battle.

"Clara, good morning."

Contrary to the rest of the people, Fred's demeanor is somber.

"Hi. You don't look as bubbly as the rest."

"I don't like how things are evolving."

"The rest of you seem to disagree. I've never seen them this happy."

"They are narrow-minded people; they don't think of the consequences further ahead. They are thinking with their stomachs, without considering how deadly this coalition could turn out further down the road."

"What do you mean?"

"Once the gobblers attack the humans, they won't stop until they destroy us all."

Fred's fears are justified. Once the gobblers

eliminate what remains of the Council, they could turn against the rebels. Far outnumbering them by a great many, the gobblers could erase humanity in a sneeze. They could go even further and fight off the mongrels who would be unable to defend themselves.

"They are taking advantage of human divisiveness to destroy us. The natives are ingenious. I can't blame them. We have caused them too much pain, turning a peaceful race into a hateful one."

"Not all humans are equally responsible for what's happening."

Fred is referring to the Council's role in these atrocities.

"Agreed. However, when you are aware of an injustice and do nothing to stop it, you are equally guilty. We are selfish. Take your group as an example; were you fighting to resolve all Tranquility's inequalities or just your own?"

"The group certainly didn't care about others, but I had hoped that once in power, we would look into the well-being of Tranquility as a whole."

"You are not alone. A few of us were exploring peaceful ways to revert these inequalities. We were trying to develop a plan which would render your rebellion unnecessary. Unfortunately, we ran out of time."

"Even if we wanted, I doubt the Council would negotiate when having the upper hand. Somehow, they have allied with the mongrels. Can you believe that? They were fighting each other less than a year ago. I guess the mongrels are willing to do anything to get you back."

"Fred, you are giving me way too much credit.

Tranquility's fate doesn't revolve around me."

"I thought so too. But the latest events keep contradicting my previous beliefs." Fred's gaze lingers on me for a second before looking away. Later, in a much softer tone, he adds, "Although I understand the attraction."

I fix my gaze on the floor as my cheeks become hot as a burning stove. Disregarding my shyness, I seize the small window of opportunity.

"Please, let me go. I'll find a compromise."

"Do you still have everyone's interests at heart?"

I nod silently.

"Unless we act soon, our presence on this planet will soon become extinct."

****

Tomorrow the rebels will deliver me to the gobblers. For a week, the insurgents have forced me to eat three times a day for fear I would not survive until the exchange takes place. It played out perfectly, as I had already decided to eat as much as possible to gain the energy required to carry out the plan.

Tonight, I will escape from this prison. I do not mind the risk. I prefer to die rather than help the rebels exterminate all humans. Fred is on board with the plan and will make sure the Hatch is open once the lights go off.

I keep up my gloomy pretense. Fred is staying apart to ensure nobody figures out we are in it together. The rebels need him as their leader. He will steer them in the right direction if my escape proves successful.

Since the agreement, nights have been eerily quiet. During the last two nights, Fred has allowed nightly visits to the outhouse, and he has volunteered as a guard. He had used these opportunities to survey the area for gobblers. He is confident there are no natives in the vicinity. Fred believes the gobblers are resting for the grand occasion. Still, I must be extra careful.

I do not have a map, but Fred gave me a detailed description of the terrain. All I have to do is walk west toward Trappist rising. Not a big deal. I am quite proficient at reading the sky.

The thought of breathing fresh air fills me with anticipation, and I can hardly contain myself. Wrapped up in my thoughts, I walk to the kitchen to wash my plate.

"Clara, are you feeling a bit better?"

Rose welcomes me with a huge smile.

"Me?"

I should be more careful. I must return to my cot immediately.

"I'm glad you are up and about."

"I have accepted my imminent death, I suppose."

Rose turns around and continues peeling vegetables in silence.

I hurry back to bed to remain the rest of the day facing the rock.

****

Time passes slowly, especially when my body aches from being stuck in the same position for hours.

When it is almost time to sleep, I turn my head a tad to check on the rebels.

They are still gathered around the tables. Fred is chatting with a small group of men. He appears at ease, but he can't stop cracking his knuckles.

Five minutes later, people settle down. Even when in my proximity, they do not bother to hide their excitement about my imminent departure.

Nobody cares if I live or die. Sorry to disappoint, but I won't stick around for the grand finale.

Once everybody has settled down, Fred heads to the door. Like every other night, he turns off the lights and says, "Goodnight."

I turn around and follow the light of Fred's flashlight as it zigzags across the crowded sleeping quarters.

The minute he arrives at his bed, he turns the light off, leaving the refuge in absolute darkness.

The moment I have dreamed about for so long is about to arrive, and I feel way too anxious.

Fred keeps tossing and turning in bed.

Is he having second thoughts about going behind his comrades' backs? What if he changes his mind?

Stationary as a log, I wait for an hour to pass. Once everyone is in a deep sleep, I sit up and listen for sounds.

Yesterday, I spent hours memorizing my way out of this crisscross of cots. I even walked it once, counting the number of steps after each of the turns.

But now, as my mind tries to remember the numbers, I am drawing a blank.

I grab the bed frame to anchor myself. Still, I can't remember the steps. Feeling nothing but blind terror, I sit down and grip the mattress with both hands. However, the stillness is even more upsetting.

I am about to sabotage my only chance of surviving this ordeal.

Suddenly, Fred sits on my bed and holds my hand tight.

I take it with desperation, hoping it will give me

the courage to continue with the plan.

Fred seems equally nervous about the fallout of my imminent departure. Disregarding Marten's teachings, he slides closer until our sides are touching and puts his arm around my shoulders to embrace me with tenderness.

Although we have never shared such a close relationship, I do not move away—his proximity calms me.

The next time I concentrate on the steps, my mind delivers a detailed map of the room.

I should leave before it disappears again.

I am about to stand up when Fred draws me closer to hold me tight in his arms. I would much rather remain within his embrace than attempt the escape, but Fred has no way to stop the rebels from handing me over to the gobblers.

The same type of reasoning must be going through Fred's mind because a few seconds later, he releases his hold.

Before my anxiety handicaps me, I follow my mental map one step at a time. But less than two minutes later, the map becomes blurry.

I quicken my pace to avoid getting stuck in the labyrinth of beds. By the time I have covered seventy percent of the maze, my state of mind has deteriorated to the point where each step I take becomes a betting game.

The next time I step forward, my right foot gets stuck on a cot's leg. The rough movement awakens the man, who turns over mumbling.

Paralyzed by fear, I wait for the man to sound the alarm.

Fred emits several fake snores, trying to cover me. Although well-intended, I doubt his lame tactic will distract the man in the slightest.

However, the man on the cot soon settles back into a deep sleep, and I am free to continue with my escape.

The severity of the situation forces my mind to bypass fear and regain the clarity required to complete the task without further complications.

Fred has left a gun by the door, but when I grab it, the metal burns my hand like a hot coal, so I set it back in its original spot.

Can a place be both a prison and a shelter?

Navigating the sea of cots has been an ordeal, but the real trial still lies ahead. I shake my head to stop myself from worrying about what could go wrong. Whether I like it or not, I hold the key to human survival, and it is time to walk the talk.

Chapter 29

It takes extra caution to close the door without waking the rebels. Then, I hustle to the outhouse, sliding over the rock to avoid detection from gobblers who might be guarding the refuge.

I find the coat Fred left by the back wall. The jacket is stiff from cold, but I still put it on right away. It feels uncomfortable at first, but the heat emanating from my body soon thaws the fabric until it molds to a decent fit.

I look up to the sky to find the most recognizable star, Mikala. Instantly, a wave of enthusiasm floods me.

Home, here I come.

The night is strangely silent, which could only mean two things: there are no gobblers in my surroundings, or they are guarding very quietly. My sense of self-preservation compels me to act as if the gobblers were watching.

I tiptoe toward Mikala, struggling to avoid the many rocky spikes on the ground. Though the terrain is not atypical for Tranquility, I have never seen these many spikes this close together. In the last five minutes, I have already fallen three times. At this pace, daylight will find me unprotected.

I sit on the ground and remove my shoe to rub my foot against the soil.

After ten minutes of full contact, the pain becomes

bearable. I am about to stand up when I hear shouts nearby. Filled with fright, I lie flat on the ground to wait for the inevitability of being found.

I lift my head to look up to the sky. The night is dark, and my range of vision is minimal. When the terrifying shrieks fill the air, I spot the source—two gobblers are flying straight at me.

Wasn't I supposed to light up Tranquility?

I almost laugh aloud at how little did I know about the generalized dissension brewing on this planet.

Good luck to whoever dares disentangle this mess.

As I consider giving myself up, the loudest of the pair accelerates his flight, grabbing the second one by the legs. The gobbler attempts to loosen his grip, but they both fall hard on the ground a hundred yards away.

I remain immobile while the gobblers wrestle with each other. When the giant gobbler is about to win the battle, he stops and roars with laughter. Next, both gobblers take off, disappearing from my view.

I dust off my clothes while searching the sky for my guiding star. I then race ahead, my heart still bursting inside my chest.

The trek becomes less rugged, and I gain ground at a faster pace. However, darkness is vanishing, and with it, my ability to follow Mikala. Thankfully, I soon find another identifiable landmark in the topography. Just below Mikala stand three similar mountain tops—The Trinity—Tranquility's most recognizable landmark.

By the time Trappist is high up in the sky, the throbbing in my foot is too intense. Still, I keep a steady pace toward a destination that remains unaltered no matter how much I try to reach it.

When I am almost sure nothing could worsen my

mood, a drone appears on the horizon. A glance at my surroundings reveals no hiding spot, but I still dash to the nearest hill.

A small opening appears thirty feet away. Drawing energy from an unknown source, I accelerate my speed and arrive at the hole in seconds. However, the drone has already spotted my movements and is heading my way at a scary pace.

I dive inside the cave without much hope. The cave is tiny but allows me enough space to hide from the drone.

The machine halts by the opening and hovers above the entrance. The operator must be wondering if the device fits inside such a restricted space.

I take my jacket off and get ready to smack the drone as soon as it ventures inside. Nevertheless, whoever manages the machine must have decided I am not worth the risk because the drone remains outside. Relieved, I collapse on the ground to wait for the drone to depart.

For a little while, I let myself fantasize about Mom watching the drone's footage and organizing a rescue mission. I even visualize her face when witnessing the recording for the first time—pure joy.

I do not disrupt my fantasy. I more than deserve a fleeting moment of pleasure. However, my fantasies morph into different versions until they present one where the person at the other end of the recording is Rem. His image makes my body convulse, and the awkward movements return me to the present moment in a flash.

Is the drone gone? Should I venture out?

****

Since my encounter with the drone, my senses have been on full alert. I am continually checking my surroundings for perils that could find their way to me.

According to Fred, it would take sixteen hours to reach the complex. Though I feel blessed for having covered half the distance already, an additional eight hours of trekking still lie ahead, and I am exhausted. Nonetheless, I allow myself to believe I will make it back home unharmed for the first time since my escape.

I am in my happy place, not checking my periphery as frequently as I should. The next time I turn my head around, a drone is fast approaching from behind. I hide inside a nearby crevice, but it is small and covers my body only partially. Still, I freeze as the rock itself, hoping the drone will miss me.

The machine stops two feet away from my face.

Mama, is that you?

The drone remains in the same position for almost a minute before abruptly departing.

What just happened? Do they know who I am?

That is the only possible explanation for the drone's bizarre behavior.

I resume the journey with increased determination, hoping aid will reach me fast.

****

An hour later, the wind carries portions of a conversation. I immediately seek refuge to listen to the dialogue, but the wind is strong and blows half of the words away.

Friend or Foe? Should I risk it?

By now, Fred must have put the recovery plan we discussed in motion. Fred knew that once it became apparent that I was gone, he would have no choice but to chase after me.

They must be rebels from another cell.

I wait for the voices to diminish or increase in volume, but they do neither. The group is guarding the area from higher ground. As I survey my surroundings for a way to continue the journey, I find traces of familiarity in the terrain.

I'm close to the underground passage I once took with Rem.

As I survey the area a bit farther ahead, I notice a color change in the rocks.

That must be it.

Trappist is about to set, and a new set of problems are about to ensue as the gobblers search every inch of Tranquility for me.

It takes me almost an hour to traverse a hundred yards separating me from my target. But as soon as I am standing outside the opening, I feel relieved. The underground tunnel leads straight to the other side of the mountain and much closer to home.

By now, the voices have almost disappeared. I take a deep breath and exhale the air loudly. I am about to step forward and into the long tunnel when the awkward memories of my previous visit return.

I have no source of light. The tunnel ground is as slippery as I remember. Without illumination, I will soon fall through the cracks and disappear into the dark abyss.

Still, I have no other alternative. Hesitantly, I take a few steps forward and stop to let my eyes adjust to the dimness.

I am considering my sanity when a soft yellowish glow projects its way from farther ahead.

Is this the same cave?

I walk forward very cautiously. Thirty feet ahead, I am at the center of a pulsing fluorescent mass. I observe the beautiful spectacle, trying to figure out the source of this throbbing marvel.

An infinite number of fluorescent worms are glittering from their own weaved net. But my silent admiration for these seasonal insects comes to an end when an equally large number of curious heads pops from holes in the rock.

These creatures, I remember very well.

The number of heads bursting around becomes oppressive, and I hasten ahead. The thought of the creatures' curiosity turning into aggression fills me with worry. However, I still appreciate them as a warning system. As long as these curious animals remain quiet, I can rest assured there are no gobblers in the vicinity.

The massive number of worms produces enough illumination for my path, and I can avoid the pools of water along both sides of the track. Still, the ground is too slippery to race ahead.

My advance is slow but without interruption until I reach a fork. I stare both ways, hoping to gain divine inspiration, but I can't remember which way to go. I will have to choose at random. If I select the wrong way, I will return to this spot to take the right path.

I tear off a piece of my skirt and wrap it around a protruding rock to indicate which way to turn.

The passage is filled with glowing worms, which allows me to keep a steady pace. The curious creatures keep popping their heads out now and then. I remain vigilant in case their curiosity turns into aggression, but it never does.

The exit should be near.

I am about to savor my achievement when the creatures nesting farther ahead make weird noises. I halt to wait for the racket to pass, but the opposite happens. The animals emit ear-piercing shrieks.

Chapter 30

I race back to the split, hoping to arrive before the gobblers notice my presence. The creatures' screams are powerful, forcing me to run with my ears covered to reduce the aching.

By the time I reach the split, the horrendous shrieks have already besieged the entire passage. When the small piece of cloth flags me to safety, I still can't see the gobblers, but by the loud sound of their stomps, they are not too far behind.

Without losing momentum, I steer in the direction of the untraveled path. I am about to complete the turn when I stop dead in my tracks. Other gobblers are already approaching from ahead.

The sudden halt makes me fall to the ground. My left foot ends in a pool of water, and the loud splash alerts the gobblers to my presence. I attempt to stand in a hurry but slip several times on the wet rock. By the time I succeed, the gobblers have already surrounded me.

A few youngsters are eager to attack, but the one in command holds them back. I keep my gaze fixed on the floor not to anger them even further, but the sight of their long and pointy nails violently shakes me.

It will be much less painful to die inside this cave than to go through the torment the gobblers have planned for me, so I try to find ways to irritate the natives to the point of killing me.

With limited space to extend my legs, I can only resort to kicking them in the shins. However, I lack the power to inflict damage. When I stop to assess the result of my actions, all but one of the natives look unmoved. I concentrate my next strike on their weakest link, punching him in the chest at full strength. Oddly enough, my strategy works.

But when the gobbler is about to react, two other natives immobilize him. Their leader then orders my immediate capture. His subordinates respond at once, covering my eyes with a stinky cloth. Immediately after, one of them lifts me in the air and carries me like a child, my face stamped against his broad and hairy chest.

Unable to see, my sense of smell becomes more acute and captures every ounce of my carrier's reeking odor.

The commander leads the group to the exit, yelling all sorts of instructions. Undoubtedly, he has orders to deliver me at once. I keep using my fists to punch my carrier in the chest, but he continues his unaltered gait with no signs of discomfort.

My plan to secure human survival has backfired. The gobblers have gotten hold of me without giving the rebels anything in return. But I should not sweat it—the natives did not need an alliance with the resistance to extinguish us. They already have the numbers to do it themselves.

Still, it is difficult to worry about humanity when many gruesome images of my imminent fate keep popping into my head. I hit the gobbler until my hands hurt too much to continue. I then remain still—with my head against his stinky chest—even when he exits the cave and becomes airborne.

I pose no resistance. I let my body hang from my carrier's arms like a ragdoll. His soar is smooth—and while in the crisp air—I forget where I am and let myself experience Tranquility's pull. I imagine being released from his grasp to drift to the ground until I become one with nature.

The mesmerizing moment ends once the gobbler lands. I instantly tense my whole body, grabbing the native's neck so tight that my nails dig deep into his thick skin.

The gobbler follows his pack without any signs of discomfort. When everyone stops, he drops me to the floor and forces me to walk ahead.

The loud vocalizations of an angry mob engulf me until I am forced to a full stop.

"Ruko!" They all salute their leader.

My carrier removes the cloth, and I find myself standing in front of an enormous native. Intuitively, I jerk back, stepping on my carrier—an equally scary-looking specimen.

"You killed my son!" Ruko's shout shatters the ground. He has made an effort to learn English words.

Although Ruko's statement is inaccurate, I remain quiet. Ruko will kill me either way, and there is no point in putting Rem's life at risk.

With a swift movement of his arm, the angry gobbler grabs my neck and raises me to his level, stopping when our faces are ten inches apart. His demeanor is terrifying, and I wonder if a stare could kill.

Ruko slowly compresses his grip. I kick him as

hard as possible, but Ruko keeps his hold steady until I can no longer breathe. Hoping this is the end of my misery, I stop fighting back and do my best to relax my neck.

I am about to pass out from lack of oxygen when Ruko throws me to the ground and orders his guards to tie me to a pole a few feet away.

I resist with all my might, but it is a futile exercise.

One of the gobblers presses my chest against the pole while the second guard wraps a rope around me.

"Please, kill me," I whisper to the closest guard, but the gobbler ignores me completely.

The natives have brought me to a tiny valley surrounded by high peaks where they have set several tents against the rock. Based on their worry-free behavior, we are in a remote location where drones never visit.

The rope binds me tight, impeding all movement. I am contemplating my imminent demise when the infuriated Ruko kicks me. His nails penetrate deep into my back muscles, causing excruciating pain.

Ruko takes a few steps back to choose the right spot to target next. He stabs me in the hip. Like the first strike, I stay quiet while the nails penetrate my flesh. However, when the mourning father twists his foot before pulling the nails out, the most agonizing scream escapes my mouth.

At the sight of chunks of my flesh by my feet, I feel somewhat relieved. At this rate, I will die within the hour. Nevertheless, Ruko stops his torture and strides away, issuing an ultimatum to the crowd before disappearing inside a tent.

When Ruko is out of sight, the angry natives throw

themselves at me. I prepare myself for the end, but two enormous natives cut through the crowd to stand guard.

"I'll kill you all!" I entice the crowd to end my misery.

But none of the natives dare challenge the guards.

****

By the hour mark, my bleeding has stopped. The blood has impregnated my clothes, and I am freezing. I am about to pass out when the entire clan builds a fire. Both youngsters and seniors contribute to the task, throwing all sorts of combustible material into the flames.

One of the seniors catches my attention. He looks familiar—but in my condition—I can't remember where I have seen him before. I am looking straight at him when he fixes his gaze on me. His facial expression tells me he recognizes me too. However, he soon looks away and continues with his job of feeding the flames.

As soon as the fire is going strong, the natives dig a small circular trench around me. When they finish digging, one of the youngsters darts into Ruko's tent. Shortly after, Ruko exits his tent, holding a metallic branding iron in his hand. He marches to the fire and places the brand over the flames before facing the crowd for a lengthy speech.

The branding iron soon turns bright red. One of the guards brings it to Ruko, who issues further instructions with an orchestra conductor's smoothness.

The guards obey, lifting my skirt and removing my shoe. I resist, but their hold is strong, and the recent loss of blood has weakened me.

When the crowd quiets with anticipation, Ruko summons a youngster to approach me. The youngster

Susana Aclan

has been watching the evolving scene filled with apprehension. Still, he hurries to show me the skin under his right wing.

My stomach turns at the sight of our religious symbol branded on his back.

Ruko extends the iron brand in his possession to allow me to see it. The brand displays an identical emblem; somehow, the natives have acquired one of ours.

As Ruko disappears, I search the crowd for the only familiar face. Oddly enough, the old gobbler meets my gaze in earnest, as if wanting to provide some level of relief.

The crowd shrieks in excitement as Ruko orders his guards to bend my left knee and present my sole. Soon after, my cold skin sizzles when he presses the blazing iron against my foot.

The guards complete their job by carelessly releasing my foot, causing the sole of my foot to crash painfully against the ground.

I plant my other heel firmly against the dirt, hoping to keep it away from the guards. Then I meet the old gobbler's gaze for moral support.

But Ruko plans to savor my killing unhurriedly, and rather than repeating the operation on my other foot, he discards the brand on the ground and exits the dug-up circle.

Immediately after, the guards pour oil into the trench, filling it to the brim—the flames will keep everyone away until it is time for the next torture.

I keep my gaze fixed on the senior until the whole circumference catches on fire. The flames are not close enough to burn my skin, but the harsh environment increases the pain until I end up unconscious.

****

The gobblers have stopped replenishing the oil, and the fire is burning out. They soon gather around, and almost instantly, Ruko shows up for the next torment.

The thick wooden stick in his hand is hard to miss, and I shiver in distress. I remember seeing one of those weapons inside the refuge.

"It is disgusting! Who put those hooks in each of the spikes?" My stomach had turned when Fred showed me the long metal spikes.

"It wasn't me. I hate it as much as you do, but a few of us think differently," Fred had said, upset. He disliked working with the type of people who could design such instruments of torture.

Ruko brings me back to the present when commanding two gobblers to approach.

The oldest gobbler walks with a marked limp.

Oh, no!

The numerous hideous scars stretching along his leg serve as witnesses to the type of weapon used to inflict such brutality.

I look up, expecting to meet a hateful gaze. However, the native confronts me with shyness and apprehension.

Ruko instructs the second gobbler to turn around. When I see that half of his wing is missing, the weight of human abuse hits me with full force.

Is any of us worth defending? Am I any better?

Chapter 31

"We are monsters. Please, kill me!"

Ruko ignores me. After he has dismissed the handicapped pair, he positions himself a few steps behind.

I search everywhere for my anchor—the friendly senior— but he has vanished.

In the next moment, I experience agonizing pain in my right hamstring. Ruko has hit me so powerfully that the multiple spikes have pierced through my skirt's thick fabric and entered deep inside the muscle.

Unable to breathe through the pain, I wait for the worst to come—the yanking of the hooks.

Ruko pauses until the crowd is bursting with anticipation to deliver the grand finale. When the group finally erupts in yells, he yanks the stick from my leg.

I exhale an agonizing cry as blood drips down my leg and into the frozen ground. Two seconds later, I drift into oblivion.

****

The ring of fire is back on, which can only mean Ruko is getting ready for the next torment. Though I can't envision anything worse, I fear Ruko will soon prove me wrong.

My feet are no longer supporting my weight, and my arms are too weak to keep holding on to the post.

I release my hold. My body shifts position, but the

rope sustains it. I try to relax, hoping it will ease the pain, but the agony is too intense to make a difference. The worst grief comes from my heart. For the first time in my life, I am afraid the harm we inflicted is too grave to attain any reconciliation.

On the brink of death, I evaluate my real contribution to the crisis and conclude it has been mostly negative. My mouth opens in a silent wail—surviving this ordeal would serve no purpose. All the different factions will keep trying to use me as a pawn in their senseless wars.

With anguish stabbing my heart, I surrender to death in body and soul.

Unfortunately, the Angel of Death does not appreciate handouts. He is after fiercely fought battles.

****

The show is about to continue. As I quiver in terror, my injuries hurt even more. The gobblers have gathered around to witness the torture, but none of them looks thrilled. Whenever I make eye contact with them, they look away as if ashamed. Nonetheless, the crowd is sizable, which can only mean Ruko is forcing them to witness the delivery of justice.

From the corner of my eye, I observe a youngster entering Ruko's lodging. Soon after, the enormous leader exits the premises with the youngster tagging along close behind.

I check Ruko's hands but find them empty. Anxious, I search the crowd for something out of the ordinary and tremble when I see it.

A five-foot-tall metal rod is sticking out from the flames. The piece of iron is so hot that it shines vibrant red.

Ruko grabs the rod by its wooden handle and walks to me. As my brain struggles to figure out how he plans to use it, I notice the Followers' skull engraved along the length of the bar.

This time Ruko does not command anyone to step forward, which means no one has ever survived such torture. The crowd gapes in horror as Ruko commands the guards to lift my skirt.

When the guards approach me, I stop breathing. The lifting of the dress will be excruciating; the cotton fabric has intertwined with skin and muscle, creating a peculiar lattice that has dried together as a block.

I close my eyes to wait for the tug, which will have to be forceful enough to achieve the desired result. When the time comes, the pull's agony is too intense, and I almost lose consciousness.

With blood running down my leg, the guards proceed to remove my undergarment—the guessing game is over.

My beloved Rem instantly comes to mind. I am counting on him to guide me to the afterlife as swiftly as he has done with Lisa.

Your suffering will be over soon.

I imagine Rem whispering in my ear as I wait for the final assault.

"Touch her again, and you'll die!" This time, Rem's words resonate in my head as if he is standing next to me.

The guards release my undergarment, but they keep holding me tight.

"Get your hands off her!"

My mind is improvising.

However, I soon realize the scene is taking place

outside my head and open my eyes.

Are those mongrels?

Havoc has unleashed in the valley, and dozens of natives are flying in all directions.

As my mind processes the scene, I recognize some of the faces among the mass of beings.

In desperation, I turn my head around, but the rope impedes it.

"Rem!" But the turmoil is such that nobody hears.

Somebody lands by my side almost instantly.

Rem?

I freeze at the sight of a familiar face. He is one of the prisoners who had attacked me on the farm. When the mongrel kneels by the post, I am too frightened to lift my head.

"We were afraid we wouldn't make it in time. All of us are here." The mongrel points in the direction of the scuffle. "We deeply regret what we did to you back then."

The mongrel sounds contrite, and when I meet his gaze, he turns away as if mortified. Still, he hurries to cut the rope.

"Yank it off. It won't hurt," I lie when the mongrel stops momentarily.

The mongrel knows I am lying but pulls the rope regardless. Then he extends his arms to grab me before I fall, but two gobblers attack him at the last moment.

The crash landing causes my body to spasm in agony. When I try to stand, my legs are unresponsive.

"Rem!"

I use my palms to get out of the circumference and to the nearest tent, where I will have an unobstructed view of the battle.

It's all my fault!

My eyes fill with tears as the natives fight each other.

I am trying to figure out a way to end the madness when Ruko lands by my feet. He harshly grabs me by the ankles and drags me back to the circle where the glowing rod awaits on the ground.

With the metal rod in his hand, Ruko stares at me with hateful determination—his staged torture has concluded, and he is about to deliver the finishing blow.

When he lifts my skirt, I consider screaming for help but stop. Ruko is mighty, and he will kill anyone who tries to interfere.

Ruko is about to strike when somebody violently throws him to the ground.

"Rem!"

Rem is standing across from Ruko. Although he is massive, he is no match for Ruko.

"Rem. Stop this fight! I rescued the mongrels so they could live a better life. Don't you dare let them die!"

The pair is about to engage in combat when two of Ruko's guards arrive, and a fierce fight unravels.

Ruko soon forgets about Rem to turn his full attention on me. With deadly resolve, he searches for the rod, but the metal bar has vanished.

Ruko improvises. He grabs my ankles and swirls me in the air. His circular motion continues for several seconds until he halts and smashes me against the ground.

The terrible blow knocks me out, but I regain consciousness right when Ruko grabs me for a second time. He intends this strike to be the last.

As I search the air to see Rem one last time, a shadow approaches Ruko from behind. When the figure comes closer, I am surprised to see my anchor. He is holding the wooden stick in his hands.

Before I can even react, the old gobbler swings the rod at Ruko, impaling him in the back of the head.

The colossal leader drops to the ground without a struggle. His head bleeds profusely, even with the wooden baton still sticking out of his skull.

I can't comprehend why the old gobbler would choose me before his leader.

"I'm repaying my debt."

"Your debt?" I suddenly recognize him. He is the worker I rescued from Owen's racist outburst. "But you don't owe me anything."

The elder carries me to the nearest tent and carefully sets me down. After stroking my hair with compassion, he disappears amidst the mass of natives.

With a lump in my throat, I push my legs against the soil seeking healing. Tranquility does not disappoint, offering instant restoration.

Engulfed in screams of death that stab my soul, I place my palms over my ears. I am on the verge of unconsciousness—unable to distinguish hallucinations from reality—when I hear Rem's voice.

"We don't want to fight. We only came for the girl."

Rem has already realized Ruko is dead. But in such commotion, the gobblers can't hear him.

"Listen!" This time, Rem's yell strikes like thunder. "Stop this nonsense. We are family."

The gobblers stop momentarily to check why Ruko has not killed Rem yet. One by one, they see Ruko's

Susana Aclan

dead body on the ground. Shocked, they stop the fight.

After minutes of unnerving uncertainty, everyone settles down to attend to the wounded.

"Clara. You must drink." Rem removes my hands from my ears, handing me a cup of medicine.

"Rem? Is it really you?"

"I've been searching for you for too long."

After Rem succeeds at making me drink the medication, he holds me in his arms and rests my head against his chest. Half-unconscious and half-awake, I listen to our hearts beating in unison. Within this symphony of love, I surrender to darkness.

Chapter 32

"Sorry," Rem whispers to my ear.

"What about?"

Rem hurries to his feet, almost falling to the ground in the process. "You've been in a medically-induced coma for almost ten days."

I look around and immediately recognize the sterile settings of a hospital. I have yet to run an inventory of my well-being. However, my muscles seem to be responding to my commands with a minimum of pain.

"The nurse just brought you back from yet another visit to the reconfiguration machine," Rem says, rolling his eyes. He seems fed up with human treatments.

"Why are you sorry? You saved my life. Do you regret it already?"

"Don't be silly."

"Then, what is it?"

"I had promised myself to stay away from you, but I failed."

His words hurt like a punch in the stomach. Upset about Rem's cold response, I say, "You certainly made it clear when you left me."

"I was fulfilling my promise. You did your part of the deal, and I was completing mine," Rem says, sounding like an emotionless robot.

"Right."

"I failed at being a good husband." This time, Rem

Susana Aclan

stutters as he speaks. "Instead of protecting you from harm, I almost got you killed."

I hurry to grab his hand. "It wasn't your fault. I went inside the burning building on my own accord."

But Rem keeps staring at the distance.

"Look at me! I survived. There is no point in fretting about that night."

Now Rem fixes his gaze on the tile floor. "Truth is, I never left you. I remained close, watching you from a distance."

"But when...how?"

"Since you returned home from the hospital. It was tricky at times, and the Followers almost caught me twice."

"But why? Rem, you owe me nothing. You had already completed your duty. Plus, ours is a fake union."

It's time to let Rem go. Seeing him disappear from my life will tear me apart, but I'll survive. I've done it before.

"For me, the union was always truthful," Rem responds, surprisingly timid.

Skrish's words return to me.

"What does the phrase 'The union is truthful' mean?"

Rem remains silent, avoiding my gaze.

"Please, tell me."

Rem looks me in the eyes. "It means ours is an unbreakable bond. Our love will never weaken. It transcends time and space."

"Eternal love..." My heart bounces inside my chest, and I can't contain my urge to hug him.

"Infinite love." Rem's gaze is so intense that it

makes me tremble from head to toe.

"I thought you didn't love me…" My emotions are too strong, and I am crying by the time I add, "I've missed you so much! My heart has ached since the day you left."

Overjoyed at my love confession, Rem gets closer and kisses my lips. "Mine has mimicked your pain."

When Rem hugs me tight, our hearts melt into one unified beating machine. I am in the midst of a thunderstorm of emotions—my mood fluctuating from euphoria to absolute fear—when I say, "Never, ever leave me. I won't survive it."

****

When my family visited earlier today, I observed that my interaction with my parents has changed, probably as a result of almost losing Mom during the rebellion. Hopefully, the struggles have taught us to deal with our differences in a healthier way.

It was hard to believe how amicably Rem interacted with my parents. A few months ago, I would not have predicted them having such an endearing relationship. The image of Mom throwing a brick at Rem's forehead comes back, and I laugh with abandon.

"What is it?" Rem raises his eyebrows at my sudden outburst.

"How is your forehead, by the way?"

Rem gives me a half-smile. "Your mom apologized several times for her lack of judgment."

"Is that so?" I draw Rem close and give him a peck on the lips. We have been holding hands since my family left this morning.

"Your mom isn't too bad once you get to know her. She even calls me Son."

Rem's eyes have no traces of hatred—none whatsoever.

"Really?"

Rem remains quiet for a few seconds before saying, "I'm sure she wants to."

I laugh, delighted. Undeniably, Rem makes my heart sing.

Rem spends some time getting me up to speed. My anchor had been more instrumental to my survival than I had initially thought. He not only managed to kill Ruko single-handedly, but he was the one who left camp in search of help, striking gold when stumbling upon one of Rem's scouts.

"Once we realized the person he wanted to help was you, we organized a recovery operation. I never wanted to fight the gobblers, but when I saw them hurting you, I wanted to rip their heads off."

"Did any of the gobblers die?" I shiver as memories of the natives killing each other surface.

"Only a handful, including Ruko."

"What about mongrels?"

"None."

I spend the next few minutes honoring those killed in battle. Though a small number, their deaths will haunt me for a long time.

Rem had searched for me since my disappearance, but each time he found new clues, they turned out to be dead ends.

"Everyone you know helped at some point."

Rosh had excelled at the art of tact and diplomacy, convincing their Council to make a truce with the remaining members of the Follower's leadership. What had started as an unpredictable and unstable alliance soon turned into a precious one, succeeding at keeping the rebels at bay. With time, the two factions agreed to move on to the offensive, recovering lost ground and cornering the insurgents into the mountains. Still, nothing compared to the exceptional progress they achieved when Rem recovered the drones.

"The rebels had deactivated the machines. But Peter and Yuma worked endlessly to get them operational again."

Love fills me at the thought of everyone working together to get me back.

"Somehow, everybody likes you." Rem hugs me with pride. "We first spotted you entering the refuge."

"You saw me? I wasn't at all sure."

"We saw you, as well as the hundred gobblers, camped nearby. We discussed all possible rescue options, but neither your Mom nor I wanted to risk your life."

"I am so glad you didn't attempt a rescue. The Hatch is impenetrable."

"The guy guarding you seemed quite protective."

"Who?"

"You tell me." Rem's intense gaze meets mine.

"That was Fred. He is the leader of the rebels and the only reason why I am still alive. The rebels wanted to kill me, but Fred convinced them I would prove useful as a bargaining chip. He was right, even when entertaining an offer from the gobblers was not what Fred had in mind. He ended up helping me escape once he figured out a union with the gobblers would be self-destructive. Fred wants to cooperate with the Council."

"What do you mean?"

"We have his support to put an end to all this

nonsense."

"That sounds encouraging."

Rem is doubtful about the possibility of achieving peace any time soon.

Rem looks worried. I place my head on his chest and remain quiet for a few minutes. The erratic tensing of his muscles is a clear indicator of how concerned Rem is about the current unrest.

I hug him tight. The violence also weighs heavily on me, and I have no words of encouragement to offer.

Eventually, Rem snaps out of his trance and continues with the story.

"A second drone spotted you close to the caves. Once I confirmed it was you, I launched a recovery expedition. I was certain you would head for the tunnels, considering we've been there before. But by the time we arrived, you had already vanished."

"You are right. I did enter the caves, but the gobblers captured me near the exit."

"How is it possible for such a young woman to be the most-wanted creature on the planet?"

"I can't figure it out myself." I chuckle uneasily. "Tranquility is full of delusional beings, I guess."

Unfortunately, joking about an issue that has bothered me for quite some time does not make the pain disappear. All of a sudden, I become emotional. "Rem, I'm not good for you! Violence and suffering follow me wherever I go."

Rem displays his beautiful wings and surrounds me with them.

"Within my wings, I will keep you and promise to be yours forever."

I remain immobile as Rem reissues the vow he

once stated in front of Rensei.

"Love will flow your way until we turn into ashes."

This time, Rem's devotion is palpable, and I tremble with emotion. Rem expresses his love in soft tones and through the energy emanating from every cell of his powerful body.

I surrender to the inevitability of our love, which extends as far and wide as Tranquility itself. However, as I remain within Rem's protection, other needs arise in me that can't be satiated within a hospital room confinement.

"When can I leave the hospital?"

"You are almost recovered. There is no reason why the doctors won't let you go. I'll ask your mom to pick you up…"

"No!"

"No? What do you mean?"

For a few seconds, our gazes meet. Subsequently, Rem trembles like a schoolboy and says, "I'll take you home."

"What if they don't allow it?"

This time, Rem's gaze emits fiery passion. "Trust me. They will."

****

Mom had protested the idea of me leaving the hospital without proper protection. However, Rem had reassured her the mongrels would provide all the security needed.

Although I am excited about going back to the caves and seeing Rosh, the thought of confronting the mongrels makes me quite uneasy. Still, I do not voice my concerns until I am standing outside the caves.

"I don't have the Pass."

"You shouldn't worry about it," Rem says, seemingly calm. Still, he holds my hand tight as we traverse deep into the mountain.

The deserted path allows us to walk fast. We are halfway home when we encounter the first mongrel. As soon as I spot the native, I rush to hide behind Rem, hoping he will miss me.

"Greetings!" The mongrel meets Rem respectfully.

"Greetings to you."

As soon as the mongrel walks by Rem and spots me, he comes to a screeching halt.

Petrified, I wait for the imminent confrontation with my back against the rock.

"Clara!" The mongrel comes closer to bow in salutation. "It's such an honor to have you back."

The mongrel continues on his way, visibly awestruck.

"What was that?" Dumbfounded, I remain immobile until Rem pokes me forward, urging me to walk.

I am about to comply when a large group of mongrels approaches us.

As soon as the group notices me, one of the youngsters leaps forward.

I hastily turn away to avoid any potential punch.

Rem stops the youngster when he is about a foot away.

"Clara? I can't believe it's you! Can I get a hug?"

The youngster claps his hands with excitement.

Is this for real?

As Rem releases him, the youngster throws himself into my arms.

"Thank you! You saved my father."

By now, the entire group is around me. The mongrels wait for their turn to express the sincerest gratitude for rescuing their loved ones.

Cameron was right. The mongrels treasure me.

The show of affection is immense, and all I can do is stand speechless.

Like an electrical circuit, the scene repeats itself all the way home. By the time I enter the house, I am an emotional mess.

"Lovely, Clara. I can't believe you came back." Rosh has a smile plastered on her face when she gives me one of her tender cuddles.

"Rosh, I've missed you so much." I return her embrace unreservedly, my lower lip quivering with emotion.

"We were so worried about you. Yuma! Come see who is here."

Yuma has recovered from her terrible confinement and looks radiant. As soon as she spots me, her mouth curves into a smile, and she rushes to hug me.

I return her affection two-fold. When Yuma breaks the embrace, I notice Peter a few steps away—the Pass is still hanging from his neck.

"I am glad to see you." Peter gives me a bear hug, a clear indication of how the mongrels have already altered his behavior.

I enjoy every second of the reunion, the outpouring of affection nurturing my soul.

"Thank you for your determination to bring me back."

Chapter 33

"I dare say you don't need the protection of the Pass."

The way in which the mongrels welcomed me back has moved Rem deeply. Though he knew of the natives' change of heart, he never expected it to be so dramatic.

I remain silent. It is the first time I step foot in Rem's room, and my hands are sweating with nervousness.

"Your room is a mess," I say casually to distract myself.

"What did you expect? I've been busy looking for you around the clock."

As I look around the room, a book seems oddly familiar. "Is this…"

"Yours?" Rem grabs my book and hands it to me. "I found it the night of the attack."

"Were you watching me all along?"

"No, the rebels were heavily guarding the grounds. By the time I got in, the explosions had already destroyed most of the complex. I later found out you were under Cameron's protection at the time."

"How do you know him?"

"The boy worked as hard as anyone else to find you."

"Really? He is such a great friend."

"Friend?" Rem issues a fake laugh. "He is madly in love with you. But I never took him as a serious competitor. He is just a boy."

Rem's response almost makes me laugh. He is only a couple of years older than Cameron.

"Is Cameron all right? He was in pretty bad shape when I left him."

"He was fully recovered by the time I met him. We've been working together all this time."

Rem laughs aloud.

"What's so funny?"

"Cameron has been patiently waiting to see you. I might have told him you were unfit for visitors."

"No, you didn't."

"I sure did. I was feeling pretty insecure about your feelings toward me at the time," Rem says, kissing me on the cheek.

"Did you tell him we are married?"

"Not my place to tell. You'll have to do it yourself." Rem chuckles again. He is already imagining the scene.

"It doesn't matter. I'm sure Cameron has no romantic interest in me." I turn around to avoid Rem's gaze.

"Of course, he has." Rem now laughs wholeheartedly.

"It's a bit funny how you always presume everyone likes me." My cheeks burn with shyness.

"Unfortunately, your sweet personality is like a potent magnet that drives men crazy."

This time, I laugh with abandon, surprising myself with the loudness of my laughter.

"Will your Seer object to this?" Rem embraces me

from behind, kissing my neck with passion.

I turn around and kiss him back. I had renounced Marten's beliefs a while ago, vowing never to allow him to regain the power he once had. But my behavior is not meant to anger him. My life is unpredictable, and I have been on the verge of death multiple times. The probability of dying is still high, and this could be the only moment we have together.

Rem gently unbuttons my monastic dress all the way to my waist.

My breathing stops when my dress slips from my hips to the floor, leaving me bare in his presence.

Rem undresses a few feet away, revealing his muscular body and lustrous wings.

My husband is beautiful.

Rem takes two steps forward, but rather than stopping when in front of me, he circles me, caressing my body with the tips of his fingers.

I remain immobile—my eyes fixed on the floor—while my skin sizzles with his touch.

Once Rem completes the full circle, he lifts my chin to make me meet his gaze. "What's wrong?"

"I don't know how to do this."

"It's the first time for both of us."

"Seriously?"

"Unlike my predecessors, who were quick to indulge in the art of love, I take it rather seriously."

The memory of his human lineage distracts Rem momentarily. The next time he speaks, he gazes into my soul. "You are the only one I've loved in body and soul."

Memories of how Rem used to recoil at my touch come to me all of a sudden. A wide smile appears on my face.

I can't believe that I'm making love to him.

But life seems to have weird ways of teaching us new lessons.

I sit on the bed, and Rem follows suit.

"Will it hurt?" After all, Rem is part gobbler.

"I'm not certain, but we don't have to do anything you don't want to. After thinking that I lost you forever, holding you like this…" Rem says, lovingly caressing my back. "…is more than enough."

I slowly slide toward him to close the gap between us. But once I am by his side, I do not know how to satiate the thirst that consumes me.

Rem takes charge, grabbing the back of my head and slowly pulling me to him until our lips are an inch apart. His eyes are filled with ardent admiration when he kisses me on the lips.

Rem's kisses are slow and deep, and I am experiencing new sensations in the base of my stomach. Soon his kissing becomes frantic and passionate. He moves my hair out of the way to expose my neck and passionately traces my long neck and shoulders with his lips.

I use all my senses to memorize every inch of Rem's beautiful body as if my life depended on it.

When his lips reach my chest, he cups my breasts in his hands and looks at them, mesmerized. He then kisses them slowly and with total devotion.

I tremble from the sensory overload of the first time. I even gasp for air when Rem softly kisses my breasts.

When Rem notices my state, he sits me on his lap and tightly holds me in his arms. He extends his beautiful feathers and wraps them around me. Rem quivers, too, also overwhelmed by emotions.

I wrap my legs around his waist and remain immobile for a long minute, gazing at Rem's loving eyes. When a tingling sensation spreads through me, I kiss him passionately.

Rem lays me on the bed with a sense of urgency. He lies on top of me, and we roll on the bed—our desperation a clear indicator of our sexual inexperience.

My body burns with desire until the moment Rem possesses me.

The initial frenzy of the first encounter gives way to rhythmic movements as our bodies adjust to each other. Soon our motion becomes as natural as the cadence of breaking waves onshore.

A few hours later, drenched in sweat, I collapse on Rem's arms, exhausted.

****

I rest in bed within Rem's protective embrace. Rem is sound asleep, but I am wide awake. The memories of my recent sufferings have found their way back into my thoughts, and I am feeling anxious. Soon, restlessness grasps me in its grip, and no matter how much I try to relax, it does not let go.

My transition into adulthood has been too taxing. Awakening to the Followers' deceitfulness still hurts. Life in Tranquility remains chaotic, and a peaceful resolution to the rebels' unrest appears unattainable. The dark side of Tranquility has proven gloomier than I ever imagined. Tranquility's inequalities are plenty, and I dread there is still more to unravel. Though I have seen sparks of hope, permanent change will remain elusive until the powerful acknowledge their wrongdoing and initiate transformation from within the system.

I place my head on Rem's chest and listen to the rhythmic beating of his loving heart. A feeling of peace floods me as I trace his chest with my finger.

I am still in awe at the fact that I am married to a mongrel. But through all the many challenges, we have managed to stick together. Rem and I are living proof of what is possible—two different species drawn together by madness, who found friendship and love in the process.

You are my home. As long as I have you, I fear nothing.

I become hopeful.

Eyes closed, I place one hand on the rock while feeling my body rise with each of Rem's inhales. Soon, the sense of belonging expands from Rem's arms to the entirety of Tranquility, renewing my commitment.

I will leave no stone unturned to let the light shine on Tranquility.

A word about the author...

Susana lives in Canada with her husband, three children, and two dogs. She received a Master's degree from a Canadian university and had a successful career in government. Susana quit her job a few years back to write fictional stories tailored to empower the reader.

http://www.susanaaclan.com/home

Thank you for purchasing
this publication of The Wild Rose Press, Inc.

For questions or more information
contact us at
info@thewildrosepress.com.

The Wild Rose Press, Inc.
www.thewildrosepress.com